Getting Even

Gillian Pollock

Guid Publications

Getting Even
Published 2021 by Guid Publications
Barcelona, Spain

Email: guid@guid-publications.com

Cover design: Books Covered
Interior design: Daisy Editorial

ISBN:
978-84-120916-6-3 paperback
978-84-120916-7-0 ebook

www.guid-publications.com

For my sisters

Kirsty and Catriona

1

Kathy truly, honestly, and with a passion, hated social media. She looked down at the icons on her phone. Her hair flopped onto the screen and, irritated, she shoved the offending lock behind her ear. Her elbow swept her cappuccino onto the cafe floor. The waiter, used to Kathy's melodramatic, gestures, drew a long, patient breath, wiped up the mess and ordered a fresh cup for the third time that week.

Unaware, as usual, of the impact of her actions, Kathy glared at the screen. There they were: Gmail, Twitter, Snapchat, Instagram, Facebook and, just waiting to be added to the list of hated apps, TikTok. She mentally ticked them off, one by one. Dumped three times, long-windedly, by email. Four very publicly humiliating times on Facebook. She'd never forgive them for that. Twice extremely succinctly on Twitter, for which she was grateful, and once, briefly, on Snapchat, the screen flashing a quick 'fuck off'. The Instagram dumpings were varied and graphic, certainly more than she deserved, and finally, she was once dumped musically on Myspace, but that was a long time ago. This time, however, took the biscuit.

Friday evening had started well. Kathy and her boyfriend, David, had gone for an after-work walk around Kelvingrove Park. It was a bit damp; being Glasgow that was a given. The pale grey sky, the result of a recent shower, and the dark grey of the city provided a dramatic backdrop that contrasted with the bright, young green of the trees' glistening leaves. They talked, laughed and cuddled as they walked along the path admiring the flowers.

This is how it should be, she thought.

As they walked, arm in arm, she imagined how others must see them: a respectably handsome couple, at the very least. Both dark-haired. Hers long. His short. She fitted neatly under his shoulder as they walked together and, although looking adoringly up at him she could see right up his nose. He took care of himself, not a hair in sight.

"Look at that old couple." Kathy nodded towards two eighty-somethings walking ahead of them. "They're still holding hands after all these years. Isn't that cute? Do you think that could be us?" Kathy tipped her head up towards him, finally gazing, into his eyes that matched the sky.

David stopped abruptly and moved a telling few inches away from her to allow air to fill the space between their bodies. "Aye, well, no, I mean, who knows! Anything can happen. A solar flare could land at our feet, obliterate us and knock out the electricity and the internet in Glasgow for months. That could happen. Worse things have!"

"David, David, David." Kathy breathed his name and turned to face him. She reached up, took his face in both hands, and stood on tiptoes to put her face within inches of his. "Don't be afraid of happiness." She paused, and with increased intensity continued, "Don't be afraid of being with the one that you will love forever. Don't be afraid of your feelings."

Chapter 1

A slow smile spread across her face. There were defining moments in one's life and for Kathy, this was it. *The* moment. Eternal love, eternal happiness. Bliss *à la* Barbara Cartland. Kathy had found her man, her hero. His attributes were many: the most considerate lover, breakfast in bed whenever she stayed over, regular WhatsApps, even on his nights out with the boys, a trip to Corfu. A bit *passé* as a holiday destination but she didn't care; he'd paid. He'd given her one of the wheels of his sports car as a deep gesture of his love. The fact that the wheel was attached to the front left-hand side of the car meant that she could now legitimately call it *their* car!

David carefully removed her hands and rubbed his face, red from her vice-like grip. He put his left hand into his pocket. Kathy's hands flew to her face. She gasped with ecstasy. This was it! She fixated on his left pocket as his hand rummaged inside, and visualised the little black box tucked away waiting to be presented to her. She sensed David gazing at her intently and looked up.

"See that wheel I gave you?" He looked away, then looked back. "It's had a puncture. Here."

He pulled out an envelope, shoved it at her and took a few large paces backwards. His body seemed poised for fight or flight.

Kathy, shocked, took the envelope with her left hand, which had been moving towards David, ready to accept the ring she had been expecting him to produce. She looked down at it, then glanced up at David who was watching her from a safe distance. She could feel the adrenaline pumping through her body. Her heart thumping, she stuck her finger under the flap and tore it open, pulling out a letter. She took an involuntary step back. A letter? Handwritten at that. Who writes letters any more? This was going to be a first. She didn't have an app for that.

The letter was two pages long. Kathy took her time to unfold the pages and started to read slowly and carefully. Jumping to conclusions was one of her superpowers, but this time she needed to understand. Her heart bumped when she read "I love you" and plummeted with "but I love someone else more". And again with "I love you" followed by the heart-breaking "but you're just not right for me". "I love you but ..." "I love you but ..."

Kathy kept her head down and pretended to read the rest of the letter, her eyes too full to make out the words. *Not again, please, not me, not now, not him.* A profound feeling of something, of a loss of her sense of self, overwhelmed her. Her gut seemed to fold in on itself and a black hole developed, moving upwards, sucking her heart in with it, taking it somewhere she wasn't sure she would ever find again.

Kathy straightened, lifted her head and looked over towards David. He was standing a few metres away, stock still, waiting. He looked relieved that she hadn't made a scene or stabbed him in the jugular with that sharp object holding her hair up. As he looked at her, her eyes unfocused, her arms fell to her sides and the letter floated to the ground. She looked limp. David's shoulders relaxed and he started to breathe again. With Kathy's temper, limp was a very good thing. "Fancy a pint?" His attempt at cheerfulness hung uneasily in the air.

Kathy had a choice. She could scream her head off at the insensitive arsehole, which was pretty much her default mode, but she had no strength left to make any decisions of her own, and, in the end, all she managed was a quiet "*okay.*"

2

⮕

They ended up in their favourite pub. It was Friday night packed, but they managed to find room at a tiny table, sitting on stools still warm from their previous occupants, rubbing shoulders and occasional bums as people squeezed past to reach the bar. The dozen tiny, ancient, chipped tables, some shoved together, made progress towards the bar seem like a never-ending maze, the reward being the row of beer pumps pert and ready to dispense fancy local beers.

Kathy and David looked longingly at the lucky ones who'd scored one of the booths with their ample, red-covered seats and rectangular tables. Two people hogged each one, spread out, smug in the knowledge that they'd won the pub equivalent of the lottery. The din was deafening, partly because of the wooden floors and high ceilings, but also because it was karaoke night.

David was acting as if nothing had happened in a seemingly desperate effort to make Kathy feel the same. He still had hopes of getting out alive.

For Kathy, the whole situation was surreal for being so normal. Here she was with her boyfriend in their usual Friday night haunt, drinking their favourite beers, trying a few new ones, and acknowledging the regulars. They drank, they snogged, they drank, they snogged, her tears flowed. Barbara Cartland would be horrified at this turn of events. This wasn't meant to happen, not now. This was meant to be the resolution. The eternal-love part.

David didn't exactly have a clear plan of extraction and decided to go with the flow. After a few pints he became genuinely cheerful as if a weight had dropped off his shoulders and landed squarely on Kathy's.

"Come on, Kathy, you love karaoke!" He grabbed her arm and, ignoring her protests, dragged her to the microphone. "I put you on the list. You're next!"

Before she knew it, she was singing a wobbly version of Gloria Gaynor's 'I Will Survive', stopping frequently to sob. The round of applause was muted. A few whistles punctuated the air, mostly from David.

By the time Kathy sat back down, drained, David was on the very-drunk-heading-for-wasted end of the spectrum. He put his arm around her. "What's up, lass? You look miserable. What can I do to help?"

Kathy, having had a few drinks herself, was righteously incredulous. "I've been dumped! Again!"

David jumped to his feet. Fists clenched, ready to punch the offending party. "Who was it? I'll have him! I won't let anyone make my girl miserable! Go on, tell me! Who was it?"

He punched the arm of the bloke at the next table. "Oi, was it you?"

David started bouncing on his feet and feinting, as if he actually knew how to box. The man stood up, stretching to his full six foot six. As broad as he was tall. A prop forward if Kathy ever saw one. She leapt out of her seat and got in the middle of the two men before it got ugly.

Chapter 2

"It was you, you big arse!" she shouted at the top of her lungs, drowning out 'Love Is In The Air'.

David sat down suddenly, momentarily shocked. Then shot to his feet. "Shit, I was supposed to meet my girlfriend half an hour ago. Got to run. I've got a date. I mean, a thing. Yes, I've got a thing. Got to go. See ya!"

3

That was it. All dreams gone wherever dreams go to die. All the imagined forever-lasting love always ended up in that place, and it must be full up because Kathy was empty. Exhausted. She left the pub and started to walk, and walk, and walk. She walked all night. In straight lines, in circles, following the city blocks, in and out, across streets she barely even registered.

Finally, just as dawn broke and without really being aware of it, she turned into her street. A fox trotted past looking as if he owned the place. The unexpected movement made her jump and roused her out of her zombie-like state. Terraced houses, each front door sporting at least three doorbells. Some scruffy, some in the process of renovation. The house next to hers stood out, extra white as the new paint shone in the light of the dawn. She walked up to her front door. Of the four doorbells, hers was the top one.

Wide awake now and angry, she slammed the front door of the house with a window-rattling crash, hoping to waken Sheena, the owner of the house and therefore her landlord, who lived on the ground floor, because, why not? Misery loves company.

Heavy booted, she thumped up the communal stairs to the first-floor landing and threw her middle finger in the direction of the door to the first-floor flat. She heard a low growl from The Wee Besom who lived in the flat with her Beloved Master, Dan.

Kathy stomped her way up the stairs to the second-floor landing and deliberately stood on the loose board where she knew it would squeak the loudest, aware that Annie was a light sleeper. It was nothing personal, she liked Annie.

With only a tiny twinge of guilt, she took her foot off the board, letting the sound reverberate around the hallway, and finished her journey at her studio flat on the top floor under the eaves. She stood with the door open for a moment, contemplating her life. Kathy literally lived in the rafters. There was one window above her desk and the other two were skylights. One in her tiny bathroom and the other above the kitchen area.

Since Kathy had moved in, no one had seen her room. She was a private person with particular tastes that she liked to keep private. Kathy had a passion: Barbara Cartland. She worshipped her. Despite every single dumping, every single deceit, every single put-down, every single tear shed, she still completely and absolutely believed in The Happy Ending.

Barbara Cartland's books had played a key role during Kathy's tortured teenage years. She couldn't imagine how she would have coped without them. No matter the problem, Kathy never asked anyone for advice, except Barbara.

Under a pseudonym, Kathy had become a renowned authority on Barbara Cartland. Her blog had hundreds of thousands of followers. She wrote critiques, commentaries and essays on the author's life and work. She knew everything worth knowing about Barbara Cartland, and quite a lot that wasn't.

Her latest posts had garnered a lot of interest because who knew that, during World War II, Barbara had worked as a welfare officer with the Women's Voluntary Services and arranged white dresses for women in the service so that they didn't have to get married in uniform? And that she'd lent her name to a perfume? The venture hadn't worked according to Barbara because the perfume was not expensive enough. Kathy wanted the world to know the real Barbara behind the books. Hundreds of thousands of people wanted to know too.

The end result was that Kathy had turned her room into a shrine, albeit an incredibly untidy one.

Three large dolls, each one at least a foot high, all frou-froued up just like Barbara herself, sat on top of the chest of drawers. Each doll held one of Barbara's books in one hand and her white Pekinese under an arm. A corkboard pinned to the wall above the kitchen sink was covered in coloured Post-it notes with motivational phrases about love by Barbara Cartland. Next to that, her vision board included photos representing everything Kathy wished for in life. A battered old shipping trunk stood in a corner stuffed and overflowing with every book that Barbara Cartland had ever written. Dirty dishes and mugs were dotted around the room. Clothes thrown over chairs, a large carrier bag with underwear hanging out of it, ready to go to the launderette, sat by the door.

Practically falling out of the overstuffed wardrobe, the door hanging drunkenly on one hinge, hung Kathy's guiltiest pleasure of all. The pink puffy dress was the most frou-frou of all frou-frous, a veritable explosion in a pink factory. Classic Cartland. A small pink evening bag was filled to the brim with a sparkly, over-the-top bracelet, earrings and necklace and hung around the hook of the hanger. Another bag dangled half-open, strands of hair from a blonde wig spilling out. Kathy had coiffed it just how Barbara liked it. And finally, a matching plumed hat sat on the top shelf of the wardrobe. When Kathy needed advice, she would dress up as Barbara, heavy make-up and all. The sense of dignity and serenity calmed her down and inspiration would come, telling her what she needed to know.

She stomped into the studio, slammed the door shut and threw herself on the bed. The cracking sound of wood signalled the bed leg's demise as it splintered and the bed collapsed, dumping Kathy on the floor. That represented the last straw in a night of last straws. Her eyes welled up and she wept and wept until she ran out of tears.

Exhausted, Kathy fell into an uncomfortable sleep right where she had landed.

4

The alarm rang at 8 a.m. Sheena's eyes sparked open. Leaping out of bed, an act unheard of for a Saturday morning, Sheena was up and in the kitchen drinking coffee with a blank notepad and pen in front of her, her left knee bouncing in place, a blur of excitement, even before the alarm, that she'd forgotten to switch off, had given up ringing.

"Happy Birthday to me! Happy Birthday to me! Happy Biiiiiirthday to meeeee! Happy Birthday to me!"

Sheena danced around the kitchen. "Oh." Her face dropped and she sat down with a thump. "It's my fortieth." She looked briefly depressed but then perked up and, speaking to no one in particular, said, "Who cares? This party will be epic!"

At the top of the blank sheet of paper Sheena wrote the word 'EPIC' in capital letters. Her long, blonde hair flopped onto the page. She pulled it out of the way and wrote 'drink delivery 11 a.m.', 'food delivery 11.30 a.m.' and 'hairdresser 4 p.m.'. Sheena was a lawyer, although, according to at least one of her friends, she was to the legal business what Bridget Jones was to journalism – and that on a good day. Happy to have had a quiet week at the office, she'd done most of the planning and online ordering, with a few minutes here and there attributed to clients' accounts to cover the fact that she was doing arse all to earn the firm money.

The invites to the fancy-dress fortieth birthday party had gone out weeks ago. Sheena wanted a no-excuses-for-not-coming full house. Not that it was her house, exactly. Her parents had bought it and then divided it into four flats. Not only that but they were actually contributing heavily to the mortgage in the mistaken belief that one day Sheena would make partner at the law firm and pay them back. Sheena had the ground-floor flat which was the largest, its main feature being the large kitchen with full-length glass doors that looked out onto a square of dishevelled grass.

Between the kitchen and the living room, she reckoned she could get in a good sixty people. She'd invited ninety, just to be on the safe side. The overflow could huddle on the grass if needs be.

Back to the list, she added 'check fancy dress 9 a.m.' to the top. A recent visit to Spain had given Sheena the idea for the theme of the party.

"Fuck! Party decorations! Where are the fucking party decorations?" In a panic, Sheena ran from room to room looking for the large yellow bag stuffed with streamers, baubles, plastic champagne glasses, cups, serviettes and balloons. The colour scheme involved Spanish-flag yellow and red with quite a lot of random green as she'd found cheap-as-chips Christmas decorations on sale.

She started to spin on the spot until she reached a state of hyperventilation, then grabbed one of the many paper bags littered around the house. She steadied herself and took deep breaths into the bag. Sheena had a tendency for hyperventilation due to her ability to go from calm to the-sky-is-falling-on-our-heads panic in a split second, and her breathing could never keep up.

Her pulse and breathing back to normal, she recalled seeing a very fanciable version of the male species on the bus on her way home. She was so busy trying to look beguiling, interested, aloof, hard to get but easy to catch, and sexy, that she'd almost missed her stop. She'd jumped off the bus completely forgetting the large yellow bag that she'd left on the seat next to her. The man had never once lifted his eyes from his phone, making it all the more aggravating.

"A Spanish flag on that wall, red and yellow balloons hanging from the mirror, four red and four yellow lightbulbs to replace the normal ones. And streamers." She rushed back into the kitchen. "Red and yellow streamers to hang over the black bull on that wall, five red and five yellow spotlight bulbs." She added the items to a shopping list. "Download Spanish music on Spotify. And Sangria, I need jugs. Where did I put that recipe? And, oh Lord, all that food preparation. I've never cooked Spanish food in my life. What was I thinking? Why didn't I start cooking yesterday? Oh God, oh God, I'm never going to get this all done. I need help. HELP!" Sheena screamed at the ceiling. The Wee Besom who lived above gruffed in reply.

Sheena opened her front door and shouted up the communal staircase, "Dan! I need you!" then went back into the kitchen to sit down and wait for him, her best friend, to come to the rescue. Again.

The Wee Besom arrived first, tail wagging madly, ready for action, as Border Collies always are, and needing a pee. She barked at the glass kitchen door and looked pleadingly at Sheena, legs practically crossed. Sheena got up and opened the door a crack. The Wee Besom squeezed through in a rush and you could almost hear the sigh of relief as she relieved herself on the grass.

Dan arrived in boxers, bare feet and a loosely tied dressing gown showing off his muscled, smooth, recently waxed chest and stocky body. He pushed his dark brown hair back from his forehead, took one look at Sheena, realised that whatever the crisis was, it was clearly in her head, as usual, poured himself a mug of coffee and sat on the stool next to her at the breakfast bar. He checked her pulse. It was racing.

"Sheena, you're still alive. Turning forty isn't that bad. Happy Birthday, by the way." He leaned over and gave her a peck on the cheek. "So, what do you need?"

Sheena shoved the list in front of Dan and pointed. And waited.

Dan studied it in resignation. "All right, all hands on deck. I'll get Annie."

He bounded upstairs followed at a brisk pace by The Wee Besom who jumped up three stairs at a time just because she could. Leaping past Dan, their legs tangled and he almost went over the banister. Not for the first time. Recovering his composure, Dan knocked on Annie's door. Sheena's plea for help had reached her ears and, resigned to her fate, she was dressed and ready for whatever. As she left the flat, they looked upstairs at Kathy's front door.

"Did you hear her come in?" whispered Annie.

"Who couldn't have? It'll have registered on the Richter Scale. Shall we ask her to join us?"

They both took one last look at Kathy's door and shook their heads. However, The Wee Besom, who never liked being disturbed from her beauty sleep, charged upstairs and barked at Kathy's door until she heard a faint groan. She wasn't above a bit of tit for tat herself.

Within five minutes, Dan had created a flow chart, barked orders, and sent Sheena and Annie off to do their tasks while he poured himself another coffee and contemplated how to fit the huge order of beer and cava into Sheena's fridge.

5

Kathy woke up on the floor in pain. Her back was complaining, her tongue glued to the top of her mouth, her head was thumping and her eyes so puffy that opening them a slit was a Herculean effort in itself.

As she lay there, her gaze fell longingly on the kettle, willing the tea to make itself. The box of Tetley's sat tantalisingly on the countertop, peeking out from behind the dirty dishes. Kathy briefly wondered if tea fairies existed and, if they did, could they possibly make her a last cup of tea before she expired, thank you.

Her eyes rested on the Post-it notes on the wall and the messages they conveyed. Messages of hope and love. She looked away, a stab of pain going through her heart and saw the mess that surrounded her. *God, if I can't live like a responsible adult then how can I expect the Barbara Cartland happy ending? I'm fucked and I need to do something about it.* Slightly outside herself, hungover and flat on the floor, she considered how the state of her studio reflected her life. On the one hand, a life full of unfulfilled desires and passion for what, she realised, existed only in books and movies, and on the other hand, the real-life mess of her real life. Her flat was a mess. She was a mess. On top of all that, she realised that the only person who hadn't known it until now, was herself.

"Ah, fuck." If she had to learn anything from David dumping her, it was that something had to change. And she had to figure out what.

Effectively mummified by the bedclothes, it took her ages to disentangle herself enough to reach the kettle and make a cup of hot, steaming, reviving tea. Still in her clothes from last night, stinking as they were from sweat and the stale smoke that somehow lingered in the fabric of the pub despite a years-old smoking ban, she gingerly undressed and stood under the shower, tea within reach, and let the pounding of the water on her head waken her up properly. Fresher, and after another cup and the remains of a congealed bacon sandwich from yesterday, she felt better, not a lot, but better.

She dressed in her usual black, her choice since she'd decided that she'd been an abandoned child, completing the look, as always with one vivid touch of colour – a badge, a scarf, a bobble hat, earrings – sometimes blood red, green, sky blue, whatever colour matched her mood on waking up each morning. Occasionally, a huge, startling necklace, and sometimes a tiny dot of colour in her earrings that only she knew about.

She sat at the table with pen and paper at the ready, flung her arms wide, taking in everything Barbara, and asked for her help. "Here I am, Barbara, do your worst!"

She inhaled and exhaled to calm her mind, closed her eyes and wrote down the first words that came into her mind: *Ignored, unloved, abandoned* …

"For the love of fucking God! When I said do your

worst, I really meant your best. Really? I mean, really? We're going there, are we?"

Kathy could see her mother, a dedicated professional in a PR agency, speaking the words that she seemed to use most – "Goodbye! Tidy your room!" – as little Kathy stood at the front door waving her mother off on yet another business trip, trying to hold back her tears. Her mother never looked back.

Her father, a doctor – "Goodbye! Be good!" – never looked back either. At least, that's what Kathy remembered.

And the nannies, lots of them, were employed to look after Kathy and her big brother, William. Practically a queue out of the front door, the fast turnover mostly Kathy's fault. French, German, Bulgarian, Portuguese, Spanish, Argentine, Italian and Norwegian.

Convinced that her parents would rather ignore her than love her, Kathy developed a talent for acting out, each nanny presenting a new challenge. Could Kathy beat her record? How quickly could she have this one hightail it out the house? Kathy had a plan. She always had a plan.

She could, and with an alarming degree of confidence, tell her nannies exactly where to go and what to do with themselves when they got there, in whichever language was appropriate for the occasion. She didn't always know what the word meant, but she did know which ones were the most effective.

Kathy's greatest triumph came in the form of a young, naive French girl who planned to join the seminary after her little 'adventure' in nanny-hood. A sensitive girl. Easy prey. She'd not even unpacked her bag before Kathy was on the case, whispering constantly *pute, pute, pute, pute, putain, pute, pute, pute* in the poor girl's ear. She woke up in the middle of her first night to see Kathy looming over her: *pute, pute, pute*. She was gone by morning. A personal best.

The Italian nanny – *troia, troia, troia* – took longer, possibly because the number of boyfriends who climbed in and out of her bedroom window suggested Kathy's mantra was not too far from the mark. The Norwegian nanny – *jævla fitta, jævla fitta, jævla fitta* – was shocked, at first, but took it in her stride and gave as good as she got. Kathy respected that.

The Argentine nanny seemed oblivious to any and all insults. *Puta, puta, hija de puta*, and some colloquial variations which Kathy learned specially, fell on deaf ears. Kathy gave in gracefully and took note of the cultural differences.

Kathy's belief that she was ignored and unloved was compounded the day she decided that she'd been adopted. Kathy had just turned seven and was seated on a bench in the playground during break eating an orange, throwing the peel on the ground and wondering how long it would take before a teacher shouted at her to pick it up, when she caught a schoolmate staring at her. Kathy stared back.

"What?!"

"Why are your eyes different from William? And your hair? Shouldn't you look the same? I'm just like my sister. You're like someone else."

Kathy realised it was true. Her eyes were striking, different from the rest of the family, and her hair was darker. She looked across the playground at William, who was playing football with his mates. He was nine. Nearly a third of a lifetime older than Kathy. Why were they so different? Shouldn't they have the same colour of eyes? A sharp intake of breath resulted in the first of a lifetime of jumping to conclusions. *I don't belong! This is not my home! My real mother abandoned me!* She took off so fast, running away from herself, that it seemed like she'd left the outline of her body, a part of her soul behind.

Her parents showed her photos of her grandmother. Kathy was the spitting image of her, but they couldn't convince her that she belonged to the family. She was miserable and made it her life's mission to make her family, and anyone else who got in her way, suffer.

The day she found Barbara Cartland was, in her head, probably the happiest day of her life. The pure escapism took her into a different world. Someone had left a book on the bus. The cover was tantalising so Kathy picked it up and from that moment she was hooked.

Just me and Barbara Cartland. The trunk in the corner of Kathy's room was testament to that, bursting at the seams with every romance the novelist had ever written. Barbara inspired Kathy's approach to every relationship. She threw herself heart and soul into every romantic encounter. The characters from the books were shining lights of true romance in the mistaken premise that they would guide her, and guarantee that she would live happily, and dreamily, ever after.

Then she'd get dumped, unceremoniously. Kathy sighed and looked down at the words she'd written. She could not believe what insensitive lumps all her boyfriends had been. Each one had no idea how systematically, and without the grace of being aware of it, they had gone about breaking her heart. No charm, no elegant words. She glanced over at the trunk of Barbara Cartland books. She needed a new plan.

6

The party, in full swing, had divided into three main camps. The lads in the living room had converted the space and the furniture into what only beer-filled minds could easily imagine was a Spanish galleon. While an epic sea battle took place, the women had mainly taken refuge in the kitchen where they were getting blootered. A third group packed the garden, the grass well and truly trampled, the flower beds sporting a growing pile of empty bottles. A queue for the toilet wound around the flat. They were well organised, though, passing plates of nibbles back and forth while they waited.

Sheena was in her element. She'd meeted, greeted and accepted hugs, kisses and presents. Standing in the kitchen, glass of cava in hand, she was now listening to Annie pontificate.

Annie had spent the day running around, on Dan's orders, helping with the organisation of it all, and was now holding forth. Her frame was tiny and her personality oozed Zen, most of the time, and then she'd get on a roll like tonight. The subject, however, was pertinent to the occasion: turning forty. Annie had just turned forty, but like everything else she did, she had the whole decade sussed out just two weeks in.

"What I love about being forty," stated Annie, waving a carrot stick at Sheena, and in the general direction of Mary and the Nicolson twins who had found themselves gathered around her as she was closest to the food, "is that I can finally relax and do what the hell I like. If I don't feel like doing whatever, then I can say so and not agonise over it." She smiled. "What a fucking relief. Anyway," she added, "forty's the new twenty."

The chorus of derision that greeted this remark almost, but not quite, drowned out a loud crash that came from the direction of the living room. Sheena winced.

"Well, all right then," she amended. "That may be a slight exaggeration. Fifty's the new forty, and with a bit of Botox here and there it could even be the new thirty-five, so let's say that forty's the new twenty-five. We're not as old as we thought. Isn't that liberating?"

"No, no, no, no, no, no," said one of the Nicolson twins. "No," added the other, completing her sister's sentence as twins often do. They flicked their long, straight, blonde hair in unison, one to the right and the other to the left, and put their hands on opposite hips, each a reflection of the other, dressed identically in jeans and T-shirts emblazoned with "We're twins!", like nobody would have noticed.

"At twenty-five, I was just a teenager without the spots," said one of them. "I don't want to go back to that," continued the other. "And when you're twins you suffer twice as many spots and twice the anguish of adolescence," said one. "That's no fun, believe me," agreed the other.

"But you're twins. There are two of you. That's two people having spots and adolescence, right? One set of spots and one adolescence each. Like everybody else." Sheena assumed she had stated the obvious.

The twins exchanged a glance and silently shook their heads. Misunderstood, as usual.

"Look," continued Annie, "I'm all for maturity too, just not too much. Nobody's interested in a young immature woman these days. It's the times we live in."

"Yes, but you only think that because the blokes you meet are hitting forty too and they can't pull the young 'uns like they used to so they have to settle for someone a bit older," commented Mary, a woman of few, but usually very pertinent, words.

"Absolutely, I agree." Sheena nodded.

"Yes," Mary continued, surprising the group by her animation. "For example, there's nothing young and attractive about my boobs."

However hard they tried to be polite, their eyes automatically shifted towards her chest. Mary blushed. Now she regretted bringing the subject, or rather two subjects, up. She continued. "Nobody can deny that any man would rather feel a twenty-year-old's boobs than ones belonging to a forty-year-old woman, mature or otherwise. I mean, my nipples seem to spend most of their time these days staring at my feet rather than perked up, ready for action." Mary paused briefly. "You can't tell me that breasts are considered attractive by men when they're pointing in any direction but at them?"

They all fell silent. Sheena couldn't have imagined a better way to dampen the mood of the party if she'd tried.

Kathy appeared out of nowhere with a bottle of cava in hand and stood next to the group in full waiter pose, one arm tucked behind her, a white cloth over her arm and a thumb in the dent of the cava bottle ready to top up the empty glasses.

"Ladies, would anyone like a top-up?" Kathy smiled at them politely. She'd decided to be friendly and helpful. That way no one would suspect anything, even if she hadn't figured out quite what needed to be suspected yet.

A ripple of shock ran through the group. Kathy was being nice. That was unheard of. Especially to Sheena, who she served first.

"Great party, Sheena, well done. In fact, I have to say, your greatest! Happy Birthday!" Kathy slapped Sheena on the back a little harder than she should have done and cava slopped from Sheena's glass.

"Sorry! I don't know my own strength." Kathy smiled at Sheena. Sheena had never heard Kathy apologise before. She'd barely seen her smile. Annie looked at Sheena, Sheena looked at Annie, the twins looked bored, and Mary stared, depressed, at her own boobs.

Kathy realised that she'd overdone the niceness. "I mean, jeez." She picked up the conversation where it had been left off. "Following Annie's logic, she should look about, say, a mature twenty-five and without surgical intervention, she really doesn't have a cat's chance in hell of meeting that particular challenge. As for Sheena, any more operations and she'll need industrial-sized scaffolding to keep those boobs pointing in any direction at all! Gravity ain't your friend ..." She walked off.

Sheena huffed. 36 Ds were only one of many fortieth birthday presents she'd given herself. They were currently squeezed into – or out of, depending on your point of view – a very tight matador-style waistcoat she'd left open to the point where someone who didn't have an imagination wouldn't miss out on anything. She adjusted her boob job and exchanged a relieved look with Annie. Kathy was fine. It was just a brief sideways shift of the matrix which corrected itself almost before anyone had noticed.

Sheena tried to cheer the group up. It was a party, after all. "Let's look at the positive side of our situation. We may not be as perky as we used to be, nor married, but at least we're not divorced."

"Not yet," muttered Amy from the end of the toilet queue. Her husband was one of the chief instigators in the Spanish galleon scheme. The living-room door burst open and a lad fell out, ran into the kitchen, grabbed a six-pack of beer and, with a whoop, threw himself back into the living room and slammed the door shut behind him.

"Who was that?" asked Annie.

"No idea." Sheena didn't really care, as long as everyone was enjoying themselves.

"Anyway, you see?" Sheena was getting into her stride. "We expended huge amounts of energy in our twenties and thirties trying to get married, but most of those who did are now spending the rest of their lives wishing they hadn't. We're suddenly the ones they look up to. We still have the single lifestyle, but with money to throw around: we have fabulous holidays, no kids to worry ourselves sick over, or to be sick over us. On top of that, the married men are in the middle of a midlife crisis and are a nightmare to live with while the single men can indulge in whatever makes them feel, and supposedly, look younger without feeling guilty or looking quite so stupid."

"Good point," agreed Annie.

"Too true," added Amy, who sighed. "I do love him, but he can be a right tit."

Pizza arrived. Sheena had decided that whatever came

out of the Mediterranean that saved cooking time was fine by her. Once she'd double-checked the alcohol supplies, she positioned herself in the hallway close to the front door and fussed over her hair and the perfection of her make-up in the hallway mirror in tingling anticipation of one guest yet to arrive.

7

Sheena had three close male friends. Two of them, Dan and Jack, had arrived at the party early. But one was missing: James.

They were a tight group: Sheena, Annie, Dan, Jack and James. Girlfriends or boyfriends came and went but they always stuck together and confided in one another. That had changed recently. Sheena had taken a shine to James.

Once the New Year had passed, Sheena's eyes had turned to the next major event of the year: her fortieth birthday. It had been approaching at an indecent pace and she'd been boyfriend-less for some time now. One day, Sheena looked at James and saw him in a different light: his dirty-blond hair with the slightest hint of ginger, his oh-so-baby-blue eyes, his pallid skin and freckles. These attributes, the Curse of the Scotsman, now looked so cute. The freckles, she wanted to count every one; his skin, in her eyes, translucent; the ginger tinge, it made her warm all over.

In her mind's eye she ran her hands over his gym-trained body: cute pecs, not too over-developed; strong arms, all the better to be hugged by; washboard stomach which he worked hard to maintain during the week but slipped into a slight pot at the weekends as he indulged his love of real ale and curry. True, he had a tendency to be a bit careless with girlfriends. Got them, dropped them. But he'd calmed down. She hadn't seen him with anyone in at least four months. *Maybe he's ready to settle down. Maybe he's looking for just the right girl.* Sheena wondered if it could be her.

It was late, though, and he hadn't turned up. She shifted her eyes from the front door to check the kitchen clock. The doorbell rang and The Wee Besom went berserk for the umpteenth time that evening. The dog loved a good doorbell. Sheena rushed to the door and pulled it open. She could barely contain her excitement to see James standing there.

"Hi!" She was giggling, nervous. "I thought you were never coming!"

James stepped aside and Sheena felt her heart fall out of her body and go bumping down the steps onto the street to be run over by a passing car.

"Hi, Sheena, meet Lizzie. Lizzie, meet Sheena."

Sheena grabbed onto the door handle for support as her knees buckled under her. "Dan! Dan!" she screamed until he tumbled out of the living room and landed at the front door.

"James! About bloody time ... hello em ..."

"Lizzie, Dan. Dan, Lizzie."

Dan smiled a hello at Lizzie. "I didn't know you were bringing someone, James. We'll lay an extra place at the table." Dan smiled at his own joke. "Lizzie, what'll you be having? Come this way. Have you known our boy long?"

"Three months today. We went out to dinner first to celebrate," said Lizzie.

At that moment, Jack strode into the hallway, full of beans, despite the gallons of beer he'd consumed, his entire six-foot, slim-build body ready for action, as always.

"Jack!" Sheena's eyes were pleading. Jack had no idea why.

"I'm going for a piss. Back in a sec."

Dan continued the conversation as they remained at the front door, Sheena effectively blocking the way into the flat as she hung onto the door for support.

"Did you say three months? James, how did you manage to keep this quiet?" Dan looked surprised.

Sheena tightened her grip on the handle. She really needed a seat.

"You know, just didn't get around to it. Been busy. Lots on. It's not that long since we met." James had the grace to look slightly sheepish.

"Three months today, remember, James." Lizzie looked none too happy.

Jack sauntered back into the hallway. "Well, hello, James. Thank you for gracing us with your presence. And this would be?"

"Jack, Lizzie. Lizzie, Jack." James looked a bit worried.

"I'll get your drink, Lizzie." James nudged Sheena out of the way and whisked Lizzie off, leaving Dan, Sheena and Jack gawping in their wake. Sheena was devastated. Jack and Dan shrugged their collective shoulders and headed back into the living room.

Sheena wandered listlessly into the kitchen, oblivious to the revelry around her, and saw that James and Lizzie had taken their drinks into the garden where they stood in their own private bubble. Heads together, her chestnut hair flowed and blended with his dirty blond. James's head lifted momentarily in laughter then he took her face in his hands and kissed her on the nose. They looked so right together that Sheena wanted to throw up. She reached out and picked up the closest bottle of cava. Half-drunk. Just like her. She decided to complete the process.

***

After her brief appearance at the party, and still the worse for wear, Kathy had gone to bed around midnight, having propped up the broken bed leg as best she could. Ear plugs drowned out the revelling three floors below. As she turned to switch off the bedside lamp, she looked at the framed picture of Barbara on her nightstand. She studied it for a moment then carefully laid it face down, switched off the light and fell into a dreamless sleep. The kind of sleep that comes when you know that the morning will bring the first step towards a new life.

8

Up at daybreak, Kathy tiptoed down the stairs and out of the front door carrying a large box and the key of her elderly neighbour's equally elderly, but in remarkably good condition, green Morris Minor. After Kathy had got some shopping for her one rainy day, they'd discovered a mutual passion for Barbara and had numerous conversations about her books. Had she known what Kathy was planning to do, she would have tried to talk her out of it so Kathy kept schtum about the real reason for borrowing her car. After three tiptoed trips up and down the stairs and three heavy cardboard boxes all safely stowed in the boot and on the back seat. Kathy settled into the driving seat, turned the key and, amazingly, the engine started on the first try. She had indicated to pull out when she remembered something vital: matches and lighter fluid. After a final trip up to her flat and back, she headed off at a stately pace out of Glasgow, through Bearsden and Milngavie, past the reservoir and into the country on the road to Strathblane, on the lookout for the perfect spot.

Seeing a layby partly hidden from the road by trees, she parked and dumped the contents of the boxes into a pile. It wasn't so much a bonfire, in her opinion, as a pyre. Seven hundred and twenty-two books lay there, awaiting their fate. Every single book that Barbara Cartland had written. Except one. One had gone missing.

She stood stock still, staring at the pile of books, the pages flapping in the wind that was slapping her hair round her face as if it were trying to catch her attention. Focused as she was, she didn't even feel the sting. It was her heart that hurt. Broken. Again. This time there seemed no possibility of it mending. Her support system, that is, Barbara, had failed her. Again. If being a devoted disciple to romance and happy endings, tying her heart to Barbara's stories, meant failure time and time again, if it meant she had to endure this pain, well, she couldn't any longer. Kathy was done. She literally didn't have the heart for it. Time for a change.

She pulled herself together and said a little prayer for all her broken dreams, then set about sprinkling a generous amount of lighter fluid onto the pile, recalling the stories as book cover after book cover flapped in front of her eyes. She hesitated. Were they waving goodbye or pleading for clemency? Determined, she turned her back to the wind, lit a match and set the books alight. She walked round and round the bonfire lighting matches and feeling the heat from the *whoosh* when the lighter fluid caught the pages. For a moment she felt uplifted. This was all about new beginnings.

The blaze grew higher and the flames danced, blown with the wind. Sparks flew and a strong gust blew smoke into her eyes. In a fit of coughing, she dragged her smoke-smudged sleeve across her weeping eyes and backed away.

A police car, attracted by the smoke turned into the layby. The officer stepped out of the patrol car, barely the minimum age and minimum height for the force, and strode purposefully towards Kathy, surprised at the unexpected scene.

"Oi!" he shouted, and Kathy turned to face him. Hair wild, face tear-streaked, her black clothes dishevelled and billowing in the wind like a mad woman. She marched towards him, scowling and the police officer backed off before he'd even consciously registered the scene. Better to leave a woman scorned to her own devices. He climbed into his car and parked it at a safe distance to keep an eye on things. He considered calling in reinforcements but knew he'd never live it down.

***

Kathy dragged herself upstairs to the studio, her energy depleted and her ash-strewn clothes leaving a faint trail of grey behind her. The house was silent. She could almost feel the hangovers. She stood in the middle of the room. It felt strange. She felt strange. She looked over at the empty chest. On the inner lining of the chest near the top she could make out the faint childish drawing of a family. Mother, father, young girl. Kathy smothered an involuntary sob. Her dreams, gone. She had killed them, her very own dreams, with her very own bare hands.

She trailed into the bathroom, turned the shower to the hottest setting she could bear, pulled off her clothes, stepped in and let the hot water mix with her tears.

With the shower came the determination to forge a new future. She towelled herself vigorously, trying to push the past behind her. She was on her own now. She had chosen to renounce Barbara. It was time to grow up.

A clean room is a clean mind, she thought, and put dishes in the sink, clothes in the hamper and made the bed. She began to sort the papers on her desk with no greater intention than to, at least, have them in neat piles, and found the final missing book in amongst them. She picked it up and, without thinking, threw it into the now empty chest where it landed with a hollow thud. Kathy reeled as the sound resonated in her heart.

9

As the last person still capable of leaving had left, Sheena consumed her own body weight in Irn-Bru and then, girding her loins, went to check out the living room. As she walked in, the sight caused an intake of breath so sharp she thought she'd swallowed her tongue.

The two sofas had been turned over on their sides, and the long, wooden coffee table, upside-down, placed on top of them. This structure appeared to be the cabin of the Spanish galleon. The legs had been unscrewed from the coffee table and, as she'd witnessed at one point when she'd stuck her nose round the door, were later used as sabres in the battle that ensued when the crew tried to repel boarders. The velvet ropes with tassels, used to tie the curtains back, were tied to the metal rail that supported the ceiling spotlights. As she wondered how they'd managed to reach the ceiling to tie the ropes, she spotted the ladder straddling the cabin structure and sideboard, presumably used to attempt a transfer between 'ships'. The sideboard's doors hung off their hinges. Whatever its role in the battle, it had certainly got the worst of it.

She counted five snoring, beery-smelling bodies

arranged around the room. No, six. Ah no, that one had four legs and a tail. The Wee Besom was snoring in sync. She'd happily bet on all six having foul beer breath. She'd seen one of the lads pour beer into a bowl for The Wee Besom.

"Jings, crivvens, help ma Boab." The chances of the flat ever fully recovering from the devastation of this party were most likely nonexistent. "God help me. Well, I did say it was going to be epic," Sheena muttered to herself.

She put down the now empty can of Irn-Bru and picked her way across the room. She looked down fondly on Dan and The Wee Besom. A friend had left the puppy and gone off to Crete for a two-week holiday, and in true Shirley Valentine-style, fell in love and stayed behind, leaving a four-month-old hyperkinetic, over-hyperactive puppy (if there is such a thing as being over-hyperactive), effectively homeless. So, Dan had kept her, and, despite the fact that she drove them all mad, she did have the most adorable grin when she greeted them, and they always forgave her antics. She'd eat anything. Except potatoes. She had recently celebrated her eighteen-month birthday yet showed no signs of calming down. Sheena dreaded the Terrible Twos.

The Wee Besom lay nose-to-nose with Dan. Both, no doubt, inhaling and exhaling each other's noxious fumes. The Wee Besom's incipient beer belly almost rivalled Dan's. Why they'd crashed out on the floor when they could have crashed out in their own comfortable beds in Dan's comfortable flat just one flight up didn't make much sense. The stairs must have been too much in their collective inebriated state. And it wasn't as if The Wee Besom had her own key.

Sheena adored Dan. The two had been best friends since primary school. They were inseparable as children and then later as adults. They'd only argued once when they'd both fancied the same boy at the same time, and Dan had won. He'd been gay since the day he was born, but he went through a phase of experimentation, wanting to be sure, and Sheena was there to support him. Being the handsome lad that he was, he ended up breaking a few girls' hearts, before concluding what he knew already that, yes, he was definitely gay.

He looked so cute lying there dressed as Agnetha in his ABBA Do Spain costume, the wig skew-whiff over one eye. Dan had only one fancy-dress costume: a blonde wig, shiny blue halter neck top, mini skirt and knee-high boots. He wore it to every fancy-dress party, regardless of the theme, adding whatever he considered appropriate for the occasion. In this case, he carried a pair of castanets and his red and yellow Y-fronts represented the Spanish flag, with the Spanish emblem in the middle covering his *cojones*.

Sheena caught a glimpse of herself in the gilt-framed mirror above the fireplace. A long night of partying in a smoke-scented, beer-soaked room with a bunch of drunkards (and that was only the girls) had taken its toll. As she stepped over Dan to get a closer look in the mirror, her heel cracked on an empty bottle of lager and she sank down onto Dan's hip. He didn't stir so she stayed there, straddling him.

She turned her attention to her shoe and checked the heel of her newly-purchased-for-the-occasion four-inch heels from the currently trendy 'Ye know it's no' Manolo' shop in the Gorbals. "Ah well, for twenty quid what do you expect."

"For fuck's sake, Sheena, give it a rest and go and get some sleep. I'm dealing with a serious hangover here. I don't need your demented mutterings penetrating my brain at a moment like this." Dan massaged his forehead. "By the way," he continued, "dogs don't have the Terrible Twos. Now get off me, you weigh a ton."

"I don't weigh a ton! I'm …" Sheena suddenly realised Dan had heard her talking about The Wee Besom but she'd have sworn blind that she hadn't said a word out loud. She tried to review her thoughts of the last five minutes to see if she'd said anything incriminating, but found the effort too taxing.

Just at that moment a loud anguished wail followed by a scream of "You wee besom!" emanated from the hallway. Someone had left the front door of Sheena's flat open and the screech echoed down two flights of stairs into her living room.

The Wee Besom looked up, startled, and Dan calmed her, stroking her head.

"Sounds like Annie's discovered you've drunk her stash of Irn-Bru," he said.

"Oh, bugger. I'd run out and I thought she'd crashed."

Dan opened a startlingly blue eye and squinted at Sheena. "You'd better nip down to the Wee Shop when it opens at six, otherwise your life's going to be hell. And mine by association," he added.

"God, I don't think I can stay awake that long," she said, peering down at Dan and admiring her new 36 Ds in the process. "Don't you think my new boobs look fabulous?"

"Oh yeah. I became a gynaecologist," Dan said, "because I'm fascinated by the female body and its workings. It truly is the most amazing thing of beauty and practicality. Silicone insults woman and womanhood. You should never have had the operation. Your breasts were just fine."

A shiver of what appeared to be disgust ran through Dan's body as he dislodged Sheena. He turned over and immediately started snoring again.

She picked herself up awkwardly, struggling with her crotch-gripping bull-fighter-style trousers. Imagining an elegant matador striking a pose as he rose to meet a bull head-on, she tried to do the same, but elegance really wasn't her thing. She hauled her ungainly self to her feet.

Limping over to the mirror, broken shoe in hand, Sheena decided to evaluate how the rest of her birthday presents to herself were faring. She moved two empty bottles of Rioja on the mantelpiece out of the way of the antique gilded mirror, and planted herself in front of it.

Not bad. Nice eyes, decent nose, no unsightly kinks, attractively shaped face framed by hair styled by the top man at the currently in-fashion hair salon that promised you hair that would look a million dollars (and had cost much the same). But right now, staring in the mirror, she wanted her money back.

Sheena focused on the collagen. She was all mouth. She could practically see bubbles floating out of the side, such a perfect image of a guppy she made. She'd swear that her doctor had got a deal on a European collagen mountain and had injected the lot in her lips.

"A hatchet man with a degree." She glared at herself in the mirror.

Sheena's doctor was, in fact, her friend William, Kathy's brother, who had strongly advised her not to have the procedure the day before the party because her lips would be swollen before settling down. But had she listened? No. Absolutely not. She was a lawyer after all.

William was an excellent doctor. He inspired confidence through his quiet manner. She'd always liked him even though they weren't as close as she'd become with his two partners, James and Jack. The three of them had studied together and shown a preference for cosmetic surgery.

They'd called themselves 'The Hackers' during their training and set up what had become a thriving and well-respected cosmetic surgery practice in Glasgow's West End. They'd wanted to call the practice 'The Hackers' but fortunately, thanks to Sheena and a pub full of punters, common sense intervened in the nick of time.

Turning back to her 'Mirror, Mirror on the Wall' contemplations, her mind clicked into gear as depression stared back. Now she remembered why she'd overdone the cava. Not that she needed an excuse, but it was always handy to have someone else to blame for the hangover. Come hell or high water she was going to find out why James had kept quiet about Lizzie. She also wanted to know how much he was really into her for her own personal research. To see if she still had a chance.

"Whatever's going on," muttered Sheena to herself, "I'm going to wring it out of him on Monday night."

As she turned, she knocked over the hearthside utensils and they toppled over with a clatter. A round of groans emanated from various points in the room. The Wee Besom, with a gruff woof, lifted her head off the floor and gazed at her, balefully, before letting it drop again. *Now, there's a dog with a hangover if ever I saw one*, she thought, realising that she hadn't.

Sheena picked her way across the living room and around the prostrate bodies. Two she recognised as friends of Dan and Jack, the other two could have been anybody. She tried to avoid impaling anyone with her remaining shoe. She weaved her way around the debris that continued into the hallway, stuck her head out of her front door and shouted up the stairs, "I'm just popping out for some Irn-Bru, Annie!", even though the shop was still closed. She went straight to bed.

10

While Sheena was evaluating the damage of the Spanish galleon in her living room, James found himself happily at home with his hands full, just the way he liked it on a sunny Sunday morning. He poked his nose out from under the sheet to look out the window. The rain was coming down in lumps. He returned to his search for oblivion, Nirvana, or both, in Lizzie's ample, plump, soft breasts. James adored breasts: all kinds, all shapes, and all sizes. He loved helping women be as beautiful as they could be, inside and out. He treated his job as a mission, a true vocation, and a work of art: his work was precise and loving. The ultimate professional on the job, but on a date, as lascivious as the next man. This morning he was revelling in Lizzie's glorious, luscious, heavy breasts and enjoying every second of it.

"Hmmm," moaned Lizzie.

"Is that an erotic '*hmmm*' or an 'I'm going to be sick again '*hmmm*'?"

Lizzie responded by pushing James away and, leaning over the side of the bed, retching into a bucket.

"Damn that cava," she groaned. "What do these bloody Spaniards put in it?"

"Catalans, actually. Anyway, you were well stocious at the party. I practically had to carry you home."

"I didnae have that many glasses," she groaned between retches.

"You were drinking it out a pint glass, sweetie," said James, tenderly.

"It wisnae a pint glass. It was a half-pint glass."

"A minor detail, considering the result."

Grimacing from the unpleasant noises at the head end of Lizzie, he focused on her pale, round Scottish bottom that was pointing up in the air where the covers had fallen off. It was very, very white, with that pale bluish tinge that only comes with never-seen-the-sun Celtic skin. He gave it a loving pat and noticed some cellulite dimples. He prodded one then pinched her buttock. Lizzie attempted to swat him from her vulnerable position hung over the edge of the bed by flinging her arm back, but missed by a mile.

"Leave my cellulite alone. I've told you before. You're not getting any medical instrument on my cellulite!" she croaked, between groans.

Lizzie heaved herself back onto the bed and tried holding her breath. She didn't have the strength to pull the covers back over herself and James rubbed his hands together as he sensed an opportunity to pick up where he'd left off.

Lizzie pushed him away weakly. "Hell, I have to go to work," she moaned.

"But it's Sunday!" squeaked James whose plan of spending an entirely sinful day tucked up under the covers with Lizzie and her glorious body had just gone up in smoke.

"Dad wants to go through the accounts today. It's the only time he can do it. I promised I'd be over there by noon." She dragged herself out of bed and wove gingerly towards the bathroom, stepping on, over, and around her clothes that were scattered all over the floor. She rubbed her freshly pinched buttock. "For a doctor," she said, "you can be a right pain in the arse."

He fondly watched her lovely plump backside as it wobbled towards the bathroom. She had the look of a woman from a different era, a Land Girl he could imagine toiling in the fields in 1940s wartime, in a floral print dress and apron, thick brown tights and brogues with a scarf covering her hair. Lizzie was short and curvy, with a pale, round face, pretty in a homely kind of way. Not at all the kind of girl he normally went out with.

Hearing that Lizzie had made it to the shower in one piece, James reluctantly got out of bed. On his way past he admired his body in the large mirrors on the wardrobe doors. A previous girlfriend, a feng shui expert, had said that mirrors in the bedroom were a big no-no. James didn't care, he needed the daily reminder. The day he couldn't face himself in the mirror would be the day he'd submit himself to the surgeon's scalpel. Either that or get rid of the mirrors. He went to make coffee.

"Lizzie," he shouted from the kitchen in the general direction of the bathroom, "how about bacon and eggs, or I've got a lovely piece of Lorne sausage you can have in a roll if you like?"

The sound of Lizzie retching was her clear response. "It'll be the dry toast then." James stuck a slice of wholemeal in the toaster and prepared fresh coffee. Right on cue, on the dot of eleven, the screech of a set of bagpipes being warmed up came blasting through the window. He winced and then grinned at the effect that was going to have on Lizzie's hangover. James loved the skirl of the bagpipes as much as anyone else but his neighbour's Sunday morning practice was hell. The offending party had nowhere else to go, and was therefore forgiven by the rest of the building's occupants for the unholy noise. James suspected that the main reason no one complained was due to the energy required to get up and shout at the man while hungover and shattered, and by Monday it was forgotten about, until the following weekend.

He carried the coffee and dry toast into the bedroom where Lizzie had gathered her clothes together and was getting dressed.

"What on earth is that?" James snapped before he could stop himself, staring at Lizzie.

Lizzie looked up. "I know, I know. *That* is my normal underwear. My good underwear is in the wash. I was hoping you wouldn't see."

"Your *good* underwear?" He still couldn't stop himself.

"Yes, you know, for nights out, dates, weekends. I can't afford to wear matching underwear every day. Don't you have *good* underwear? Calvins, boxers and maybe an M&S classic Y for those don't-know-what-to-do-with-yourself days?"

"But, I mean, your pants have bits of thread hanging off them and your bra's grey." James ploughed on, unstoppable, into uncharted territory. "That's not really a colour, is it?"

"I'm hardly going out in them alone. I will have clothes on, you numpty." Lizzie paused. "What's wrong with them?" Then. "Ohhhhhhhhhhhhhh, that's it! I'm not like your posh girlfriends. I guess you aren't used to seeing *normal* underwear. The any-day-of-the-week underwear of your average working-class woman. You only go out with the rich girls who have nothing better to do than spend their time and money on their *lingerie*." Aggrieved, Lizzie turned away, then back, her hangover forgotten in a flash.

"Are you trying to tell me that I'm not classy because my underwear isn't top rate? Are you telling me I don't have class because I can't afford posh underwear and I don't have a posh accent? Is it because my Dad's a butcher and I work in his shop every day? Has this to do with the fact that none of your friends knew of my existence and you'd hardly let anyone talk to us last night? You've not introduced me to any of your friends since we met three months ago. Last night was the first time, if you can call what you did last night as *introducing* me to your friends." She paused, thoughtful. "Up till then I'd thought you were a workaholic. You'd never mentioned anyone and now I suddenly realise you've loads of friends."

She was teetering on the verge of a full-blown rant.

James stuttered. "No, no. It meant nothing. No more than an idle comment. It didn't mean anything. Honest." He held his hands up in surrender while offering a silent prayer to the Gods that he'd get away with having planted his foot in the *merde*.

No chance.

"The thing is, James, I've just realised that there *is* something going on here. I just never saw it before." She continued. "Are you a snob, James? Too used to going out with classy, professional, educated women?" She teetered across the room pretending to be wearing high heels and preening herself. "It's odd, after all, a good-looking bloke like yourself, a surgeon no less, attracted to someone like me. You asked me out one day when you came into the butcher's. I had my hand up a chicken's arse, up to my elbows in giblets. You'd seen me a hundred times before. What made you ask me out at that particular moment? Am I an experiment? A bet to find out what it's like to shag a working-class girl? Your bit of rough?"

"No, no, no," begged James. Desperate. "It's not like that at all. Look, I really love you. I really do!"

The bagpipes stopped. James's loud proclamation, over the noise, came out almost a shout. He didn't know where to put himself. Lizzie was staring at him. James thought how the neighbours all now knew his business. Lizzie was still staring at him. His discomfort turned his cheeks crimson.

Lizzie's voice went all soft, almost a whisper. "You love me?"

James's discomfort rose a notch to DEFCON 2. He'd entered fight or flight mode. He took a deep calming breath and another and a final one. He looked at Lizzie, who was watching him very closely, waiting for one false move, then he confessed, his voice quiet. "I do, I really do. I just haven't had the nerve to say it before." The pause was long but sincere. "But I'm saying it now."

Lizzie's heart melted as she watched James struggle with his emotions.

"Well, I love you too." Lizzie smiled as she walked into James's arms. She snuggled up for a whole five seconds then pulled away, with a glint in her eye. "But don't think this gets you off the hook. I'm not that daft. You're ashamed to be seen with me in public." Lizzie searched his face for confirmation. James held her gaze, rigid, terrified. She turned away. "In the meantime, I've got work to do." She finished dressing, grabbed her coat and left.

James's head dropped into his hands and he let out a groan of despair, then another, in time with the renewed mournful strains of the bagpipes. The piper clearly knew what James was going through. He pulled himself together and decided to take a shower. He berated himself for his stupidity. "Idiot!" He lathered himself with soap. "Stupid!" He shampooed. "Stupid fucking idiot moron!" He rinsed the shampoo. "Aargh!" He got soap in his eyes and slammed his hand on the tiled wall in sheer aggravation.

11

Jimmy's Greasy Bucket was calling his name. All James needed now was a mate to join him. He called Dan to check on the state of his hangover.

Dan answered, although no greeting was offered.

"Fancy the full works at Jimmy's Greasy Bucket?" James enquired cheerfully.

"Eeearghcht."

"Ah, I see." James oozed sympathy. "I'll call Jack. Do you think he'll still be with that girl from last night?"

"Eeearghcht," repeated Dan before hanging up.

James rang Jack's mobile and, after establishing that Jack was on his own, Jack himself uttered the magic words. "Fancy the works at Jimmy's Greasy Bucket?"

"You took the very words out my mouth. Get on your bike and see you on the corner in five minutes."

James glanced outside. The rain had stopped, probably a brief respite, and it looked fresh and blustery. A bike ride would blow the cobwebs away.

Catching sight of James as he rounded the corner, Jack, full of energy, as usual, shouted, "Race ya!" and shot off without waiting for an answer. James was particularly slow on the uptake this morning. The loser had to pay for the food and James nearly always had to cough up. Jack charged ahead. He won easily and was in Jimmy's seated at a table by the time James arrived, panting. "This place is heaving. You were lucky to get a table."

"A couple were messing around with their coffee, gazing into each other's eyes. I told them to get a room and leave the table to us. They did."

"Good on ye, man." James laughed.

Jimmy's was a basic, but extraordinarily popular, greasy spoon. It catered for all types, although its weekday clientele tended to be of the humbler variety than the Sunday brunch crowd of professionals who liked its atmosphere and fabulous food: solid Scottish fare. The large plates were piled high with fried everything. The food had just the right amount of cholesterol-raising fat to taste great, but wasn't swimming in it. A delicate balance. The owner's temperament was as changeable as the Scottish weather. An Italian Scot, born and bred in Rothesay, he liked to keep his customers on their toes. A favoured customer could find his bill doubled one week, perfunctory service the next. It was a lottery, and part of the fun. However, James and Jack didn't need to worry: Jack had operated, successfully and for free, on his daughter's cleft palate. The owner treated them like royalty and always refused payment, although they left the correct amount tucked under a plate anyway.

Once settled in, the boys took less than a minute to decide on their order.

"So, that'll be two fried eggs, two sausages, three slices of bacon, black pudding, beans, a fried tomato and a round of healthy wholemeal toast, then?" repeated the waiter.

"That's right, and buckets of coffee," said Jack.

"Heavy night was it then?" said the waiter.

"That it was." James grinned. "I'll have the same and bring plenty of butter for the toast. Thanks."

The coffee arrived, and as James took a sip, Jack spoke. "OK. Give. You've been holding out on us. That's not like you. Come on, spill."

"What?" said James, trying to look innocent. "There's nothing to spill."

"Aw, come on, ye think my heid buttons up the back? James, I've known you for longer than I care to remember. Come on, give. You need to get your story straight because Sheena'll be on your case tomorrow night. Just tell me, I promise to be gentle." Jack smiled, pointing his fork at him.

"I'm in love," said James. He looked stricken.

Jack sat back, shocked at such an honest answer. "And you look miserable because ...?"

"Because she's not the type of girl I ever expected to fall in love with. She's not educated, she's not sophisticated, she's pretty and very natural but she doesn't have style. She works in her father's shop, a butcher's, surrounded by blood and raw meat and gristle all day long."

"And you're not?"

"Ha bloody ha."

"So, what's your problem?"

"That. All of the above."

"So, you're not in love with her then." Jack crossed his arms. Smug.

"How can you say that? Yes, I am in love."

"No, you're not."

"I tell you, I am." James's voice was beginning to rise.

"You're ashamed of her."

"I'm not, honest."

"Aha!" crowed Jack. "You are, so ye are."

"Look," said James, holding his hands up in the air.

"She's not the kind of girl I go out with normally. I just don't think she'd fit in with the group."

"Have you tried?"

"I took her to the party."

"Ah," said Jack in mock pensiveness, hands together, forefingers tapping his mouth, eyes staring into the middle distance. "The party, yes. I noticed how hard you tried to integrate her into the group. The two of you spent the night alone in a corner. A social experiment, was it?"

James looked heavenward, exasperated.

Jack continued. "Do you know why you're annoyed with me right now? It's because I'm right. If you were in luurve, you'd be parading her around even if she wore giblets for jewellery. You can't reconcile her with your innate snobbishness."

"Well, I don't see *you* going out with women that aren't stunningly beautiful."

"Ha! You admit it then."

"No, I don't." He drew a breath. "OK. She's giving me grief about it too. But, I repeat, I don't see you going out with anyone below ten on the gorgeous scale."

"You're absolutely right but that's just the circles I move in. I haven't met anyone else. I wouldn't care if the woman were educated or medicated if I loved her. Anyway, this isn't about me. Don't try to change the subject."

The food arrived, giving James a breathing space. This wasn't going as planned. A lads' get-together to talk about yesterday's matches and to forget the grief he was going to get from Lizzie and, as Jack had reminded him, from Sheena tomorrow night, was all he'd been after. A simple bloke looking for a simple Sunday morning's hangover cure: a mate, the Sunday papers, the footie, and fried food. That was all.

As Jack tucked in, he continued, waving a forkful of black pudding in James's face. "The point is," he mumbled, his mouth full, "you think everyone's as judgemental as you are. They're not. She looked like a really nice person. We'd all have loved to get to know her better. Well, the girls would have anyway. My mind was on the body of that gorgeous model I had with me. Anyway, I have an idea for you: if you need to prove that she can fit in, what better than to take her to the Scottish Plastic Surgeons' charity dinner in Edinburgh?"

James looked horrified. "I couldn't."

"You could have a weekend in Edinburgh. She'd love to be whisked away for a romantic break in a posh hotel. I'm sure she'd forgive your general stupidity, and at the very least, it'd be a good distraction. It's either that or therapy, mate."

James didn't like the look of either idea. "I'll think about it. Now back off."

"Great! Now we can get on to proper manly conversation." Jack picked up the sports section of the Sunday paper.

James was still distracted. "By the way, do you think Sheena's taken a shine to me? She's been looking at me strangely lately."

Jack didn't look up. "Oh, it's probably a bit of a crush. She'll get over it. It'll be all to do with her hitting forty, a midlife crisis. You know what women are like." He held up the sports page of the newspaper. "Stoater of a match, wasn't it?"

12

Kathy woke up on Monday morning after a wild night of dreams, exhausted from all the frenetic mental activity. In the movie that ran, over and over again, in her dream, the heroine was shot, but, wounded and bleeding, she picked herself up and carried on until, triumphant, she got her man. It repeated itself at least five times. It left Kathy physically shattered and her mind in a heightened state of perception, on the edge of hallucination.

As she ate a pedestrian poached egg on toast and prepared sandwiches for lunch, Kathy allowed herself to feel optimistic, to imagine that independence from dependence on Barbara could be good for her. The dream was telling her that she could do it. She could get her man. She could go it alone.

But could she? Barbara had always given her the inspiration to carry on. Could she do it alone after all? She wondered if there would be a moment when she would just give up.

On her way to work, all the non-important things in life receded into the background, highlighting what was left. None of it was what made life worthwhile. It was the injustices, the little cruelties that one human casually played on another. The slights thrown by one man at his wife: he in a business suit with a small, probably empty except for the newspaper and a sandwich, briefcase in one hand, walking next to his wife who was struggling with everything she had to carry while holding her young son's hand and pushing a stroller with the other. Calling her stupid and useless because she'd forgotten the child's school lunch. Then striding off to work, leaving his wife struggling, weary and downtrodden, behind. The disdain shown by a woman, dripping in jewellery, to a man, begging, by her side. All he wanted was some change. "I'm not an addict, I'm not a drunk, I'm just homeless and hungry. Just a few pennies for my breakfast, love, please." The angry shout by a father to his son who just wanted his father's attention, and acting out was the only way he could get it.

Something has to be done, thought Kathy. *Life is shit. Life is not fair.* "It's not fair!" Kathy's childlike exclamation was accompanied by a solid kick of a can into the middle of the road where she watched it instantly flattened by the wheel of a passing car. *There are those who get what they want and those, like me, who don't get the happy ending. We try, we struggle and yet, most of the time, it's denied us.* Across her mind flashed images of her childhood disappointments, her belief in her adoption, her relationships that always ended in tears, regardless of her deepest Barbara-inspired wishes. All Kathy could think about was that she had to do something about it. She just didn't know what, yet.

For the last two years, until six months ago, Kathy had worked as a private nurse through a temp agency. Her last job involved a rich octogenarian with wandering hands. She was at her wits' end and on the point of chopping off all of his wandering appendages when William had called.

Jack desperately needed an assistant nurse at their practice. On the one hand, she was desperate to get away from the octogenarian's hands, and on the other hand, her own hand, she was a bit nervous about working with Jack. She hadn't seen him in a long time, and, after what had happened between them, she really didn't fancy being around him all day.

On the other, other hand, she was just going to be a nurse. It wasn't as if she'd be with him all day every day. And then she needed to consider James. She hadn't seen him for some time either, and wasn't too chuffed about the prospect of being around him too. But, on a final count of hands, she decided that she needed a change and the job at the clinic wouldn't be too taxing. Almost a holiday. Just what she needed.

The final decision was made even easier for her when William put her in contact with Sheena, and she moved into the studio at the top of the house.

After seeing the can flattened in the middle of the road, the rest of her journey to work was focused on what she could do to change her life. None the wiser, when she finally settled down behind her desk, the sense of not being quite all there continued.

At times she was completely unaware of the business-as-usual activities of the day, totally absent-minded, and at other times hyper-aware of every detail. Without Barbara, she was a ship without an anchor. She shook herself, trying to feel herself again. She realised how dependent she'd been on Barbara. "Well, that's going to stop!" Kathy muttered to herself. Jack raised an eyebrow at her as he walked past her desk. She gave his back the finger, the petty action she did every time his back was turned. It was childish but it always made her feel a little better.

Except this time, it didn't.

Kathy wasn't the only one having a somewhat interesting start to the week.

13

Sheena had just committed the crime of the century, and it was barely 8 a.m. Its name was fuchsia. She'd decided it was time to break a few rules.

As a lawyer in the stuffy, old-fashioned Glasgow law firm, Dun, Miles & MacDonald, Sheena was traditionally condemned to black, shades of grey, and mud. And white shirts. She looked at herself in the full-length mirror to get the full effect. The fuchsia front-buttoned coatdress was elegantly pinched in at the waist and a suitably demure knee length. She'd left the lowest button undone for ease of movement. What it revealed when she sat down left precious little to the imagination. The perfect combination of serious and sexy, in her eyes. With heels higher than normal and jewellery brighter than usual, Sheena was very pleased with her forty-year-old self.

She strode into the kitchen to find Annie having breakfast. Raiding Sheena's kitchen was not an unusual occurrence. Most weeks it seemed like she was feeding the whole house, along with the neighbourhood mice. Annie's mouth dropped open, revealing her choice of breakfast fare: toast and marmalade. She forced it closed again, chewed rapidly, swallowed, then spoke.

"You look amazing. Why so glammed up at the crack of dawn on a Monday?" A pang of apprehension tinged Annie's tone. "Don't you have work to go to?"

"I do and I chose this outfit to brighten up that boring old office. Anyway, I don't have any meetings scheduled," said Sheena, trying to look casual.

"No, no, no! Please, God, no!" Annie sprinted to the foot of the stairs and let out an ear-splitting shriek. "Dan! Get down here quick!"

Sheena glared at Annie. For someone normally the most Zen of individuals, requiring a certain stable and meditative character for her job as a chiropractor, Annie sure as hell was doing a lot of shrieking these days.

Dan came flying out of his bathroom and down the stairs attired in only the tiniest of hand towels, which he held decorously in front of himself; the other hand waved a shaving brush around as if it were a weapon. "Where's the fire?"

"It's, it's ..." Annie put her hand over her eyes and pointed at Dan's bits. "Please ..."

Dan unhooked an apron from the back of the door and tied it on. "Better?"

Annie peered through the space between her fingers. "Sort of." Then pointed at Sheena. "Look."

Dan looked Sheena up and down. "You look very smart, Sheena," he said. "Good for you. So, where's the fire?"

"Sheena plans to go into the office dressed like that. You have to stop her," pleaded Annie.

"Ah, that's all? Well, that's her problem." Dan turned to go, his bare buttocks wagging cheekily at them as he walked off.

"Wait, Dan. If she gets herself fired, as she may well do ... I mean, it's been a long time coming, after all." Sheena gave Annie the evil eye. "Then she'll be mooching around the house all day long, bored, worse, broke. How will she pay her part of the mortgage? Will her parents pay it all or kick her out through sheer disappointment?" Sheena's gaze intensified. "They might decide to sell the place and kick us all out. Where will Sheena go? Where will we go?"

Dan turned back. "You have a good point there," he agreed, using the dripping shaving brush as a pointer. He turned to Sheena. "Why are you doing this? You know it makes no sense."

"I'll be fine. I want to brighten the place up a bit, that's all. I'll bet we'd get more clients if we had a cheerier outlook. See it from my point of view. My clients tend to be serious. Wouldn't they feel better if I was upbeat?"

Dan looked at her, worried. "This fortieth birthday stuff has addled your brain. You're *supposed* to look serious. That's how clients know you can do your job. They don't want frivolous. Fuchsia is frivolous. You'll probably find a law dated circa 1619 stating that lawyers are forbidden to wear fuchsia."

"Oh, don't worry about it," waved Sheena dismissively. "Nice beer gut you're developing there, Dan." She patted his pot as she crossed the kitchen to pour herself coffee, deftly changing the subject, knowing that Dan would take the bait.

"I know," he groaned. "It'll be double time in the gym every day this week, and no booze, to get my six-pack back." He wandered out stroking his abs worriedly.

Annie followed him. "Now I'm going to have to meditate to calm down and prepare myself for work." She gave Sheena a final once-over from top to toe. "You've totally destroyed my equilibrium."

Muttering to herself as she stuffed stacks of papers into her briefcase, Sheena prepared to leave for the office. She stood erect, her surgically enhanced chest out, shoulders back, chin in, just like her primary school teacher had taught her. Sheena was prepared to fight for her right to wear fuchsia.

14

♋

The lift door pinged as it opened at the second-floor offices of Dun, Miles & MacDonald and Sheena walked into reception humming tunelessly. Her heart sank. It always did. The reception area was what the word 'uninspiring' was invented for. The walls could only be described as 'insipid' and the reception furniture was as grey as the receptionist, although, admittedly, Margaret's blue rinse did add a touch of colour.

Sheena paused briefly, then with a muttered 'here we go', she marched across reception. Margaret observed her over the top of her half-moon glasses. She had never taken Sheena seriously as a lawyer. Her expression, disapproving as usual, appeared particularly intense this morning: the lips were that bit more pursed, the brows more tightly knitted together.

"You're late," squeaked Helen, Sheena's secretary, hysterically, as Sheena approached her office.

"So? I don't have any meetings today."

"Well, you do now," said Donald MacDonald as he walked into the office and stopped dead at the sight of

Sheena's attire. He shielded his eyes with his hands. "Help, I'm blinded by a colour that I think is banned in this office."

"Ha ha," said Sheena. "Don't tell me you don't like my new look."

"I'd say it's the fastest way you've come across yet to get fired, especially as Mr Dun wants you in a meeting with him right now. There's a partners' meeting and no one else is free. You need to get your arse in that conference room and pray that Mr Dun forgives you."

Sheena threw her briefcase and an evil look at Donald then set off at a trot, as best she could in her high heels, for the conference room. She opened the door and stopped short. It was a sea of black suits. All the partners were in the room along with several other lawyerly types and one very chiselled chin with eyes, those eyes ... Donald came rushing up behind her, grabbed her by the shoulders, swivelled her and gave her a gentle push down the corridor. "The other conference room, Sheena."

"What's going on?" she mouthed to Donald. Even she could tell that this was no ordinary meeting. Donald ignored her and with an apology to the group inside, closed the door and joined the meeting, leaving her outside

As Sheena entered the other conference room, her bright attire seemed to make the stuffy furnishings look gloomier than usual. Floor to ceiling bookshelves were filled with not recently dusted legal books. The conference table was made of dark oak. It was solid and imposing with solid and imposing chairs surrounding it. The ancient beige wallpaper could probably have told incriminating tales of meetings there. The lower halves of the windows were stained glass which only allowed in a brownish-yellow, shitty light. The overhead lighting only added to the gloom, undoubtedly another inspiration from the same architect who had designed the reception area. Miss Haversham would have felt comfortable here.

Sheena dared a quick glance in Mr Dun's direction. The senior partner was staring, shocked, at her dress. He and the new clients were dressed in dark suits, dark ties and white shirts. Sheena stood out like a tart at a funeral. She sat down and pulled her dress as demurely as possible over her knees. Squaring her shoulders and trying to look professional, ignoring the stares, she dug out her Montblanc pen and sat with it poised over her legal pad, ready for action.

Mr Dun gave Sheena a last questioning look loaded with disapproval and annoyance; it promised retribution while tinged with the tiniest bit of resignation, demonstrating that this was not the first time that Sheena had provoked this reaction. "Sheena, I'd like to introduce you to Mr Hugh McNally and his friend Mr Charles Campbell. They are colleagues of a distinguished client of the firm."

Hugh McNally stood up and stretched his wiry body to its tallest, which was still, nevertheless, considerably shorter than Sheena's high-heeled frame, as she stood to greet him. He extended a small, thin hand. "Aye, hello there, pleased to meet ye. Call me Shug, everyone else does. Ah dinnae mind. And this gentleman here is Charles."

The chair rumbled back as Charles stood up. He extended a giant hand towards Sheena. She almost cricked her neck to look up at him. "Good morning, pleased to meet you." His polite Edinburgh accent was a shock against Shug's Glaswegian.

As they settled back in their seats, Sheena looked from Shug to Charles and back, her eyes open wide in surprise. They didn't fit the profile of their typical client. They looked like thugs or something dodgy. Sheena coloured as she glanced over at Shug just in time to see him drag his eyes away from her over-exposed cleavage, so out of place.

Shug internally reproached himself. *Ah am an honourable man, ah respect women but sometimes they jist fling it in yer face. What can ye dae?* He shifted, uncomfortable.

Sheena tried to get a grip on her embarrassment and focused on Shug's face, a veritable unfinished Picasso. She fixated on the burst blood vessels on his nose. The longer she stared, the clearer the shapes appeared in the red lines; like cloud shapes, she saw what looked like a rabbit with long ears holding a shovel. She snorted involuntarily, so engrossed in the strangeness of it all that she forgot she was in a meeting.

Mr Dun rapped his knuckles on the table. "Sheena!" Her trance broke and she cleared her throat and smiled sheepishly at Shug. "Pleased to meet you, Mr McNally. My apologies for not being up to date on your case. Perhaps you could briefly recap your situation?" She gave him a winning smile, designed more for the purpose of calming Mr Dun down than flirting with Shug.

"Well," started Shug. "Ma wife—"

"You're married?" Sheena said, incredulous, eyebrows raised high. "I mean, I'm sorry, for how long have you been married?" She wondered how on earth someone who looked like that had managed to get married when she was still working her way through the male population of Glasgow at forty.

"Ma wife," Shug repeated, looking somewhat tense, "cheated on me. Not only do ah want a divorce but ah want tae sue the milkman for emotional distress. Ah read that ah can do that." He sat back with his arms crossed.

Sheena drew a deep breath and held it for a few seconds

to try to control what could easily turn into a guffaw. "You want to sue the milkman?" she squeaked. "Were his deliveries not up to standard?"

"Oh aye, and there were a few more deliveries than ah'd asked for given directly tae my wife, if you see what ah mean." Shug glared defiantly at Sheena.

Sheena struggled for control. "You mean that the milkman was having an affair with your wife? What kind of emotional distress did you suffer?"

"Ah caught them at it. Doin', ah don't like tae say, things with milk products that you could never imagine. Ah was shocked. Ah am a traditional man. The idea that my wife was doin' it with the milkman was bad enough but with whipped cream ..." Shug stopped, unable to continue. Charles put a comforting hand lightly on Shug's bony shoulder while throwing a warning stare in Sheena's direction.

Sheena was helpless. The guffaw that emanated from way below her tonsils could be heard a block away. A dog howled in sympathy. Her hands flew to her face, too late, in an attempt to stifle it. If Mr Dun had looked horrified before, then he was apoplectic now. Sheena snorted and then couldn't hold it in. She howled with laughter. She couldn't stop. She tried, really tried to contain herself but only became hysterical.

Charles slammed his hands on the table and leaned forward, his nose inches from Sheena. She shrank as far as she could into her seat.

A sepulchral silence echoed around the room.

Charles's voice, Fettes-educated, was low and menacing. "You do not treat Mr McNally like that. I will ensure that you, and your firm, are brought to task for this."

Shug stood up and pulled himself up to his full five feet two inches. "Ah was told that this was a respectable firm. You," he pointed, arm extended at Sheena, "and your colleagues have no' heard the last o' this. You dinnae insult a McNally and get away with it." At that, Shug marched out the room, the door held open by Charles whose last icy glance at Sheena as he walked out turned her pale.

He slammed the door. Sheena and Mr Dun jumped.

Mr Dun turned to Sheena. "Get out. I don't want to see your face again today. I want you in my office at 9 a.m. sharp tomorrow morning. I need to work out what to do with you." He put his head in his hands with despair as Sheena got up to leave and, with a furtive look outside to make sure that Shug and Charles had gone, closed the door very, very quietly behind her.

15

⌁

As a point of principle, Sheena never rejected an invitation, even if it meant running between events on the same night. But Monday was stay at home night and, to liven it up, she had invented Gossip Night. It provided an opportunity to discuss the weekend's events, gossip about anybody and anything and complain about whatever they liked. No one was allowed to be judgemental, (aye, right), and they were supposed to be caring and sharing or else they didn't get invited back. Gossip Night had only one rule: no dancing around the details, no holds barred.

James, Jack and William often joined Sheena, Dan and Annie. Occasionally, others of their extended group of friends were invited, but only if they had particularly juicy news.

At 8 p.m. Dan wandered through the hall on his way to the living room with three empty glasses and a bottle of Rioja while Annie went to answer the main door. She could see James standing outside, nose pressed to the glass making faces. He held up the obligatory bottle. As Annie ushered James in, William came rushing in behind them waving a pack of beer. Entering the living room,

Dan could still smell the beer and cigarette smoke despite having helped out in a listless post-party cleaning session on Sunday.

Sheena had had a head start. She was sitting on the living-room floor surrounded by cava bottles and looking pie-eyed. She'd exchanged her fuchsia dress for a tight, white T-shirt, tracksuit bottoms and purple four-inch stilettos. The Wee Besom was at her feet with a worshipful expression on her face. Sheena was feeding her ham sandwiches.

Sheena picked up a near-empty bottle and waved it in greeting at Dan, while trying not to spill her over-full glass in the other hand. Carefully placing the bottle back on the floor with the wobbly precision of a drunk trying to avoid a breathalyser, she pointed at her shoes. "D'ye like my new shoes? I got them today but I have to break them in – they're digging in at the side there." She moved to indicate where it hurt, splashing cava onto The Wee Besom's nose in the process.

Dan took one look at Sheena. "What's going on?" And, remembering her earlier attire, he said, "Oh God, what have you done now?"

Sheena ignored his comment and made an attempt to get up onto the stilettos but failed and flopped back onto her bottom and leaned against the sofa.

At that point, Annie appeared with James and William. Sheena gave James a big, leering, drunken grin intended to look flirtatious. He grimaced and looked away.

"Come and sit next to me, James." She smiled, patting the floor next to her.

James loosened his tie, took the glass of Rioja that Dan proffered and looked around for a seat out of Sheena's line of sight. He finally slumped onto the sofa Sheena was leaning against so she couldn't see him without twisting around.

William settled himself on the sofa opposite and Annie folded her petite body in one corner next to him and pulled her hair back into a ponytail, ready for action. Dan handed her a glass of cava.

"Right," said Dan as he made himself comfortable. "Let's get down to business. Sheena, without a shadow of a doubt, you have to go first."

Sheena related her version of the events that had taken place in the conference room that morning. Finished, she looked around, hoping for, expecting sympathy. They looked, without exception, shocked.

"Aw, come on, guys," she slurred. "You have to admit it was funny. I mean, the milkman and the whipped cream and the husband who looks like a gargoyle."

"You were in a business meeting," said William. "Where's your self-control? Imagine if I fell about laughing every time a client came in with a ridiculous request or a huge, knobbly nose, or whatever. Do you think I'd still be in business?"

"Well, no," admitted Sheena. "But this was different. I mean, no one with any sense could have maintained their cool under those circumstances."

Annie shook her head. "You've really blown it this time, haven't you? You've been fired, haven't you?" Annie threw up her hand in disgust.

"So, it was really only a matter of time, Sheena." Dan articulated what the others were thinking. "I don't understand why you do this to yourself. You're a good lawyer when you want to be."

Sheena hung her head in shame, briefly, then looked up brightly. "Oh, I don't care. Anyway, I haven't been fired. Mr Dun wants to see me in the morning. I'll probably just get a warning and I'll have to promise to behave from now on. Something like that. Cava, anyone?" She leaned over, grabbed a full bottle of cava and proceeded to take off the foil cover, concentrating hard to keep her eyes in focus.

Just in time to relieve the tension, the doorbell rang. The Wee Besom knew exactly who it was and rushed to the door for all the world as if, one day, or maybe even today, she'd be able to open it and launch herself at one of her many favourite people, Jack. As it was, all she could do was wait, barking, just in case no one else had heard the doorbell. She took that responsibility very seriously, and grinning, in that special way that Border Collies do, hopped from foot to foot in impatience like a dressage horse prancing around a ring, until, finally, James opened the door for her.

After a solid minute of "Good girl", "Who's a good girl?", "Who's a gorgeous Besom then?", "Who's a good girl?", "There you go", "That's it, calm down", and with a final "Will you sit down?!", The Wee Besom finally got over all the excitement and sat down next to Annie. He could always rely on her for an ear scratching, her third favourite thing after a good back scratching, that bit just above the tail that she couldn't reach herself, and a belly rub, both of which came in at number one.

Glass in hand, and after a brief update on Sheena's state of affairs, Jack's only comment was: "For the love of God."

Annie made one last plea. "Sheena, please stop drinking now otherwise you're going to feel awful tomorrow morning."

"Nah, I'll be fine." Sheena emptied her cava glass and raised it in a salute to Annie.

Annie shifted, making herself comfortable, and provided a welcome change of subject. "I have a confession to make."

16

Annie waited until she had their attention then continued. "I was trying out a new man last night when —"

"Hold on a sec," said Dan. "Stop right there. What do you mean 'trying out a new man'?" His fingers made air quotes. He glanced over at Sheena. "Take note, Sheena. This is the kind of gossip we're after." Sheena gave him the finger.

"Well," Annie began her story, "things haven't been going that well with Sandy lately. You all know I've been a bit bored, so I was eyeing up this guy at the party on Saturday night. I don't know who he'd come with as I hadn't seen him before but, anyway, we exchanged phone numbers."

"But you were with Sandy at the party, weren't you?" Sheena tried to remember if she'd seen him in amongst the crowd.

"Yes, but he wasn't really paying me much attention and it was late in the evening when he was too drunk to notice. I mean, this guy was really cute. Maybe you remember him? Tall, deep, dark eyes, and dark hair, very Italian."

"I remember him," said Dan. "Great sense of dress, like all Italians. I spoke to him for a while. His name was Marco, wasn't it? But I don't remember you being with him."

"My dear Dan," interjected Jack. "For most of the night you were *far* too busy to notice what was going on around you."

Dan looked puzzled for a second then smiled. Once the galleon battle had been done to death, and Dan had gone in search of another beer, he'd spotted an extremely cute twenty-three-year-old, a friend of a friend and definitely someone whom Dan intended to keep in touch with.

Annie continued. "That's the one. Marco. Well, he phoned me yesterday and we arranged to go out to dinner. We went to the Chip and had a lovely time. He sat next to me at the table and was very romantic, not at all like your average Scot. He had such a cute accent. 'I wanna curdle you', he kept on saying to me."

"Curdle?" questioned James.

"'I wanna curdle you alla the night.' Oh yes. The man likes to curdle. He kept kissing my hand, my arm, my neck. We hardly ate. We were too busy curdling. It was one of those situations where food became superfluous and dessert promised to be a really good shag."

Dan let out a whoop.

Annie continued. "Sandy hasn't been delivering the goods recently so I thought I'd take my try-out a step further and go to his place. We paid the bill and as we were walking out of the restaurant, we had to pass a table where," she paused, "you'll never guess, Sandy was seated snuggling up to his ex!"

The boys roared with laughter and Sheena clamped her spare hand in front of her mouth and hiccuped gleefully. The Wee Besom did a victory lap around the coffee table and then flopped down at Dan's feet and stared at him in adoration, tongue lolling.

"Brilliant stuff! This is the best gossip we've had in

ages. Tell us what happened next." Dan leaned forward, not wanting to miss any lurid details.

"What happened was terribly British, terribly stiff upper-lipped. We exchanged polite smiles. I introduced Marco to Sandy and Sandy introduced that slag of an ex-girlfriend to Marco and then we left. But, God, I was spitting. I didn't know he was seeing his ex, the bastard. No wonder he wasn't delivering the goods. He was too busy delivering them elsewhere."

Sheena pointed an accusing finger at Annie. "Pot, kettle, black. You can hardly call Sandy a bastard unless you include yourself in that statement. You were cheating on him too, you know."

"I wasn't exactly cheating on him. I was just testing the market. Anyway, at that point I hadn't shagged Marco."

"You were leaving the restaurant for the sole purpose of a good shag!" exclaimed

Sheena, taking a large swig of cava. "And I think snogging someone who's not your current boyfriend comes under the category of cheating."

Annie continued. "I'm thoroughly pissed off with the man. That's the relationship over. Shit. I wasn't really ready to break up with Sandy. All I'd wanted was a back-up plan."

"Well, maybe that was his plan too. Why don't you call Sandy and sit down and talk it out with him? Maybe you can fix this if you're both willing," said William. "How much will the tickets be to sit in on that conversation?"

Annie swiped him with a cushion. "Do you want to hear the rest of the story or not?"

"You mean, there's more?" they chorused. Annie paused, gathering her thoughts. Sheena pulled herself up onto the sofa and sat sideways on it to continue to smile flirtatiously at James. Seeing what she was up to, James pulled up a chair and sat out of Sheena's line of sight.

Annie continued her tale. "Remember, Marco is gorgeous. He has that clean-shaven, really handsome look about him that is *so* my thing. I'd completely forgotten about Sandy and his ex by the time we'd got to his equally gorgeous flat. He's an architect and it was really stylish in a kind of minimalist style, all light and airy and with a great view over the Clyde. So, there we were, and it was all getting a bit heated and then ..." They all leaned forward, gripped. She took a long slow sip from her glass and then, assured that they wouldn't miss a word, continued, her voice low. "He went to the bathroom and came out naked."

They all sat back, confused and deflated. The Wee Besom looked at Dan, and raised one eyebrow questioningly. Dan responded with a Gallic shrug of his shoulders. They both looked back at Annie.

"What's so awful about that I hear you ask? Normally, nothing. But he was as hairy as a gorilla. And I mean *really* hairy. His entire body was covered in thick, black hair: his back, his chest, his arms, his legs, even, like, tufts on his *bottom*, for Christ's sake, and do you know how I know that? Do you? Do you know how I know that?" Annie's voice rose. Simultaneously they chimed in, "No, Annie, I don't."

Annie looked at each one in turn. "He did a twirl. He was that proud of himself. It was horrible." Annie put her head in her hands. "'Let's make lurve,' he said. 'Let's make lurve alla the night.' He just stood there, hands on hips with a huge grin on his face. I couldn't tell if it was because he thought he was well-endowed or, or what, because I can tell you, what was sticking out through all that hair was really nothing to write home about. Mind you, I could hardly bear to look. And it was like he expected me to be happy."

"Annie shagged a shag pile," snorted Jack. Annie ignored him and continued. "He obviously shaves himself every morning to make sure that nothing is visible around his collar or wrists. Anyway, I just couldn't touch that hairy Italian specimen. I couldn't wait to get out of there. I left him standing there, naked." She shivered. "I'm still traumatised."

Dan screwed up his face. "I can't understand why men don't just wax."

"I haven't heard from him since, which is hardly surprising, and now I don't even have Sandy." Annie looked sorry for herself. William gave her a reassuring pat on the leg.

The main front door slammed and all heads turned.

17

Everyone held their breath. Kathy was invited, as a member of the household, to Gossip Night, but her absence was usually more welcomed than lamented. They waited, not sure if she would come in. Kathy marched, heavy booted as usual, up the stairs and into her studio and slammed the door shut behind her. They exhaled in a collective sigh of relief as the echo came down the stairs.

Jack asked, "Does anyone know what's up with Kathy? She was positively spaced out all day. She had this weird kind of half-smile on her face and patted my hand several times. I think she was channelling my grandmother."

"There was definitely something odd in the air today. My secretary almost got me sued. I had to fire her, again," William added.

"There you go, Sheena!" Annie said. "William has a job for you if you get fired!"

William tried hard to hide the look of horror on his face.

"Well, I mean, when I said that I'd fired her, it was only a manner of speaking. I'll keep her on for a bit. You know, second chances and all that." William wiped the sweat off his brow.

"Third, fourth or is it the fifth time?" James grinned.

"It'll be fine. It'll be fine." William looked pleadingly at James.

"OK," slurred Sheena, now seriously drunk. "James!" She twisted round into his line of sight and waved an accusing finger at him. She attempted to mark the points off on her fingers. "One: that whatshername, girl? Why'd you," she waggled her finger at him, "I mean, we, not know about her? Two: eh, why'd you bring her to the party if, if, em, you didn't want any of us to talk to her?" The effort of thinking and talking at the same time was almost too much for her. "Three: what's the secret, her secret, your secret? Four: em, oh, whatever. Just tell us *everything*."

James didn't look happy at the prospect of an interrogation. Sheena was looking at him intently, if blearily. He stood up. All eyes focused on him, expectant.

"Jack's already been on at me about it. I don't need you all sitting in on judgement too. I'm off."

There was a chorus of "Hey, that's not fair!" as James strode out of the room.

"I know the story," said Jack, grinning. All eyes turned to him. "I'll tell you for the price of a pakora and chips supper. I'm starving." Without hesitation and with a nod of confirmation from Annie, Sheena picked up the phone and speed-dialled the Taj Mahal.

18

Kathy was glad that her Monday was nearly over. She slumped into a chair in her studio. Her energy tank had ticked down to zero. She looked listlessly over at the empty chest. That one lone book sat in the bottom. She could just see the cover. *Running Away to Love.* She remembered that raging story of love and secrets, hardship, passion and despair, loyalty and deceit, the grit and strength of character it took for the heroine to get her happy ending, and surprised herself with the wave of nostalgia that swept over her.

Only a day had gone by since she had burned the books; even so, she now knew what life without hope was like. She realised that she still wanted to feel these emotions, both in fiction and in reality. She really, really missed the books. She missed Barbara.

"Oh, God," Kathy spoke out loud. The sensation felt like a punch in the stomach and she doubled over. "That's it. No boyfriend, not even the prospect of ..." She looked at the chest and was stricken. "I can't even live vicariously through Barbara's books now. What have I done?"

She made herself a cup of tea, sat back down and,

staring at the book cover, she realised that alone, without hope or joy in her life, life itself was too ordinary. She didn't want ordinary. She wanted extraordinary. Preferably of the male variety. A man of grand gestures, of breakfast in bed, surprise weekends away and flowers on a Monday morning. Barbara's books may have gone up in flames, but all those chivalrous heroes still burned in Kathy's heart.

She realised that she was in danger of losing her faith in romance, in the happy ending, and that if she lost that, she'd have nowhere to go and no one to be. Kathy jumped up and shook her entire body like a wet dog that had chased a duck into a muddy pond. She had to figure out what to do, what needed to be fixed, and how to fix it, and then she could move forward. Kathy had thought that she'd given up on love but she realised that she wasn't done.

There and then, as a form of atonement for the sacrilege she'd committed, Kathy lit a candle as a prayer of apology to Barbara along with the promise that she'd buy all seven hundred and twenty-two books again. The question was: what now?

19

Sheena almost cried at the piercing sound of the 7.30 a.m. alarm. She grabbed the clock and launched it across her bedroom where it hit a vase of flowers, knocking it over. Clock, vase, flowers and water crashed to the floor, increasing the noise level exponentially.

She dragged herself out of bed and, barely taking her head out of her hands, managed to swallow two paracetamol without throwing up. On any other day she would have invented an illness to avoid having to go into the office, but today her career hung in the balance.

Dan and Annie had come to see her off. Dan was in the hallway as she wove her way to the bathroom but failed to acknowledge him. He went into the kitchen where Annie, wooden spurtle in hand, stirred a large pot of porridge clockwise, as tradition dictates, to avoid summoning the devil.

"I hope for both our sakes it works," commented Dan, glancing at the porridge as he spooned ground coffee into the Italian coffee pot. He believed that rocket fuel was the only way to start the day.

As Annie stirred, she looked into the pot's gently

bubbling grey depths and hoped that it would work its magic. She believed that porridge cured all ills: physical, mental and spiritual. A tranquil atmosphere prevailed in the kitchen as Annie contemplated the mysteries of life.

Dressed and cursing quietly, Sheena walked into the kitchen. She let out a quiet moan on seeing Dan and Annie. Annie made encouraging and sympathetic noises and poured the porridge, steaming hot, into a bowl for Sheena. Annie and Dan exchanged looks. If Sheena lost her job, things around the house would change. A depressed Sheena was not likely to be fun to be around, and, at her age and with her reputation, she'd never get another decent job.

Silence reigned as Sheena sat at the kitchen table and peered into her bowl. Albeit adorned with cream, red berries and brown sugar, the luxury, special days-only version, beating skimmed milk and white sugar hands down, Sheena suspected that Annie was trying to bribe her into behaving herself and not losing her job. From Sheena's point of view, if Annie had really wanted to bribe her, she would have served Eggs Benedict and champagne. Now, that would have done the trick.

She touched her throbbing forehead and ate her porridge, knowing it would line her stomach, if she could keep it down. All the while Dan and Annie looked on like two concerned parents preparing their child for her first independent school trip. As she went back to her bedroom, large mug of black coffee in hand, she could feel their eyes boring into her back.

In her bedroom, Sheena kicked off her slippers to put on black court shoes to match the conservative work suit she'd chosen for the office. No sooner had she put on the shoes than she kicked them off, cursing. They were soaked through from the spilled water. She turned round and saw that Annie and Dan had followed her out of the kitchen and were silently observing her from the doorway, for all the world a picture-perfect Glasgow version of American Gothic, without the pitchfork. She kicked her bedroom door which closed with what seemed like an unnecessarily loud crash. Sheena winced, and, with what felt like a superhuman effort, changed out of her black suit into a brown one she could match with a pair of court shoes which were dry.

The suit reminded her of her school uniform. She avoided wearing it precisely for the memories it evoked but it seemed particularly suitable for the occasion. In the mirror she could see herself with her head bowed standing in front of Mr Dun's desk as he told her to hold out her hands for a good belting.

She realised that with having to change her outfit she was running late. She hurried past Dan and Annie, who were still standing silently just outside her bedroom door. "Be good," Dan shouted after her.

20

By 9.30 a.m. Sheena was sitting in the reception area of the law firm, like any client or new recruit. She didn't dare go to her office as it meant passing lawyers who surely had heard all about the previous day's events. Margaret, the receptionist, glanced in her direction every now and then but Sheena ignored her.

Donald MacDonald walked through reception and, as he saw Sheena, quickened his pace.

"Donald!"

He turned towards her, reluctant. "Hello, Sheena, I hear you've been summoned."

Sheena waved dismissively, "More importantly, what was that all about yesterday? Who were these people?"

"Nobody and nothing." Donald hurried on through reception, leaving Sheena surprised by his brusque reaction.

As she was summoned to Mr Dun's office, Annie walked into reception. She'd come to offer moral support. Sheena gave her a wan smile as she turned towards Mr Dun's office, the look of the gallows on her.

Thirty minutes later, Sheena walked back into reception, head down, her gait slow and lacklustre, her fingers twisting a used Kleenex in her hands. She walked towards Annie and, with her back to Margaret, her face transformed into a big grin. She grabbed hold of Annie's arm and dragged her into the lift. She gave Annie a hug and a thank you for being there for her as the lift descended but refused to say a word until they were in the cafe on the corner, coffees on order.

Once settled, Sheena, with a large cappuccino and celebratory dollop of extra cream on top, related the events of her meeting.

"I told Mr Dun that my behaviour was a defence mechanism against all the unhappiness I have to deal with in the course of my work. I handle a lot of wills, as you know, and it's hard dealing with the family after a death. Especially if the estate isn't what they expected. It really is hard. Honest. So, I told him that I was feeling depressed and considering psychological help to get me over this period which also coincided with turning forty and all that that implied. I apologised profusely." She looked at Annie. "Of course, it's all a load of shite but I thought it was worth a try." Grinning, she dug a dollop of cream out of her coffee with a spoon and licked it.

Annie looked at Sheena, concerned. "You know, I think maybe you really are going through a depression. You need to see a professional before it gets serious."

Sheena made the sign of a 'W' with her fingers and dragged the word out, "What-e-ver. Anyway, Mr Dun took it all in and gave me two weeks' paid leave to relax and recuperate. Mind you, the man's not daft. I'm not sure he believes it entirely but I think he has a slight soft spot for me because I'm kind of open and spontaneous in a way he never could be. I think he's a little envious of me." She licked at another dollop of cream.

Annie's expression changed to incredulity. "I'm not sure

who's the bigger idiot, him or you." She stared into her decaf skinny latte and glanced over at Sheena's cappuccino. "Pass me a dollop of that cream will you, I need cheering up."

"Oh, come on, you should be happy for me. I've still got my job." Sheena gleefully poked Annie in the ribs.

Annie looked at her intently for a moment. "Yeah, but for how long?"

21

↶

The next morning, Kathy woke up refreshed, but with no specific plan other than to take a day off to think. She called in sick and could hear the barely disguised relief in Jack's voice.

Having maxed out her credit card on Amazon and still a long way from buying back all of Barbara's books, appreciating that it was going to take quite a few salaries to get there, she decided to go and see them in real life. Maybe hug the ones she couldn't afford to buy just yet. She knew that Barbara would help her figure out what she had to do to, to take that step forward into a new life. She just needed to be nearer to her books.

Kathy barged through the doors of Waterstones and swept past a man laden down with books he was taking to the window display. The books went flying, scattering a table display by the front door. Not only did Kathy not hear the aggravated "Oi, you!", she was oblivious to the devastation she'd left in her wake. She was on a mission.

She marched straight to the Romantic Fiction section, having made a pilgrimage to these shelves many times before. She would come just to look at Barbara's books, all there neatly laid out on the shelves, in order, unlike the unruly pile in her chest. She'd run her fingers over the spines, admire the colours, reacquaint herself with the titles. One would often stand out to her as if it were telling her to reread it and find the message Barbara wanted to communicate to her. It was like her personal recharging zone. Some people needed to get back to nature, Kathy needed to visit Barbara.

After five minutes of meditative scanning, a woman gently nudged her out of the way which brought her back to herself. The contemplation had yielded no insights.

"Fuck! Barbara's punishing me for burning her books," Kathy muttered to herself. "Now what do I do?" She looked around and after a moment decided that, as she'd made the effort to come all the way here, she might as well have a wander and see if inspiration struck elsewhere.

She had no idea what she was looking for but she was determined not to leave until she'd found *the* book that was going to save her life, even if it meant sleeping in the Philosophy section all night. *Best section for the sleep deprived*, she thought. On her third trip around the ground floor weaving in and out amongst the shelves, an assistant offered help.

"I'm looking for inspiration." Kathy shrugged helplessly.

"That would be in the Inspirational section, then. I personally find it very inspiring. Or Religion, which is next to it. Or Self-Help. That might do the trick." The assistant pointed Kathy in the right direction.

Kathy went down the back stairs in search of Religion and Inspirational and found a larger and more varied section than she'd imagined it would be. "Oh, for the love of Barbara! What am I supposed to do here! It's too much! For fuck's sake, Barbara! I said I was sorry!"

Chapter 21

An elderly woman passing by stopped to pat Kathy on the hand. "Don't worry, dear, I'm sure Barbara will forgive you."

Kathy was startled. "Oh, uh huh, yes, I'm sure you're right," she mumbled and moved away.

She allowed her eyes to run over the wall of books without really focusing on any one in particular. After a quick glance around, Kathy said quietly, "Barbara, I need your help. Give me a sign. *Please.*" She let her mind go blank and her eyes do the work.

She shifted slightly and suddenly a word stood out. At first glance, it appeared to be the result of a divine light shining on it, but it turned out that it was just the striplight glinting off the gold leaf lettering on the book. Still, she liked to think that it was propitious. The word 'vengeance' leapt out at her.

She mulled over the word. "Vengeance. Ven-geance. Ve-n-geance. Re-vengeance. Re-venge. Revenge. Ha!"

Kathy tried high-fiving herself. She stood there with her hand out until a young priest, who'd been browsing Religion, high-fived her back. *Oh, God, if only he knew what I'm thinking*, thought Kathy. Revenge. It all made sense. Her purpose in life right now was to get even. Once she'd done that, she could put the past behind her, once and for all, and she'd be able to move on.

"But how would it work?" she muttered under her breath. "And would I really feel better? Would it really transform my life?" She thought for the briefest of moments. "Well, duh!" she exclaimed rather loudly and received a shushing as if she were in a library.

The effect was immediate. She felt lighter, almost joyful. Kathy practically skipped out of the shop and straight into a wall of rain. *Damn, blast, shit, hell – rain in Scotland.*

Who'd have thought it? Kathy stomped down Buchanan Street keeping close to the buildings and the scant shelter they provided, along with those others who'd also carelessly left their homes on a sunny June day in Scotland without an umbrella. A couple of Mexican stand-offs were quickly resolved by one look, a glare that would have had Mike Tyson quaking in his boxers, duly forcing her challenger to step out into the rain and walk around her. She reached Argyle Street and after a ten-minute, clothes-drenching, hair-ruining wait, got on a bus and went home.

She walked into her studio and straight over to her vision board on the wall in front of her. Her dream car: Maserati. Dream home: Château Marouatte. Dream man: Ryan Gosling. She picked up a thick marker pen and wrote in large blood-red letters across the board: Vengeance. She even added bloodlike drips running down from the letters for effect. And smiled. An evil smile.

22

The rest of the week sauntered by at its own steady pace. Kathy couldn't, no matter what she did, make time go faster. She resigned herself to having to show her face at work on the basis that a living had to be earned and found herself, without thinking, efficient, respectful and pleasant, completely unaware how much easier being nice was in comparison to her default mode: suspicious, angry and generally snappy. Her brain, however, was elsewhere.

In her mind's eye she could see what appeared to be a tangled ball of wool suspended in space, strands flying everywhere, unruly and generally uncooperative. The first strand that she grasped gave her the focus of her plan. It happened while she was making a cup of tea in the kitchen at work. "Got it!" she exclaimed, startling Jack who scalded his hand as he was pouring boiling water over a tea bag.

Kathy sprinted back to her desk and wrote it down. *The punishment must fit the crime.* It was that simple. She stared at the words in wonder. Everything that Kathy had been hyper-aware of on her way to and from work on Monday, she realised, along with her own foot stomping *It's not fair!* were the signs of long-term suffering and passivity.

That acceptance of what is not right and fair without any prospect of getting even. Those careless taunts, put-downs, deliberate insults, bullying, complaining, the weary, world-worn look on that mother's face when her husband called her stupid, flinching every time he turned to her. Enough. Enough! Kathy came to the understanding that getting even wasn't a mission for her alone. She was to be the avenging angel, with the ability to transform people's lives. Starting with her own.

23

It was first thing on Saturday morning when Kathy finally sat down at her computer. She wanted to start fresh and devote her weekend to figuring out the details of her plan. The imaginary tangled ball of wool had been unravelling all week, a strand here, a strand there. Now she needed to gather these strands and turn them into a plan that made sense. Contemplating the task ahead of her, she'd bought a catering-size box of Tetley's to make sure that she was adequately fuelled for the task.

She opened Excel and added three sheets, each one with the name of an ex on it. Appreciating that getting even on every single person who had upset her, insulted her, treated her badly, elbowed past her on the street, looked at her the wrong way, or dumped her, would be a lifetime's work, she chose the three men she considered had committed the gravest of crimes and had dumped her in the worst ways possible. As an afterthought, she added David, her most recent ex. He deserved whatever he got for being such a complete shit.

Taking into account her new status as avenging angel, Kathy had found a photo of an angel attired completely in black with huge black wings, in front of a stormy backdrop, and had stuck it on her vision board.

As the day progressed it became clear that she wouldn't be able to take revenge on her four exes on her own. It would be too big an undertaking. She considered the thought that, if she found people to help her out, she could help them get their own back on their exes, current partners, work colleagues and miscellaneous arses who had crossed their paths. Kathy smiled to herself, her smile grew into a bigger and bigger grin until she bellowed with laughter at the whole mad idea.

She clicked onto Chrome. The Wi-Fi was fucking down! Rage screamed out of her body as she flung open her door and shouted over the banister.

Sheena was vacuuming the hell out of the living-room carpet, not a task she enjoyed, but it needed doing. Not only had it not quite recovered from the party but she'd just dropped the contents of an entire crisp packet on it. She switched off the vacuum cleaner and Kathy's furious strangled screeches reached her.

"The fucking Wi-Fi is off! Switch the fucking thing back on!" The Wi-Fi barely reached Kathy's studio, but it saved her having to pay for her own. A poor signal was better than nothing. That said, no signal at all was not fucking on!

"Keep yer wig on!" Sheena unplugged the vacuum cleaner and plugged the router back in. "There ye go! It'll be fine in a minute!" she bawled up the stairs.

"Stupid woman," Kathy muttered to herself.

Finally connected to the internet, Kathy, still fuming and red-faced, logged on to Facebook. It seemed like as good a place as any to start. After five minutes of deep thought, she set up a profile under the name 'Screaming Minnie'. Kathy was renowned for her uncontrollable temper, but it didn't mean that she wasn't aware of it. She kept as much information as private as possible while she set up the page. This had to be a secret. Getting even was a serious business.

Three YouTube tutorials later, Kathy had begun to realise how bloody complicated Facebook advertising was. She had to change the type of page she'd set up before she could even create an ad, and that was only after she'd added her payment details and managed the deadly dull and boring admin side of it. Exhausted from the effort, Kathy took time off to make a salad lunch and contemplate the content of the ad she wanted to write that would attract the right sort of person.

Refreshed, Kathy wrote a cryptic ad:

> *Is your past not in your past? Want to get past your past or change your present? Do you want to help others who will help you? Join us, together we can make your past wish they'd never been present.*

She hoped that the text was subtle enough to get through Facebook's review process but clear enough in its intention.

Apparently, Kathy discovered, ads performed better if they had an image, so she wasted another hour trolling through Google images and Pinterest. Finally, she settled on the image of a fly standing on a table with a giant boot hovering over it. It came out a bit Monty Python but, in her opinion, got the point across. She set the ad to appear in the Glasgow area only, which seemed to make the most sense, and the target audience to adults between the ages of twenty and sixty-five. The exotic amount of five pounds a day would have to do as the ad's maximum spending limit. Starting immediately. She waited excitedly for the ad review process to finish and her ad to go out but she got bored and turned her mind to the issue of finance.

Finance was not a strong point of Kathy's. She made yet another cup of tea and, with a large piece of paper and a pen decided to meditate on the subject and lie on the bed. Thirty seconds later, she was snoring gently.

When she woke up and drank her cold tea, she thought she would try word association to see if that would give her some ideas. She began with the word 'money' and followed it through with a stream of consciousness:

> *Money*
> *Work*
> *Boring*
> *Pointless*
> *Fired*
> *Poor*
> *Hungry*
> *Food*
> *Charity*

She stopped dead on 'charity', not sure why.

24

Kathy woke up at 8 a.m. on Sunday morning with a plan fully developed in her head. The word 'charity' had bounced around her brain all night. She was exhausted from her restless night but excited that she'd figured out how to finance the whole shebang.

Cup of tea by her side, she got to work.

She needed to create a website. As she'd set up the Barbara Cartland blog by herself with only Google and YouTube for help, she calculated that the website for GIVE! wouldn't pose any problems.

GIVE! was designed to be a one-stop charity shop for those with plenty of spare cash and good intentions but no inclination or time to choose where to place their donations. GIVE! would then, in theory, allocate the donated money across different charities. However, Kathy had other ideas. She would use the money to fund her and her group's revenges. Needless to say, nowhere in the website would the true meaning of the word GIVE! be revealed.

She was delighted at her own deviousness. The idea was brilliant in its simplicity. In Kathy's eyes, the whole project was, anyway, a charity designed to help people to move on with their lives. It wasn't as if she, or anyone else, would be taking a salary. It made her wonder about the possibility of setting herself up formally as a charity. She'd get tax breaks that way.

She put that thought to one side and focused on the website. It took all day to set up a simple website with bold colours, the perfect text and the perfect photos. With a bit of a struggle and a variety of plug-ins that would allow online payment, the resulting webpage looked pretty professional and credible. As a first stab at it, Kathy was satisfied.

She ran out for a takeaway and nodded in passing at Sheena when she bumped into her at the chippie. She had neither the time nor the brain space for chit-chat.

Later, with her new-found knowledge of Facebook advertising, she created ads for GIVE!, setting the whole of the UK as her target market, for starters, and noted the budget on her expenses sheet. A fiver a day would have to do. She wasn't made of money, after all, which was the whole point. Not only did she need to pay for the advertising for recruitment purposes and to get people on the website donating money, but they'd also need funds for props and services that may need to be employed in the exacting of revenges. And then, finally, she needed money for the Grand Reveal. And then she'd give it back. Honest, guv.

25

On Monday morning, Kathy got up, fresh as a daisy. She had her poached egg on toast, just as pedestrian as the previous week, a cup of tea, always a pleasure, and made sandwiches for lunch.

Once at the clinic, having done the absolute minimum necessary to avoid getting fired, she logged on to Facebook and in to the 'Screaming Minnie' page, and found that she had 116 requests to join the page along with the same number of messages.

It took Kathy two full days of research to complete an initial vetting of her potential candidates. She searched their social media profiles, googled phone numbers and contact details and whatever other information she could find out, and soon realised that an awful lot of people were way more screwed-up than she was. She hadn't intended to imply that murder was on the books but a few had decided that it was an option.

Kathy discovered that she enjoyed nosing in people's lives, despite the fact that it could be considered virtual stalking, but she didn't care. As far as she was concerned, she was a potential employer looking for suitable candidates for the job. She was surprised to find that three of her potential candidates, including one she was sure she'd gone to school with, were offering online video sex, two others organised weekend swingers' parties, and one schoolteacher had a fetish for brogues. When she came across a potential candidate, she contacted them through Messenger and arranged to meet them in an out-of-the-way coffee shop on Wednesday afternoon.

Kathy couldn't wait to meet her potential partners in crime. What could possibly go wrong?

26

Sheena couldn't believe that she'd already arrived at Wednesday morning of her second week of paid leave. Monday was just round the corner; she'd be back at work and, potentially, facing the music. The thought was depressing. She'd had a high old time devoted to the art of shopping.

In an attempt to mix things up a bit she joined a gym. Based on the fact that she was now in her advanced years, she couldn't just jump into the whole gym. She had to approach it like a wild beast: slowly, carefully, and appropriately attired. An enthusiastic, muscled, extremely fuckable, fifteen-years-younger-but-who-cares trainer gave her the tour and Sheena signed up gladly, if only to give her the opportunity to flirt with him on a regular basis. Motivation was a key element for creating an exercise routine. Everyone knew that. What Sheena also knew was that the only way she'd be brave enough to return to the gym was to spend at least 150 quid on gear.

Combining her love of shopping with getting fit seemed like the perfect day out. After three hours in the Nike store, an exercise routine in itself, she realised that the technical top, whatever that was, was too technical to get on and perhaps technically a size too small or too large or too whatever because the body shape it was meant to fit certainly wasn't hers. The rest of the gear just wasn't her style in general.

She dumped the huge pile of kit she'd tried on into the arms of an aggrieved shop assistant and headed to a vintage store. By the time she'd finished, she was 300 quid lighter and looked like a 1970s gym goddess with a touch of *Flashdance*. That was more like it. One 1940s swimsuit and a flowery swimming cap were added to the top of the pile and she was ready for action. She even went out of her way to buy nose clips just in case she could join a synchronised swimming class. She fancied herself in that.

27

Kathy had chosen a cafe in a neighbourhood where people knew not to ask questions and the owner, although raising his eyebrows on a few occasions, remained silent as Kathy dealt with the constant stream of characters who joined her.

The first interview was nothing if not alarming. No sooner had she sat down in a corner with her cappuccino than she found herself, in spite of her dedicated research, seated opposite the type of character she would normally cross the road to avoid. And yet here he was, sitting there, staring at her intently. She looked back, hesitant. Out of the corner of her eye she saw the cafe owner shake his head in disbelief as he polished a glass and kept his counsel.

The man, Jock Mackie, had a face like a bag of spanners. He lacked two front teeth and smelled alarming – basically, he looked like an escaped convict. *How amazingly different people can be to the personas they present online*, she thought, slightly terrified.

"Right, I can tell that you might be lookin' for somethin' a bit different but I reckon that you'd get nowhere as a bunch o' amateurs. I've come here to offer ma services."

Kathy sat back a little, partly to get away from the stench

but also to facilitate a quick exit if needs be. She was glad she'd paid for her coffee already.

The man settled himself comfortably. "I am," he bowed his head humbly, "a professional pyromaniac. I come from a long line of pyromaniacs. You will find no man more qualified than me." He puffed out his chest with pride.

He picked up his briefcase. Kathy hadn't noticed it when he arrived. It was so incongruous when set against the rest of his battered appearance, she was surprised that she hadn't spotted it. He pulled out an extremely smart, professional folder with a picture of a blazing building on the front. He opened the folder, positioned it for Kathy to see better and leaned in towards her, causing the equal and opposite reaction from Kathy. The first page had the title in bold letters *The History of Pyromania in Glasgow in the 20th and 21st Centuries as Pertains to the Mackie Family.*

"This, here, is ma credentials, the family history, if ye will." He lowered his voice. "Not many people consider the absolute efficiency of a burnin' buildin' to send a message to their competitors. There's nothin' better than the smell of smoke and seein' the client watchin' his business burn, sobbin' his wee heart out. Burnt rubber is one of ma preferred smoke blends, although, I must confess, no' the most profitable." He sat back, giving Kathy a brief respite from the stench, and drew in a deep breath as if inhaling smoke were life-enhancing.

"Nothing? There's nothing better? Are you sure?" Kathy tried to show interest.

"Positively. Look. This buildin' here." He pointed to two photos, the before and after of a five-storey building. The first photo showed a pristine, modern building, the second, a pile of rubble. "The owner had a choice. Two broken legs, each broken in two places, or the insurance money on the buildin'. He chose the buildin'. We're that good the buildin' insurance company was completely oblivious. Our clients were happy to have the debt paid and the building owner got to keep his legs intact. That service on the price list, I'll leave you a copy, is our 'Towering Inferno' service."

The next photo showed a burnt-out car. "This is a cheaper option. It's a wee warnin'. I call that 'Candle in the Wind'." He looked up and squared his shoulders at Kathy. "So, what d'ya think?"

Kathy smiled nervously. "Thank you, that's, eh, very enlightening. I'll definitely get back to you if something that needs burning crops up. Can I keep the folder?"

To her immense relief he didn't hang about. He snapped his briefcase shut and left quickly, looking around shiftily and without paying for his double espresso. She didn't mind. Sometimes discretion really is the better part of valour.

Kathy waited nervously for her next interviewee, keeping her fingers crossed that the next candidate would be less terrifying. Two people walked in. They looked like a couple but the man went to a table at the other end of the cafe and sat facing them. The woman strode up to Kathy and, before saying a word, carefully hung her umbrella on a spare chair, undid each button of the emerald-green Harris Tweed cape that she wore, hung it over a chair, unbelted the long brown cardigan, smoothed down her sari and sat down facing Kathy.

"Good afternoon. My name is Sonia, and I'm from India." Her voice was sing-song, articulate and fully accented, with just a tiny hint of Glasgow. Her tone was efficient. "I'm a fully qualified physician but my husband won't let me practise as he says he needs my help in the restaurant. We've been here five years already and the restaurant is going extremely well. We have five uncles and three cousins helping us. I'm not needed but my husband wants me there. He's just being selfish. I was born to heal people. My husband needs to learn that I have to live my life too." Her direct, intense, gaze showed Kathy that she meant business.

Kathy thought for a moment. Sonia's request wasn't exactly in line with the concept of vengeance but she needed brain cells in the group and a doctor might come in handy. Once Kathy had agreed that Sonia's participation would be valued and that her request concerning her husband would be met, Sonia thanked her, got up, smoothed down her sari, and retied her cardigan belt. She swept the tweed cape over her shoulders, closed the clasp at the top and then fastened each button one by one. She picked up her umbrella – a woman who didn't take chances with the Scottish weather – and a medicine bag that Kathy hadn't noticed she'd brought with her when she arrived. As she left, with a long and efficient stride, followed by the man who'd arrived with her, she looked like a cross between Florence Nightingale and Mary Poppins.

The next interview was just plain depressing.

28

Kathy's next candidate nodded at the owner as he strode towards her. Clearly a local. The owner glanced at Kathy and shook his head, again.

He presented himself better than the pyromaniac and, happily, didn't smell bad. Kathy was thankful for small mercies.

He gave her a bone-crushing handshake. "My name's John Tennant, pleased to meet you." Then he turned the chair opposite her around and, straddling it, wasted no time in getting to the point. A professional-looking folder appeared in his hand, titled 'Thugs 4 U'. Kathy's heart sank. It crossed her mind that Glasgow criminals had specialised business coaches to help them sell their services.

"I used to be a police officer, recently retired ..."

"You look too young to have retired already." Kathy meant it as a compliment, but the air went icy.

"Aye, well." He paused, his eyes boring into hers. Kathy kept her mouth shut and tried to slow her heart to less than 200 beats a minute. "I'm here to offer you a social service. It's supported by the Criminal Rehabilitation department." He handed her the folder.

Kathy looked at him in surprise. "This," she waved the folder, "is a government initiative?"

"No, no, it's an informal initiative supported by the shadow Criminal Rehabilitation department. When I say shadow, I don't mean in the political sense, I mean not in the formal sense, if you catch my drift."

Kathy certainly caught his drift.

"What we have here," he pointed at the folder, "are recently released criminals who have served time for grievous bodily harm who we've taken into our programme of rehabilitation. We put them in weekly group therapy and, partly as a means of paying their way, we hire them out on a strict once-a-month basis to, shall we say, solve all your problems."

Kathy opened her mouth then closed it again. She had no idea what to say.

"It's part of the therapeutic process. A kind of aversion therapy. The idea is that these thugs will gradually grow to detest this kind of activity, whereas if we had prohibited it, they would only crave it." He gave Kathy the once-over. "If you've ever tried to cut chocolate from your diet then you'll know what I mean."

She hadn't and she didn't.

"Here, look at wee Wullie here. He's a specialist in what we call 'A Wee Scare'. He'll stalk the client's victim, break into their home or place of business and steal a couple of things. Small but disturbing acts designed to unsettle the client's enemy. The price list is here at the back." He pointed to the folder. "Big Jim here." He took the folder from Kathy, opened it at another page and handed it back to her. "Big Jim's our specialist for the service we call 'Shit Happens'. This service is on the upper end of the price scale as the result requires permanent damage."

Chapter 28

Kathy slowly and carefully closed the folder and handed it back to the retired police officer. With a forced thank you she declined his services. He swept out of his chair-straddling position like a Wild West cowboy and left with a slightly bizarre "toodle-oo" and a tip of an imaginary cap. Another coffee left unpaid. This was going to be an expensive afternoon.

Happily, the next ones to arrive turned out to be suitable for her requirements. The entire cafe seemed to breathe a sigh of relief. Just as Kathy was beginning to think she'd been stood up, her final candidate arrived.

The cafe door jangled as it opened and revealed a very well-endowed chest. The body attached to it seemed to arrive a few seconds behind. All eyes swivelled as the woman walked or rather floated, across the room towards Kathy. She was petite, well, most of her, and she wore her blonde hair in a pixie style that framed her stunning, delicate face. Her clothes were frumpy in what appeared to be a desire to disguise the undisguisable. There was something about her, not just her chest, a kind of invisible magnetic attraction that drew people to her.

She extended her hand towards Kathy. "You must be Kathy. Pleased to meet you, I'm Ella." Her voice was breathy and quiet with a slight lisp which sounded extraordinarily sexy.

Kathy forced her mouth closed from the slack-jawed position it had been in since the door opened. She managed a reply. "Eh, hi, yes, please, sit down."

As Ella went to sit down, a waiter flew over from where he'd stood rooted to the spot, pulled her chair out, fussed over her, and then took her order.

"I used to be a regular here," complained Kathy. "And

he's never served me that quickly. Waiter, waiter! I'd like another capu ... oh, forget it." The waiter had gone to personally supervise the making of Ella's latte.

"I seem to have one of those faces that make people think I'm famous." explained Ella. "People fawn over me all the time and I hate it. I just want to be left alone. I don't know what to do." Ella's eyes filled up. The man at the next table practically fell off his chair as he leapt out and put a comforting arm around her shoulder.

"There, there, you look so sad. Can I help?" He patted her head.

"Bugger off!" Ella's words and strength of tone had the man's bottom flat on his seat in a flash. She looked at Kathy, resigned. "See what I have to do to get some peace and quiet?"

Kathy reached out to pat Ella's hand then thought better of it. "Tell me all about it."

"Ever since these," Ella waved her hand in front of her chest, "developed, I haven't had a moment's peace. School was a nightmare. I covered myself up as much as I could but the boys would taunt me and the girls would make stupid remarks. I hated the Wednesday gym class. The worst day of my life was when the gym teacher bought exercise trampolines. All that bouncing up and down. I felt like the freak show at a circus. I even heard one of the boys taking bets on whether or not I'd get a black eye from my flying boobs."

Kathy smothered a smile. The man at the next table turned his head away quickly.

"I'm an introvert by nature but I want to be an actress. I've taken classes, and the skills I've learned are really helping me to come out of my shell a little bit. I have a talent for accents." Ella's voice changed into an authentic southern drawl aimed at the man at the next table. "Well, hello, Mister," she breathed. "I come from the deep south of the U-S of A. Would you be so kind, sir, as to get me another cafe latte?"

The man jumped up and rushed to the bar.

"Excellent," Kathy said. "I'm sure accents will come in handy. So, what do you do and who do you want to avenge and why?" Kathy looked intently at Ella, pen poised to take notes.

"Oh, I'm a barmaid until I get a proper acting job. Glasgow isn't exactly Los Angeles, I know, but I do my best. Who do I want to avenge? Mankind maybe? God, for giving me enough boobs for three people? Do you know the looks of hatred I get from flat-chested women? Do you? Do you?" Ella's voice started to rise.

Kathy held her hands up in alarm. "No, I don't, but I can imagine. Oh, you poor soul."

"Don't you poor soul me!" Ella shouted, rising from the table.

Oh Lord, she's got a worse temper than me, thought Kathy.

She sat back down, composed herself, and continued. "I just want to be me. I want to be respected as a human being. I don't want to be pointed at, stared at, groped and treated as if I can't have a brain just because I have these." She waved her hand across her chest again as if Kathy wouldn't know what she was referring to. "I'm a good barmaid, I'm a fast worker and I never make a mistake. My boss loves me because I attract the punters and the gawkers, and they buy more beer. And the drunker they get, the more beer they buy and the worse they get. My bum's permanently black and blue from the pinching. My boss practically encourages it. He certainly doesn't try to stop it. He and the punters need a lesson in manners. That's what I want."

"Well, I can certainly get on board with that idea," said Kathy. "I think we should leave mankind in general and God in particular out of it and focus on your boss and the punters at the pub. How does that sound?"

"Sounds good to me."

Ella got up, they said their farewells, and she made her departure looking for all the world as if she didn't know that lattes cost money. As she reached the door, it opened and in walked a small, pockmarked face accompanied by a scrawny body. His eyes almost literally went out on stalks as Ella made to walk past him. He held the door open for her and, as she walked away down the street, he pulled himself up to his full, on a good day, five feet two, his arm stretched out with fingers extended as if he wanted to stay close to her for as long as possible. He was smitten.

30

He dragged himself back to reality and gave the cafe the once-over. People were looking, but not how they had looked at Ella. He was no oil painting. He walked over to Kathy.

"Hullo there, you'll be that Screamin' Minnie wumman, am ah right?"

"Eh, ah, yes, eh? How do you know? I'm not expecting anyone else." It seemed to be the day for Kathy to be caught on the left foot.

"Everybody knows."

"Everybody? Who? Who everybody?" Kathy was alarmed, envisioning an avalanche of exes turning up en masse. She glanced over at the door. Just in case.

"Ye've met Jack and John, right?" Kathy nodded yes.

"These are the sorts of people that know. Dangerous people. Puttin' an ad on Facebook lookin' for thugs and murderers. What were ye thinkin'?"

"I, I, I wasn't thinking anything. I mean nothing. I mean, nothing like that. Honest!"

"Well," he said, "those that need tae know, know, and those that don't, they know as well, see? And then in this neighbourhood tae." He stopped to look around.

Chapter 30

Kathy interrupted, braver, "But I used to live in this neighbourhood. It's OK."

He ignored her. "It's no' advisable. You need protection."

"I do?" Kathy's stress levels rose so dramatically she almost levitated.

"Anyway, ah'm in," he said. "Just count me in and ah'll make sure ye're no' bothered. Ah have a story tae tell but that's for another day. Me and ma man here can help ye out. We have connections, if you know whit ah mean." He tapped the side of his nose and winked at Kathy. He sat down revealing a giant of a man behind him who Kathy couldn't believe had been standing there the whole time without her seeing him. He politely extended his hand for Kathy to shake.

"Good afternoon." The voice was cultured Edinburgh. "I'm very pleased to make your acquaintance." He sat down and let out a long, sad sigh. The body rumbled. The muscles were Schwarzenegger, but the countenance definitely Eeyore.

"Ah, dinnae fash yersel', she'll be back soon."

He looked at Kathy. "Ma man here and his wife have known each other since primary school. They've been together ever since then but she's upped and gone off to find hersel' or some nonsense like that. He's no' been the same since." He gave the big man an affectionate pat on the knee which provoked another long, rumbling sigh. He turned to Kathy. "Got to go. Places to be. People to see. Ah'm a busy man."

They got up to leave. "Wait! I don't know your names," said Kathy.

"It's Shug," the short one said, bouncing on the balls of his feet like a boxer.

"And I'm Charles," said the tall one before following Shug out of the cafe.

31

Having exhausted herself buying gear for the gym, the following morning Sheena found herself striding confidently out of the changing room and into the main workout area. She stopped short when she realised that she had entered uncharted territory. Those machines needed to be approached with caution. She felt quite lightheaded, and decided to go upstairs to the cafe, where, with a cappuccino and cream-filled croissant in hand, she could sit comfortably, look over the balcony railing and observe the scene from a safe distance. She saw Donald MacDonald, her one ally at the law firm, dressed and fresh from a post-workout shower.

"Hello! Hello! Donald!" Sheena shouted from the balcony creating an echo around the cavernous space. Donald saw her and quickened his pace to the front door and left with a perfunctory wave in her direction. *Oh, Lord, if Donald won't even talk to me then I must really be in the shit*, Sheena thought to herself.

She turned her attention back to the heavy weights' workout station. A few men were there, grunting, faces puffed out in the effort to lift weights that looked heavier than them. It all looked really unpleasant. She wished that she'd brought opera glasses, nevertheless; she could see that a few of them looked quite hunky when they didn't have their constipated faces on. Maybe this would be worthwhile after all.

What with the sugar rush, all those muscles, and these dangerous-looking machines, Sheena's heart was pounding and her palms were sweaty. This gym stuff was hard work. She needed a change of rhythm and left the cafe in search of the jacuzzi and sauna. She reckoned she could handle that.

Two hours later Sheena emerged from the gym, her face glowing, swearing that she'd never sweated so much in her life. She wasn't entirely sure that she'd go back, though. It was all a bit of a palaver.

32

At home, recovering from her exertions, Sheena answered a call from Mr Dun's secretary who told her that she must present herself in his office the very next morning at 9 a.m. sharp. After she put the phone down, Sheena did a little dance of joy. She could feel another week off coming up, thanks to Mr Dun. She just knew it! Donald MacDonald wasn't ignoring her in the gym. He must just have been in a rush to get to a meeting. She needn't have worried.

What she did need to do, though, was not look too cheerful at the meeting. Tired and depressed would be the order of the day. Considering a whole new wardrobe to evoke that feeling, it didn't take her long to realise that all she had to do was put on her normal work clothes and think about work. Tiring. And depressing.

A party would cheer her up. A brief investigation of the contents of her fridge revealed a pile of mince, a couple of onions and a green pepper. Her store cupboard provided her with two tins of chilli beans, a couple of tins of tomatoes and a full bag of rice. The freezer offered two frozen sticks of ready prepared garlic bread. The wine and beer supplies were a bit low but that could easily be remedied. Between one thing and another she reckoned that she had enough ingredients for a giant chilli con carne, always a popular classic, with garlic bread that would feed around fifteen people. Taking into account Dan and Annie, if they didn't already have plans, but not Kathy who she didn't want spoiling the atmosphere with her moodiness, that left twelve WhatsApp invitations to be sent. Three hours later the house was buzzing.

Much to everyone's surprise, Kathy showed up. Living in the studio for the past three months had given her the perfect opportunity to make Sheena's life miserable on a regular basis. Kathy blamed Sheena, at least in part, for one of her dumpings. She felt that Sheena should have warned her and saved her the heartbreak.

She walked into the kitchen and found Sheena in deep conversation with Annie about the benefits she was feeling from her visit to the gym. Looking out on the tiny garden, Sheena commented, "Thinking about it, I could squeeze a jacuzzi in there between the nettles and the bit that the foxes use for a loo, and the sauna over there."

"Hell," interjected Kathy, "with the amount of hot air you produce on a daily basis, I'm surprised your skin isn't permanently glowing."

Sheena, stung, looked hurt.

"Come on," said Annie, "there's no need for that, Kathy!"

"Whatever. It was just a joke. You're so sensitive, Sheena, you must have the string of your knickers halfway up yer bum." Kathy picked up a glass of wine and walked off.

Sheena's eyes sparked with tears.

The Wee Besom had her lead in her mouth and was going from person to person offering it to them, hoping that someone would take pity on her and take her out. Sensing that Sheena was unhappy, she went up to her and offered her the lead. But Sheena, distracted, shooed her away.

Annie watched Kathy walk away. "What is up with that woman! She's always having a go at you!"

"I know," said Sheena, glum. "I have a feeling I know why and I don't think there's much I can do about it." She reached for the gin.

33

If Sheena had had the energy to kick herself, she would have done. The gin that she had turned to for solace was still swirling around her bloodstream when she got up the following morning. Looking tired and depressed was the least of her concerns as she dressed in brown, brown and brown while trying not to vomit. It was exhausting.

Dan and Annie were nowhere to be seen. Sheena had been so upbeat about her meeting with Mr Dun that they'd gone off to work unconcerned. No porridge and hot coffee waited for her this time. At least the dry toast matched her outfit.

As Sheena stepped out of the lift into reception, she was struck sober. Margaret, the disapproving receptionist, was glowering at a blonde, perky, bosomy young woman sitting in her chair. Jimmy, the office handyman, was unscrewing the company name plaque from the wall behind her.

The perky receptionist gave a chirpy "Welcome to Scott, Jameson, Miles and MacDonald! Do you have an appointment?"

Without a word, Margaret pointed to the appointments calendar on the desk.

"Ah, Sheena, oh, that Sheena?" She looked up at Margaret for confirmation, who, wordless, nodded her head in the direction of the waiting Sheena.

"Oh, OK, em, Sheena, please do take a seat. Mr Dun is no longer with us and your appointment is now with Mr Scott, the Managing Partner."

Speechless, all Sheena could do was nod. She remained rooted to the spot until an 'excuse me' and a slight nudge shifted her from her position in front of the elevator.

Sheena finally found her voice. "That's OK, Miss em ..." Sheena looked for the receptionist's name plate on her desk.

"Margaret. I'm Margaret too! Isn't that fun?" The new receptionist was far too perky for the original Margaret.

"Ah, OK. Miss Margaret. I'll just go to my office to catch up on my mail while I'm waiting."

"No," the authoritative Margaret intervened. "You've to wait here. Mr Scott won't keep you waiting long."

Taken aback and confused by the turn of events, Sheena took a seat in reception.

After five minutes, another blonde, perky secretary approached and ushered Sheena into Mr Scott's office.

Mr Scott's chiselled features were sombre. "Good morning, Sheena. May I call you Sheena?"

Sheena had come over all unnecessary at finding herself in front of such a perfect specimen of mankind, and a work colleague to boot! She managed a stuttered, "Of course."

"Please, take a seat."

Sheena went to sit down, barely able to drag her eyes from his sparkling, sky-blue, summer's-day-in-the-Italian-mountains, eyes. By the time she'd figured out the right shade of blue, she'd sat awkwardly on the edge of the seat. Too close to the edge. The seat toppled over. Sheena's arms flailed, trying in vain to grab onto something, anything, and swept a full glass of water sideways across the desk, over Mr Scott's papers and onto the floor, splashing Mr Scott's perfectly shined shoes. Sheena followed suit, landing on the floor with a thump, bright pink knickers exposed for those sky-blue, summer's-day-in-the-Italian-mountains eyes to appreciate.

As Sheena lay on the ground, dazed, she squeezed her eyes shut, hoping that it was all a dream.

The next thing she knew she'd been yanked to her feet and sat on the up-righted chair. Before she could apologise, Mr Scott put a finger to her lips, said a quiet "Shhhh" as he moved closer to her, going in for a deep passionate kiss.

No, what really happened was, when she dared open her eyes, she was, indeed, upright on the chair but Mr Scott had settled behind his desk, papers back in order, if a tad damp, and the water mopped up.

"So, I recall your accidental entrance to our meeting earlier this month. You were not in regulation law-office attire. Fuchsia, I believe." Mr Scott looked at Sheena, who blushed. "And here we are, another entrance providing proof that you are all I've heard about and more." He raised an eyebrow. "A walking disaster. The most un-lawyer-like person to work in the profession that I have ever come across. I also know that Mr Dun rewarded your bad behaviour with two weeks' holiday. Well, I can tell you, that ends today. We've bought out the law practice and are making structural changes to the company. Mr Dun has retired and you are fired." He sat back in his chair and waited for Sheena's response.

All Sheena could think of was that she'd made a mistake. His eyes weren't, summer's-day-in-the-Italian-mountains blue, they were the colour of evil, the sky blue that the devil makes when he paints hell to make it look like heaven to trick poor souls into believing they are going to a good place but once the scenery is pulled down, the roaring of the fires of hell terrifies these same poor souls into a catatonic state. *Exactly that kind of blue*, Sheena thought.

"Well?"

"I'll just clear out my desk then." Sheena got up and left the office, gathering what little shred of dignity she had left around her. What else was there to say? With a Tesco bag full of bits and bobs from her desk, Sheena left the building for the last time and headed for home in a daze.

34

Kathy liked the cloak-and-dagger feel of a midnight rendezvous up a dark alley. The only problem was that it was dark. A courage-fortifying G&T in the pub around the corner didn't help so, acknowledging her inner wimp, she called Willie, a neighbour and chess addict, who also happened to be secretary of the local chess club, to meet her in the pub. A random conversation with him in the queue at the local off-licence had given her the idea for the perfect venue for her meetings.

She'd arranged for the members of her Get Into Vengeance! group to meet for the first time at the club behind the Mitchell Library. It was based in an old shop space and shared between chess and ballroom-dance enthusiasts. They had designated nights when each club could use the space and they did their utmost not to coincide. Willie said that they had, one night, and the result hadn't been pretty.

Kathy looked around as Willie put the lights on. The room had been cleared and the chess sets, tables and chairs shoved into a corner as Saturday night was ballroom-dance class night. On a trestle table stood a kettle, sugar, powdered milk and plastic cups. The only other decorations were the rival posters adorning the walls. On one wall, an ancient faded photo of Garry Kasparov showed him in deep concentration as he played against Deep Blue in 1997 along with a poster advertising a world chess boxing championship in Berlin. "Whatever next?" muttered Kathy in the general direction of Willie. "Chess ballroom dancing, I suppose." Willie shrugged his shoulders. On another wall hung a poster curled up at the edges of, no need for an introduction, Scottish ex-rugby international, Kenny Logan, kilt swinging, dancing the Paso Doble with his partner on *Strictly*.

The group members started to arrive, one by one. They milled around as Kathy and Willie pulled eighteen chairs into the middle of the floor, and placed them in a large circle, giving it the air of a group therapy session.

Ella stood outside the door, watching through the window. She took a deep breath and then another one, and then another one, and kept going until she felt slightly light-headed. As a natural introvert, the moment people saw her for the first time was always difficult for her. Whichever god decided that she had to be not only stunning, but well-endowed, combined with having low self-esteem and shyness, should be shot. She was stopped at least once a day either by model agency scouts or psychopathic murderers posing as model agency scouts. She'd used her pepper spray so often that she'd been ticked off by the police. Her neighbours approached her rarely and only with extreme caution, having decided she was an exotic creature best left alone. The Indian owner of the local late-night supermarket ducked under the counter every time she walked in even though she'd never pepper sprayed or tongue lashed him. He'd seen her do it and knew profoundly the value of discretion. He always waved her out from the safety of under the counter, without paying. It kind of worked both ways.

With one final deep breath, Ella walked in. She looked round. The scene was like Pompeii just after Vesuvius erupted. The entire group frozen in position, their heads turned towards the door. A few jaws had dropped, most of them male.

"Oh, for heaven's sake." Ella's fingertips slapped shut one mouth with a force that made teeth rattle. The sound brought the group back to life and, after a few coughs, and 'excuse me's they settled, seated, into the circle, eyes averted.

Sonia arrived in a rush, her emerald cape flying behind her, and, once she'd stored her umbrella in the umbrella bin, unhooked the clasp and removed her cape, untied her cardigan and smoothed down her sari, she added a selection of pakoras, onion bhajis and samosas onto the table next to the Jaffa Cakes and chocolate digestives, for which she earned a round of applause and was practically knocked down in the rush to grab her food.

A man Kathy didn't know, but recognised from the cafe, sat down exactly opposite Sonia. "Excuse me! Who are you?"

"I'm Sanjit." He spoke to Kathy without moving his eyes from Sonia.

"And what the hell—"

"He's my husband."

"But, why—"

"He's my husband. We do everything together."

"But you want to—"

"I know."

"So, he knows?"

"Of course, he does! He's my husband."

"But won't that—?"

"It doesn't matter."

"What's the point ...?"

"Exactly. It's a point." Sonia decided to start making her point and announced to the group, "I am a qualified GP and this is my husband Sanjit, who owns an extremely well-reviewed Indian restaurant in Glasgow which I'm sure you all know, but this is not about my husband, for once." She looked pointedly at Sanjit who remained impassive. "My husband believes that it is essential that I should continue to work in the restaurant and that I cannot be replaced. Flattering as that may seem, that is not my vocation. I would like to impress on my husband that it is now time for me, as a woman, to have the career that I was trained for." She sat down to a second round of applause.

Kathy stood up and cleared her throat. That was as far as she got. The door slammed open and Shug, full of his natural nervous energy, charged in. Behind him Charles appeared, dragging his feet, shoulders slumped. Shug pulled up short at the sight of Ella, transfixed. It was clear that he was going through an inner struggle: one part of him wanted to sit next to her and adore her from up close. The other wanted to sit opposite her just to gaze in wonder at her beauty.

They all froze in position, again. It wasn't the beauty this time, but the beast. Shug's features needed time to be absorbed. This wasn't a glance-and-look-away situation.

"Oh, for the love of ..." Ella assumed the sudden change in atmosphere was connected to her until she followed the stares and her eyes landed on Shug's face, an unfinished Picasso. She scanned it, trying to make sense of it until their eyes connected. Ella was taken aback. Most people stared at her chest rather than look her in the eyes. Now, this was interesting. Shug, bashful, couldn't handle the intensity and looked away. The spell was broken. Normal conversation resumed.

Shug found a seat directly across from Ella. He'd decided to adore her from afar. It was less stressful.

Kathy cleared her throat again and, after a quick look at the door, began. "Good evening, ladies and gentlemen. Welcome to GIVE! Get Into Vengeance! We are here to take charge of our lives once and for all. We are here to avenge those who have hurt us. We are here to wipe the slate clean, to start our lives afresh and free of baggage." Her chest swelled with pride. The tone was political rally.

Her voice lowered and she nodded gravely. "It has been a long, difficult and, at times, tedious process of selection. All of you here tonight bring together the requisite combination of intelligence and creativity required to create, and carry out, the perfect punishment to fit the crime committed." She paused.

A series of murmurs and self-congratulations rippled round the circle.

"As this is our first formal meeting and the first time you've all met in the flesh, so to speak, please introduce yourselves one by one using first names only and state the reason you are here." She looked round the circle. "I know a lot of people find it nerve-racking to speak in public so, instead of going around the group consecutively we'll play 'sudden death' where I randomly point out the next person to speak. It's easier that way." She smiled.

Gasps of horror and scrapes of chairs suggested that not everyone enjoyed being the centre of attention.

"Can we get some tea before we start?" interjected Ella. "I've just got off work and I'm gasping."

"Aye, guid idea. Ah'm spittin' feathers," commented Shug. He followed Ella a respectful two steps behind and let her get her tea before making his own. He was too shy to initiate conversation with her.

Kathy watched Shug as he poured milk into his tea. She had only a vague grasp of who he was and what he did. She had a feeling that it had to be dodgy judging by the presence of Charles who was apparently his minder.

Charles, man mountain, started to carefully unwrap, with his massive fists, a delicate china teacup and saucer. He looked up, noticing the stares.

"I dislike drinking out of plastic cups," he stated politely, his educated Edinburgh accent only drawing more sideways glances. "My name is Charles, by the way."

Kathy called the meeting to order.

35

Kathy waited until she had their attention. "Right, are you all settled now? Got your tea? I'll begin. My name is Kathy but you all know me by my Facebook name 'Screaming Minnie', and I'm the instigator of this wee gathering. I decided to set up GIVE! when I realised that I could only move on with my life once I'd got my own back on the three men who'd dumped me, who hurt me badly when I was younger, and whom, I now realise, are the source of my general unhappiness and inability to move forward. I believed, and was proven right, that I wasn't the only one in this situation. I am convinced that if we work together as a group, we will be healed of our traumas and become happier people." Kathy looked at each member of the group, one by one.

"My first act of revenge will be on a man who, in fact, by sheer chance, is currently my boss. His name is Jack." Kathy stared off into the middle distance. "Let me paint you a picture of this man. He's a doctor, a cosmetic surgeon. He's tall, dark-haired and has deep, deep blue eyes. He's as fit as a fiddle and always full of beans." Kathy briefly smiled, then shook herself back to reality. "He's known as an all-round good guy. But he hurt me. Badly. Now I can see just how immature he was. He didn't treat me like a whole person, just a collection of body parts, even though I didn't realise it at the time, until he found another set of body parts he liked better. I trusted him." Her shoulders slumped at the memory. "I thought he loved me but, no, it was only my body. He really didn't care for me as an individual at all." Kathy allowed herself the indulgence of being pulled into the memory. "I saw Jack for the first time when I'd arranged to meet my brother, William, at the bus stop. He appeared with the most handsome man I'd ever seen. I was totally star-struck from the moment our eyes met. He reminded me of the heroes in my favourite author's novels. Jack asked me out that same afternoon and we spent the next two months living between my bed and his, when we weren't studying or working."

Stuart, gripped by the story, clapped his hands. "Go on!"

"I was convinced that he loved me. I used to dream of him sweeping me off my feet and how we'd live ecstatically forever after."

A few wishful sighs floated round the room.

"We spent a wonderful weekend on Mull in a B&B in Tobermory. Imagine the romantic walks, hand-in-hand around the harbour, wrapped up against the sea breeze, eating fish and chips out of newspaper while looking out to sea. I was convinced that Jack was the one. But then, when we got back to Glasgow, everything changed. Jack was distracted and preoccupied. He told me that he had to get his act together and catch up on his studying. Eventually, I realised that he'd obviously just got tired of me. When he dumped me, he didn't even bother to do it properly."

Kathy paused to gather her thoughts. They all leaned in, eyes focused on her.

"I was late for work, as usual. Jack knew that I was always late. I saw him waiting for me at the bus stop. He came up to me and said, 'I'm sorry, but I don't love you any more. I only want to see you as a friend from now on.' He turned his back on me and walked away just as the bus came round the corner. I had a choice: lose my job for the sake of a futile argument or get the bus. I got the bus." Kathy's eyes filled at the memory and her head dropped.

Sonia broke the silence that had descended on the group as each one identified with Kathy's misery, and in a compassionate voice said, "You were both young. It's hard for a young man to deal with such a difficult and emotional situation. He probably did the best he could."

"He did not! He had no right to play with my feelings like that! I'm not going to let him get away with it. Immaturity isn't an excuse. He broke my heart." Kathy took a moment to steady herself and continued. "Now, Shug, would you like to introduce yourself?"

Shug stood up and looked around the group. "Hullo there. Ma name's Hugh McNally, Shug to ma friends, and ah'm an alky." He laughed at his own humour. "Only jokin'."

Everyone stared at his face, the broken veins an apparent testament to years dedicated to hard drinking. He continued: "Ah'm no' really an alcoholic, ah've a medical condition called rosacea which isnae caused by alcohol, although can be worsened by the consumption of said beverage. I hardly drink nowadays, do ah, Charles? Ah mean, ah like a wee bevy now and then but that disnae make us an alky or nothin'. Charles looked up that rosacea for me on the internet. It's no' common knowledge that it can be caused by other things. W. C. Fields was known for his red face and big nose, which fortunately I don't have."

He fingered his nose. "And people thought it was because of the drink. It wisnae."

"You're absolutely right, Shug," interjected Sonia. "If you'd like, we can discuss treatments to improve your condition. As I mentioned earlier, I'm a qualified GP." Sonia looked over at her husband. Sanjit looked back.

"Thank ye, Sonia, ah'll make an appointment. Can ah take your surgery's details after?"

"I'm afraid," said Sonia, her eyes not leaving her husband, "it will have to be a private consultation for the moment." She paused. "No charge, of course," she added when she saw Shug's face.

Shug continued. "Anyway, before ah begin, ah just want to say that Kathy's right. Revenge is what life's all about. Solve your problem and move on, that's my way. After all, you're a long time deid."

"Deid?' Joanna came from south of the border and was a recent addition to the Glasgow population.

"Dead," supplied Charles.

"Oh."

"Ah had a hard upbringing in a housin' scheme and ah had to become one o' the hard boys just to survive."

Drawn up to his full five feet two, Shug looked as hard as nails. He was in his mid-fifties, thin and pointy: thin body, pigeon chest, face like a gargoyle, pointy nose, pointy chin.

"Right, so, as ah've said, ah've had a hard life but that disnae mean to say that ah don't have feelings. My wife cheated on me. Caught her in bed with the milkman. The milkman! He was making deliveries to ma wife that ah hadnae ordered!" Shug stopped and looked round the group, defying them to react. Faces turned away. Hands covered mouths. Shug continued. "Humiliatin' so it was. Ah went fur the wee toerag. Kicked lumps out of him. Ah don't understand it. He wisnae great lookin'. Face like a melted wellie. Ah just cannae grasp what she sees in him." Shug shrugged his pointy shoulders. "Any road, ah have to get ma own back on the missus. So, ah am thinking reckon this group is perfect for my needs." He sat down.

"Thank you, Shug. Now, Charles, would you take the floor?" asked Kathy politely.

Charles looked up, teacup in one hand, right pinkie extended, the saucer held up delicately in his left hand. Everyone stared. He looked embarrassed. "I'm really only here to support Shug. I don't know how much use I can be. I have joint degrees in English Literature and History at Edinburgh University and a PhD in 'The History of the Art of Pugilism as Practised in the Inner Cities of Scotland in the First Half of the Twentieth Century'. I also have several heavyweight boxing trophies and I teach yoga to the pensioners at the local community centre on a Saturday morning."

"Aye, he's the man," commented Shug, looking on proudly.

Charles continued. "Personally, I have no grudge to bear on anyone. I've known my wife since we were at primary school together, but," Charles stifled a sob, "she's taken a notion to go and 'find herself'. Someone has put ideas in her head and I'm lost without her." Charles paused and looked even sadder. "I miss not being able to put my head on her shoulder at the end of the day."

Charles bowed his head and a single tear stretched out and fell, with a gentle plop, into his cup of tea. Hankies were pulled out and noses blown. No one said a word as a low sigh emanated from the depths of Charles's chest and rumbled round the room.

36

Kathy discreetly wiped her eyes. "It's getting late. The rest of you, please be brief."

Three were too shy to speak in public and another three were less than articulate as they'd spent the evening in the pub prior to the meeting, which left a British Airways flight attendant, Stuart, to describe the string of male lovers going back decades that he wanted to avenge come hell or high water for no reason that was apparent to anyone.

Joanna, a secretary who worked at a temp agency, had given up her life in London to come and live with her boyfriend in Glasgow, who then dumped her just three weeks after installing herself in his flat.

Dougie, a lawyer, was sick to death of his high-flying wife, who seemed to be better than him at whatever she turned her hand to, and, therefore, according to Dougie, deserved her comeuppance.

Fiona, the traffic warden, had had enough of the abuse she got on a daily basis, but one person in particular got right up her nose every single, fucking day. She'd had it.

Alison, a psychotherapist, was fed up of listening to people whinging on about their lives when her own was in such a mess. She'd found out that her husband was having an affair. Once she'd got her own back on him, she had a list of at least a dozen people she'd enjoy making sure lived to regret the day they'd met her.

And, finally, Ella, gave a brief but graphic description of the treatment she received from men in general and her boss and punters at the pub she worked in, in particular. Shug had his full attention on Ella.

"Now," said Kathy, "let's get to work. I need a team to work with me on Operation Body Shop to revenge Jack. Ella, we're going to put those breasts of yours to work."

This gave everyone, finally, the permission to stare at what they'd tried to avoid during the entire meeting. All except for Shug. He had no idea of Ella's physical attributes below the neck. He didn't really see her properly at all. All he saw was a bubble of beauty and magic emanating from her. Ella raised her eyes to the heavens as a form of supplication while they stared, and, again, they crossed with Shug's. He was looking at who she was, not what she was, she realised. Shug, bashful, broke the gaze and started to whistle tunelessly. Ella smiled.

Kathy continued. "I can't have you looking frumpy. Do you have *any* decent clothes?" Ella looked offended and picked at her jumper. "OK, tomorrow we're going shopping. I need you to look elegant and sophisticated on Monday."

"Shug?"

"Aye, Kathy, whit can ah do ye for?"

"You wouldn't happen to have fake police credentials by any chance, would you?"

"Strangely enough ah do." He smiled. Charles also, sadly, nodded his confirmation.

"Excellent," said Kathy. "I need Ella and Shug in one group to work on the Body Shop. Fiona, you, Dougie and

Stuart can work on Clamp City. Joanna, I need you to work with me on Up Yours. And Shug, do you need any help with Dung Ho!?" Shug shook his head.

Kathy continued. "I have to warn you that money's tight. The webpage for GIVE! hasn't had much time to build up business so, please, keep your ideas on the cheap and cheerful side and we'll have a whip round later to see what we can contribute. Now, Charles, what's your superpower apart from the ability to break bricks with your hand?" Kathy cocked her head, to make sure that Charles realised it was a joke.

Charles smiled back. "I'll manage the logistics. Once a team has the overall plan organised, I'll break it down to its essential elements, timed to the second."

As inevitably happens when there is a doctor in the house, various members of the group took the opportunity to ask Sonia about their aches and pains and show her various body parts. Sonia had become the team medic.

At 3 a.m. Kathy drew the meeting to a close with a pledge. "Ladies and gentlemen! I'd like your attention, please! I'd like us all to make a solemn vow, a commitment to this process, to this healing act of revenge and to its successful conclusion. We pledge to commit these acts of revenge within a ten-day time period and conclude—"

Stuart interrupted. "Can we have a party to celebrate when it's all over? I love a good party."

Kathy stared at Stuart, incredulous that he would interrupt her in mid-flow. "A party? Just a party? What I have in mind will not be a party. It will be the event of the century. And all your targets will be there too." She smiled. "We're not just going to get our revenge and run away without them knowing who was behind it. We will stand up to those cowards and tell them to their faces. Yep, when this is all over, it's going to be one hell of a party."

She raised her glass of water and looked towards the heavens. "For the love of Barbara!"

Confused but swept up, regardless, in their leader's fervour, the group members raised their glasses and said in unison, "For the love of Barbara!"

37

Sheena woke up early on the Monday morning after her Friday firing. She lay in bed, with no reason to get up, and the enormity of her situation finally sank in with a resounding thump in the bottom of her stomach. Claiming that she felt under the weather, she'd avoided all social contact over the weekend. What was she going to tell her parents? What was she going to tell her friends?

Recognising that she needed to accept the pure facts of the matter before she could figure out her next move, she got up and, as she made coffee, repeated the phrase out loud over and over again. "I've lost my job. I've lost my job." She seriously contemplated a shot of brandy to steady her nerves.

"You've done what?" Dan was standing in the doorway, Annie a step behind.

"Oh my God, Sheena, what have you done?" Annie's hands flew to her face.

"I haven't done anything! It was done to me! The company has been taken over. There's a whole new group of senior partners and they fired me for no good reason! Well, I mean not a good enough reason, at least, in my eyes ..." her voice tailed off.

Chapter 37

Dan's tone was dry. "Do you think, maybe, possibly, if you'd done your job properly you might not have been fired? Any thoughts on the matter?"

Sheena just stared into the bottom of her cup, avoiding eye contact.

"Have you told your parents? And what are you going to do about the house? Do you expect your parents to continue contributing to the mortgage when you have no prospects? Are you expecting them to pay it all when you've disappointed them? And have you started looking for another job to sustain yourself? Have you spent the weekend planning or just plain wallowing?" Annie poured herself a coffee and waved an accusing croissant at Sheena.

Sheena was dismissive, and half-hearted. "I don't know. Something'll turn up."

"To have something turn up, you have to do something to make it happen. You can't just sit on your arse waiting for the world to come to you." It was Dan's turn to wave an accusing croissant. A chocolate one.

Sheena straightened up and tried to look decisive. She looked Dan straight in the eye. "Don't worry, Dan. I really wasn't much of a lawyer anyway. It's time for me to find a career better suited to my personality. It'll be a blessing in disguise. I'm sure I have hidden talents. Do you know what? I could be a personal shopper. I'm very good at that."

Dan threw his hands up in despair.

"What?"

"Nothing. I have to go to work. See you later."

"So, what are your plans for the rest of the day?" enquired Annie.

"I don't know. Maybe I'll have a look round the shops."

"For the love of God, Sheena! Don't you get it? You have no income! You can't go around spending money! Don't you dare buy anything! I know you!" With a waggle of the banana she'd taken from Sheena's fruit bowl, Annie left to look for some peace and calm before work.

"It's research!" shouted Sheena at Annie's back and briefly considered changing the locks.

38

Jack's day had started badly, then got worse. He'd forgotten to set the alarm. When he finally woke and realised that his lovely long sleep was just that, long, he went into overdrive. Rushing, he cut himself shaving and wasted a valuable five minutes stemming the flow of blood with toilet paper. After throwing on his suit and, with a perfunctory run of his hand through his hair, completed his grooming, he dashed out the front door.

His brisk march through reception with bits of toilet paper stuck to his face, did not go unnoticed by the waiting clients. Raised eyebrows and disapproving glances in his direction suggested that his skills with a scalpel were being brought into question. He gave Kathy a look that ensured she kept her comments to herself and shut himself in his office.

Kathy had hardly slept all night. She'd been too excited about putting Operation Body Shop into action.

When she'd walked into the cafe to meet Ella for an early breakfast and final briefing, she had to admit she was a bit jealous of what she saw. Ella no longer looked stunning in spite of her clothes. Ella was now a film star receiving film-star attention. The cafe was buzzing. Customers jostled and elbowed to get selfies with her and ask for her autograph.

Ella had chosen to wear simple, elegant, straight-legged black trousers which accentuated her slender shape. High-heeled black sandals made her legs seem to go on forever, even on her tiny frame. On top, she wore a form-fitting bright-red shirt, the top buttons tantalisingly open down to that particular button which, straining and looking ready to pop, gave more than a hint of what was to be found below and, Kathy could imagine that every man, and a few women, in the cafe wanted to rip open. Her jewellery was understated and looked real enough for the occasion. Her carefully applied make-up, the smoky eye shadow and liner, made her deep grey eyes look enormous, framed by her pixie cut. Her lips were painted a shirt-matching, luscious red. It was a lot to take in for the cafe customers first thing on a Monday morning.

Ella actually liked her look, the attention not so much, but as an acting opportunity, she was playing up the supermodel film-star role for all it was worth.

When they sat down at a table and the customers finally returned to their cooling coffees, Kathy tried to attract a waiter's attention. He rushed to the table and, looking at Ella, asked her what she would like.

"A cappuccino, if you please," interjected Kathy.

"Here." Ella handed her a cappuccino. The table was littered with every kind of coffee imaginable.

"What's all this?"

"I don't know. They keep appearing out of nowhere. I haven't actually ordered. Anyway, take your pick. I only want a latte."

After she'd established that Ella had rehearsed, as an actor would, the various different scenarios, Kathy went to work. Ella would arrive for her appointment at 11.30 a.m. By Friday, Kathy had already known what Ella would be doing on Monday morning, even if Ella wasn't going to find out until Saturday night, and Kathy had added her name, Ella Kay, to Jack's appointment diary.

On the way to work, Kathy called Shug, waking him up and receiving an earful of insults as a result. He clearly wasn't a morning person, but she did manage to confirm with him that he had it all organised, ready to go. She arranged a lunchtime get-together to review Ella's morning appointment with Jack, just in case Ella had any information that Charles and Shug could use for their afternoon visit. She'd interrupted Charles in the middle of his morning yoga, and despite being in the middle of the crow pose, he still managed to answer his mobile. As polite as ever, he confirmed the time and venue for lunch and that he was ready. Kathy hung up just as she heard his deep Eeyore sigh.

She was at work and well settled behind her desk by the time Jack marched in with a patchwork of toilet paper stuck to his face.

At 11.30 a.m. on the dot, Kathy brought Ella through to Jack's office.

39

Kathy opened her mouth to introduce Ella but Jack beat her to it.

"Ella! You haven't changed a bit!" A huge grin appeared on Jack's face. "I did wonder if it was you. I recognised the name but, you never know, you might have married and changed your surname. I wasn't sure. But I'm wrong. You have changed, you look even more amazing. I can't imagine why you're here."

Ella stood stock still, paralysed, in shock.

"Anyway, it's so nice to see you again! Come in! Come in!"

Ella walked slowly into the middle of the room trying to figure out what to do next. With her best face she greeted Jack enthusiastically and they talked about their days at university before she'd dropped out, how long it had been since they'd last met and obvious allusions to the fact that they had gone out. During this exchange Kathy looked on in her own state of shock. She stood behind Jack and gesticulated madly at Ella, desperate for a sign, desperate to know what was going on, placing Ella in the difficult position of having to continue her conversation with Jack while Kathy semaphored in the background.

Chapter 39

Jack invited Ella to sit down and, as he sat across from her, he got down to business. "So, Ella, what can I do for you?" he said, smiling at her, using his professional tone.

Ella hesitated then took a deep breath. "Well, you can imagine, I'm sure. I've had enough of these breasts for a lifetime. Apart from all the attention I get, which I hate, my back's killing me from the weight of them. I want them reduced. You can do that, can't you?"

At this point Ella wasn't acting. The idea of not having to lug around these two weights on her chest every day sounded actually like a pretty decent idea. "It'll be a relief to be normal."

She sat back, conflicted. She hadn't given it much thought at the time, caught up in the group energy, but, sitting there in front of Jack, she worried about the impact of her actions. She liked him. If she'd known it was Jack that Kathy wanted to avenge, then she wouldn't have agreed to play this role. That said, Kathy was a slightly terrifying character, and hard to refuse. She glanced over at her. Kathy stared intently at Ella, willing her telepathically to keep on going. She didn't want to find herself on the receiving end of one of Kathy's revenges, and after a brief inner struggle, convinced herself that she had to go through with it. She pulled herself up straight and focused.

"Honestly, Ella." Jack reached out to hold her hand in reassurance. "I wouldn't rush into it. You may regret this later."

"I don't know how much each of these things weighs but I suggest you find out. Strap two equivalent weights to your chest and see how your back likes it!" More quietly, she said, "Please, Jack, I need you to help me out."

"OK. Well, we'd better take a look then and I'll explain your options to you."

Ella started to unbutton her blouse.

At that point Kathy said, "Oops. I forgot something. Back in a jiffy." She left Jack's office and loitered around her desk for five minutes before returning to the consulting room just in time to see Ella put her blouse back on.

"I've changed my mind," said Ella and, throwing an angry look at Jack, she stalked out of the room.

"What happened?" said Kathy, struggling not to smirk.

"I don't know." Jack looked perplexed.

40

⮁

Desperate to know the story between Ella and Jack, Kathy ran out of the office at the stroke of one to the cafe around the corner where they'd arranged to meet for an update. Before even sitting down she burst out, "What the hell is going on? Why didn't you say you knew him?"

Ella was defensive. "You didn't give me his second name and there's more than one Jack Trainer in the world, you know. I didn't expect to meet a doctor I'd gone out with twenty years ago. I did what you asked. That's all that matters, isn't it?"

"Don't worry, hen," said Shug. "It'll all work out fine." He went to pat her on the hand, but changed his mind. "Ah'm sure we can make use of the information. Good to know." Shug rubbed his hands together. He couldn't wait to get his hands on Jack.

"Thank God for that," said Kathy, relieved, as she sank down in the seat.

***

Back at work, Kathy was as jumpy as a scalded cat. Every sound and she leapt out of her skin. Even Jack, who was preoccupied by Ella's odd reaction, noticed and asked her what had got into her. She looked at the clock constantly and James caught her muttering to herself. William, knowing Kathy better than anyone, took one look and gave her a wide berth.

The previous Friday she'd surreptitiously rescheduled all Jack's appointments for that afternoon. She wanted Shug and Charles to be seen by as few people as possible.

Outside, on the corner Shug was doing breathing and voice exercises. His *ohs*, *ahs* and *ees* turned a few heads. He was not messing around. "Come on, Charles," he said, reaching up to knead Charles's tense shoulders. "You may not be the natural actor ah am but ye'll be fine."

Charles frowned. "The man doesn't deserve this, Shug. Kathy's not right in the head, if you ask me." He tapped his temple.

"Aw, it's just a bit a fun. He might not see the funny side of it now, but ah bet he will later. He looked at his watch. "Curtain up," he said and strode off.

***

Jack's office door crashed open, breaking his concentration as he wrote up a client's file. In marched a small man, chest puffed out. Shug could barely breathe but the overall effect was worth it. Following closely behind was a huge man who closed the door behind him and stayed there in classic hands-clasped-in-front-of-balls, bodyguard pose, blocking the exit.

Kathy rushed to Jack's office looking flustered, while doing a happy dance inside, so she could apologise for the intrusion. She shoved the door open, but it bounced off the immovable object that was Charles and slammed shut again.

41

Shug stepped in front of Jack's desk and, hopping from one foot to another in sheer excitement hopefully masked as fury, extended an accusing finger at Jack. "Ye did it! Ye're just as ah expected. Ye did it!"

Jack laughed, suddenly nervous, palms extended in innocence. "If it was well done then I did it, but if it was botched then it must have been the competition." He tried to take control of the situation. "Would you do me the honour of giving me your name?"

Shug slammed his hands on the desk and leaned forward, wincing. Jack reflexively pushed his chair back away from the desk until it crashed against the wall behind him, as much to get away from the shower of spittle heading his way as any sense of being threatened.

"Ye felt her up! Ye copped a feel!"

"Who? What are you talking about?" stuttered Jack.

"Ye pretend ye don't know or maybe ye just feel up all your clients and ye dinnae know which one we're talkin' about!" shouted Shug. "Ha!" he added unnecessarily.

"This, this is preposterous!" stuttered Jack, taken aback by his own choice of words.

"*Preposterous*?" sneered Shug, dragging the word out, enjoying himself immensely. "No innocent man says that. No Scot says that unless they're a pompous, guilty eejit. Ye're a disgrace tae the nation!" He stepped back from the desk. Jack looked completely overwhelmed. He'd barely even threatened him. *Big Jessie*, thought Shug.

Jack slowly pulled his chair back towards his desk, and, in an attempt to get a sense of the situation, he took a moment to look the two men over with a professional eye. It served to calm him. The large gentleman needed major nose reconstruction work. He could imagine the supersonic sound of his snoring rattling the windows of his neighbourhood. As for the wee one, to make sense of that face would be a life's work.

"Please, tell me what exactly, and who exactly, you are talking about. But first of all, who are you?"

"Ma name is Detective Inspector McNally," stated Shug officiously. "An' this here is Detective Constable Campbell." Charles politely bowed his head in greeting, but avoided meeting Jack's eyes.

"May I see your credentials?" Jack's mind was racing. Shug passed over a police identity card, which Jack, not really knowing any better, could only assume was real.

"We found Ms Ella Kay distraught on the street corner. Said ye'd felt her up when all she'd wanted was a consultation. We take this kind of harassment very seriously."

Jack was stunned. "That allegation is totally ridiculous. I did not feel her up. It was a medical examination. It was necessary to touch her. But in a professional manner," he added quickly as it looked like Shug was going to climb over the desk and strangle him with his bare hands.

"Then ye'll have to prove to us that you didnae feel her up. And ah know, for a fact, that ye can't!" Shug stabbed a finger in the air for emphasis. "Go on, tell us about this consultation then." He crossed his arms and tapped his foot, waiting. Smug.

Jack smiled politely. "I'm afraid that information is confidential. Client–patient privilege, and all that."

Shug took his time and paced the office in an attempt to look alert and intelligent, then he took a large stride back to Jack's desk and leaned over menacingly, his face in Jack's face. "If you continue to refuse to cooperate, we will continue this little conversation doon the jile!" He sneered at Jack who had to lean away from Shug's foul breath, a result of the deep-fried haggis, black pudding and chips he'd had for lunch.

Charles spoke quietly. "It would be better for all concerned if you could describe the nature and events of that consultation at," he consulted a notebook, "11.30 this morning."

Opting for prudence, Jack spoke quietly. "OK. I guess I can give you an idea of the consultation without going into personal details as it was really brief." He cleared his throat. "Ms Kay arrived at 11.30 a.m. as DC Campbell correctly stated, requesting a consultation concerning certain changes she wished to make. I'm not at liberty to provide details of those changes. She wanted to feel better about herself. That is, after all, what we do here. During the consultation she had a change of heart and left. She was in my office for about ten, maximum fifteen minutes. That's it." Jack shrugged his shoulders and held his hands out, palms up. He looked from Charles to Shug and back.

"And ye copped a feel, taking advantage of a poor vulnerable wee lassie," accused Shug. "We found her wandering the streets. Ah don't know for how long but she was in a terrible state, sobbin' her poor little heart out." Shug momentarily forgot where he was and imagined himself a white knight rescuing the damsel that was Ella.

"She explained, *in detail*," he emphasised, "to us and a female officer, exactly what had happened and ah have to say that ah am disgusted, *disgusted*." Shug screwed up his face, disgusted.

Charles, who'd been quietly taking notes, looked up. "Ms Kay has stated that you were alone with her during the examination. There was no nurse in attendance. Is this correct, Dr Trainer?"

Jack went white. Kathy had left just as he started the examination. He hadn't thought much of it at the time, but it was true. He stammered, "Yes, the nurse did pop out for a second. But I can assure you that nothing untoward occurred." His hands started to sweat.

"Ms Kay has decided to hold off makin' formal charges for the moment. She wants tae think about it to make sure that she's doin' the right thing. She was strongly, and ah mean strongly, advised tae take legal advice and to press charges immediately, but she wants time tae think. This here is a formal warning. Ye're no' off the hook and ah'm sure ye'll be charged in the next few days. Consider yersel' warned. Keep yer nose clean and know that we are keepin' a close eye on you." Shug winked at Jack and, with a gesture of cocking a gun with his finger, left the office, followed by Charles.

42

Jack left the office without a word to anyone, went to an out of the way pub, and installed himself at the bar with no plans to leave any time soon.

In the meantime, not far from the clinic, Kathy and Ella anxiously waited for Charles and Shug in a pub whose clientele looked as if they practically lived there. Kathy knew they wouldn't bump into anyone she worked with. She liked the place. No one put on any airs and graces and, despite the majority masculine element, and the smell of testosterone, no one seemed to mind that she was now the pub pool champion.

Shug came charging into the pub, tears of laughter streaming down his face. He could barely get the words out. "Hook. Line. Sinker." He collapsed onto a chair and howled with laughter. Kathy and Ella did a victory Highland Fling round the table. Charles took himself off to the bar to order drinks. He looked glum. It took a couple of minutes for Shug to settle down enough to be able to recount the story.

"That was dead brilliant, so it was," said Shug as he took a large draught of his pint. "He questioned nothing. It was easy. Ah'm sure he's so confused now he disnae even remember our names." He leaned over and pecked Ella's cheek then sat back, his own overly red cheeks taking on a new hue.

Ella's normal reaction to an unsolicited peck on the cheek was a punch in the jaw. She forced herself to unclench her fist and looked at Shug, discomfited at his own audacity. She felt a touch of warmth towards this lost soul. Maybe as lost as she was. She smiled at him but he didn't see it, now suddenly too embarrassed to look at her.

Charles had his nose in his pint, quiet. Kathy looked over at him. "What's up, Charles? You don't think it went well?"

"Yes, yes. It was perfect. He took it all in. Deception is just not my forte. It's dishonest, but I'm doing it because it's all in a good cause, and for Shug." He looked over at Shug and they raised glasses in a silent toast that spoke volumes but said not a word. Kathy chose not to enquire. She smiled grimly. "One down, two to go."

43

The following morning, Shug got up in his tiny tenement flat and looked around. He missed a woman's touch now that he'd left his wife. He had many talents, but home decoration was not one of them. He could make a mean paper chain but that was it. The few pieces of furniture he'd bought looked sad and lost even in the confined space. He'd been dreaming of Ella. Before even his morning tea and toast he dug out the piece of paper that had the contact details of every member of GIVE!, found Ella's phone number and sat and stared at it.

The ticking of his grandfather's grandfather clock got louder and louder. It was the only major piece of furniture he'd taken with him when he'd left the marital home. The dense silence got denser. Staring at the number had taken Shug down an *Alice in Wonderland* wormhole and he found himself lost in a world he didn't truly understand. He couldn't remember the last time he'd felt any emotions for anyone other than his wife. He shook the feeling off and dialled Ella's number before he could change his mind, and without any idea of what he was going to say.

Ella didn't answer numbers she didn't recognise. Too

many weirdos called her. Lord knows how they got her number. But something made her answer this call. Silence.

"Hello?"

A clearing of the throat. "Ahhh. Emmm. Hello." Shug fought off the powerful desire to hang up and go for a lie down. The stress had his blood pressure somewhere up in outer space.

"Shug? Is that you?"

"Ahhhhhhhhh, ehhh, aye" was the best he could manage.

Ella wasn't altogether surprised at the phone call. Her voice took on an unusually gentle tone. She felt his energy so delicate that he might shatter into a thousand pieces if she didn't take care. "Good morning, Shug. How are you?"

"AAhhhhhhhhh, ehhhh, aye. Fine. Ahem." He cleared his throat. "And yourself?"

"I'm very well. How can I help you?"

"Oh, aye, well." Shug gathered every brain cell available and managed to make sense. "These set-ups are complicated. Ah mean, we're workin' together on a few and ah thought," he cleared his throat, "we should maybe talk strategy. Ye know whit ah mean?"

"You mean, on a date?"

Shug practically fainted. "Ah meant, no, but well, it's strategy." Lame wasn't the word for it.

"So, it's not a date then?"

"Well, ah, well, ah wouldn't, eh, be so forward."

"Go for it." Ella gave him a break.

"Oh, well, oh, OK. Tonight? Too soon? At 8? Stoat and Weasel?" Shug was desperate to get off the phone. He needed a lie down. Badly.

"See you later." Ella hung up the phone. She didn't exactly know what to think of Shug. She was intrigued. She'd never gone out with a man who looked quite like him. A unique specimen of the male species if ever there was one.

44

By Tuesday evening, Sheena was thoroughly fed up. Bored.

She'd left her mobile on silent to avoid the 'I told you so' that half the neighbourhood was no doubt dying to say to her. She picked at a listless pasta dinner, then bit the bullet and checked her messages. Six popped up from James which lifted her spirits. For a brief moment she imagined that he'd finally realised that he loved her and couldn't wait to tell her. But sense prevailed: even Sheena knew this was highly unlikely. She calmed herself down and listened to the messages. Each one sounded increasingly anxious. It was about Jack. He'd phoned in that morning to cancel all appointments and then switched off his mobile. This was totally out of character and James was extremely worried.

Sheena called him back.

"I've found him, finally," James said, tremor of panic in his voice. "I knew something was wrong. He's in an old haunt of ours, The Stoat and Weasel. He looks awful. God knows where he slept last night, he smells terrible. He's almost suicidally drunk and he won't talk to me. He keeps asking for you. You have to come down here now. I'll wait outside. He doesn't even want to see me."

Dressing with her usual care, Sheena headed out to the pub. She wasn't particularly concerned. She assumed that the last model Jack had gone out with had blown him off and he was nursing his dented pride. Nothing more serious than a bruised ego.

She found James anxiously pacing outside the pub. "Where have you been? I'm worried sick here. He could have killed himself by now." Sheena ignored him and looked up at the pub sign. It was an accident waiting to happen. Just then two men walked past them on their way in and one commented to the other, "What's the difference between a stoat and a weasel? I've always wondered." There it was. James couldn't resist. Sheena's world went into slow motion as she put her arm out to stop him. His voice came across to her as though through water, his features blurred. Just as she tried to articulate a loud "*Noooooooo*," James turned to the man.

"Well," he said. "That's easy. A weasel is weasel-ly recognised while a stoat is stoat-ally different." He grinned and the two men laughed as they opened the door and entered the pub.

James turned to Sheena. "See, it wasn't so bad. No blood spilled."

Sheena groaned having heard the joke a thousand times.

Sheena knew the Stoat and Weasel of old; they'd frequented it as students. Since then, it had gone through various stages of redecoration but the clientele had never cared much about the decor. One sweep of the room and Sheena saw the full range: from overalls to grunge to Armani and back to overalls. Some called it retro-trendy, whatever that meant, and some called it eclectic, but all it achieved was to offend Sheena's sense of style. She picked her way through the stench of sweat at one end of the bar to the stink of Hugo Boss at the other. She found Jack in a corner, slouched, head down, a full pint of heavy in front of him. He looked up at her with bleary, bloodshot eyes. He hadn't shaved and his dark beard was growing in fast. Sheena had never seen him in such a terrible state. He smiled up at her. "Hello, Sheena, just the gal I wanted to see," he slurred. James nodded at Sheena and indicated that he'd wait at the far end of the bar.

Jack looked like a little lost boy. Sheena smiled. In amongst it all, whatever it was that had happened to him, he still managed to look cute. It took a while for Jack to gather his thoughts. Sheena waited patiently, watching the wheels turn behind those ravaged bloodshot blue eyes. He attempted to speak then changed his mind. Started again then pulled back.

Sheena put a hand over his. "It's OK, whatever it is. You know you can tell me and I promise to keep it just between us."

"OK, but you can't tell anyone. You have to promise."

"I promise."

"I, I, I've been accused of sexual assault." Jack turned away, humiliated.

"What?" Sheena almost came off her stool in surprise. She grabbed his arm and made him look at her. "No! What? That makes no sense. You must have been hallucinating. You've been drinking an awful lot."

"No, that's it. God's honest truth." He stared into his beer seeing the events unfold exactly as they had happened. "An old girlfriend of mine turned up unexpectedly wanting a breast reduction." He continued, staring sadly into his pint. "Suddenly she changed her mind. I don't know why. I'd barely started examining her before she stormed out, and the next thing I know I have two policemen in my office accusing me of having assaulted her."

Jack's head fell onto his hands and he started to sob. Sheena looked around, alarmed. Fortunately, the music in the bar was loud enough to cover the sound, and she put a comforting arm round his shoulders.

"This doesn't make sense. Tell me every detail. Come on, Jack. I'm here to help. I'm a lawyer, well, I mean … but that's another story. Please, talk to me."

Jack pulled himself together and began a blow-by-blow account of the events of the previous day. Self-absorbed as Sheena was, she was, nevertheless, a remarkably good listener.

45

The Stoat and Weasel was probably Shug's favourite pub. It was an odd place, neither one thing or another. Shug identified with that, especially as a newly single man at his age. He couldn't believe his eyes when Ella actually walked into the snug where he'd managed to intimidate a couple into relinquishing a quiet corner table. Nobody else could believe their eyes either when they saw who this vision of beauty was meeting. A quick visit to the bar got him a gin and tonic for Ella and a Dewar's for himself and then he settled down to gaze at her. He didn't have a plan, he didn't need to talk; having Ella sitting across the table from him was already beyond his wildest dreams.

After a bit of prodding from Ella, they managed to have something of a conversation, but he was so besotted he found it hard to concentrate as long as could gaze into those deep, dark grey pools. After a while he got up to get another round. Crossing to the bar, he looked across the pub and his and Sheena's eyes met. They both panicked, but for different reasons.

Shug saw Jack sitting with her. He stopped short. If Jack looked up, he would recognise Shug. He willed Ella not to decide to go to the toilet right now as she would cross Jack's line of sight if she did.

Sheena's head swivelled, fear pricking sweat on her forehead as she looked for Charles. The last thing she needed was him to appear at her side and threaten her with all sorts of physical damage. Jack, oblivious to the events going on around him, was in no state to take on any man, much less Charles. Sheena's pulse slowed, Charles was nowhere in sight. She watched Shug hurry out of the pub dragging a startled woman with him. Sheena refocused on Jack.

"I've really done it. I'm totally screwed. I don't know what I'll do if I'm struck off. That's it. Done. The end." Jack put his head in his hands. "I committed sexual assault. I assaulted a woman. I didn't know I'd done it. I didn't mean it but I did it and now I'm in deep shit. The police said so."

"I don't get it. How this could have happened with a nurse present?"

Jack looked at Sheena, desolate. "Kathy left the room. I was on my own with my client."

"Kathy left you alone?" Sheena's blood boiled. "She's crazy! Ooh, I'll wring her neck when I get my hands on her. She knows better than to leave you alone."

"Ella's an ex. Maybe she had a grudge against me. Maybe she took advantage of the opportunity. Maybe she has financial problems and wants to sue me. I mean, she undressed and I had just started the examination and turned away to pick up my notebook, and when I turned back she was already dressing and just walked out as Kathy walked in."

"There's too many maybes. This is too weird for words."

"I think I should try and see Ella," said Jack.

Sheena paused, thoughtful. "No. I wouldn't do that if I were you. At least, not yet. Give it a few days. She probably needs time to think it through. I'm sure she'll realise that it was all a big mistake." She paused for a moment. "What you really need to do is get back to work immediately and not let it take over your life."

Jack went to take a swig of his pint, but Sheena moved it out of his reach.

He nodded. "You're right. I need to pull myself together. I don't want anyone to know, especially not James and William."

Sheena's brows raised in surprise. "But they're your partners in the practice, and your best friends. They should know. What if this doesn't go away? They have to be prepared."

Jack was insistent. "No. There's no point in all three of us running scared. Our clients would notice. We should carry on as normal."

"So, what are you going to tell James?"

"Oh, I don't know. Girl trouble?"

Sheena laughed. "Well, at least you haven't lost your sense of humour. I doubt he'll believe you but if that's the best you've got then go with it. Come on. It's time you went home and sobered up. I don't envy you the hangover but there ye go."

She gave the nod to James who came over to help. Jack wasn't very stable so, with one arm round James's shoulder, he got him out onto the street. As the fresh air hit, Jack looked like he could throw up any minute.

"He's all yours, James – take the man home."

James looked up and down the street. "No taxi driver's going to stop with him in this state. We'll take the bus if I can get him across the road. Once I've tucked him up in bed I'll check in with William and we can share his appointments tomorrow. There's no way he'll be fit for work."

"Thanks, Sheena," said Jack drunkenly. "You're a star. I love you. I really do."

"And I love you too," responded Sheena with an absent-minded pat on Jack's arm.

"No, I mean it, I really do. I really love you." Jack suddenly whirled around and vomited in the gutter.

"He's definitely all yours," said Sheena grimly and headed off down the street leaving James to get him home in one piece.

Shug and Ella were at the bus stop across the road. Shug dialled and redialled Kathy's mobile until she finally responded.

"He's got a lawyer," he practically yelled down the phone.

"Who, what?"

He saw Jack and Sheena come out of the pub and dropped his voice to a hoarse whisper. "If Jack's lawyer starts investigatin', it'll all blow up in our faces. Whit are we goin' to dae?"

"OK, calm down," said Kathy, her voice tense with frustration. "How do you know he's got a lawyer?"

"Ella and I were havin' a wee swally down the Stoat and Weasel and I saw him in there with a lawyer I met a couple a weeks ago. He's well bladdered but he must have called for advice!"

"Well, duh, that doesn't sound very lawyerly." The words 'bunch of amateurs' floated through her mind. "OK. I'm sure it'll be fine. Can I get back to my dinner now?" Kathy's breathing was strained.

Shug hung up the phone, grabbed Ella by the arm, yanked it, despite her howled protest, causing James to look in their direction, and dragged her behind the bus stop. "We've got to get away fae here without them seein' us," he hissed just as a bus rounded the corner. Shug hailed it, stepping out into the light at the last possible second and they both hopped on.

"That was close. I didnae look at the number, where's this bus go?"

"It actually takes us right to my place," said Ella. "Come back with me. I've got some of the good stuff at home. We need a stiff drink after all the excitement."

Shug's eyes widened. Alone in a girl's flat, with a girl.

46

Kathy carefully snapped shut her mobile, gathered her strength and hurled it across the room. As it smashed against the wall, the battery flew under the desk and the inert body of the phone landed in the sink. After ten minutes of intoning her most calming mantra, "Barbara, Barbara, Barbara", she got up, crossed the room, opened the sacred trunk and extracted one of the newly bought books, sat back down and focused on the cover. Concentrating, she gripped the book hard and felt herself falling through the words into a place where she could focus and think clearly, where the world didn't intervene in her thoughts.

She raised her eyes to the heavens and said out loud, "Barbara, I need you to help me to figure out how Jack might react. I need to be better prepared. What I intended to do was humiliate him, um, no, no, that's someone else ... Eh, shame, shame, that's it, that's what I wanted to achieve. I wanted him to feel shame. You understand, don't you, Barbara? That's how he made me feel when he dumped me. I loved him and he threw it back in my face."

Kathy remembered that morning. She'd sobbed all the way to work on the bus. She didn't remember how she'd got through her work day, only that she went to the pub afterwards and got outrageously drunk, and threw herself at the men in the bar, screaming at them until they threw her out.

"Hmm, that's a good point, Barbara. So far, Jack has done pretty much the same thing. I guess we're not that different after all."

Kathy also remembered that she'd told no one. The sense of shame was too strong. How could an intelligent woman like her have been taken in like that? From the next morning onwards, she'd carried on her life as normal, hiding her hurt and shame.

"Yes, Barbara, I think he'd do that too. His shame would be too powerful to let him talk about it freely. That said, he knows a lawyer well enough to meet him in a pub. That's worrying."

Mind you, she thought, *if Sheena was anything to go by, lawyers moved like molasses*. This meant that she had time to see it through before any real threat emerged. With a huge grin of relief and a "Thank you, Barbara!", she gave the cover of the book a big kiss and threw it back in the trunk.

Kathy decided that she should probably make herself scarce. Jack wouldn't be too chuffed with her right now. She took the executive decision to disappear for a few days. Packing a bag, she thought she'd go over to Ella's and see if she could bunk down there for the duration.

As she tried to slip out of the house she bumped into Dan and The Wee Besom coming back from a long walk, via the local pub. The Wee Besom, tongue lolling, almost bowled Kathy over as she rushed into the house.

"Leaving us?" enquired Dan.

"No, no, just off to the gym. See you later."

And with a cheery wave Kathy made her escape.

47

Kathy arrived at Ella's building. The main front door was just drifting closed as another tenant left, and she walked straight in. She checked the flat number in the group file on her phone and headed up to the second floor and rang the doorbell.

From the other side of the door, Kathy heard a voice she recognised.

"Shite!" Shug exclaimed, jumping up. His nervous energy, always on the point of fight or flight, got the better of him. Ella looked at him, amused, wiping splashed whisky off her lap. "Sorry, but ah was havin' such a good time ah didnae want tae be interrupted."

"It'll just be Diane next door. She's always running out of stuff."

Ella opened the door and there on the threshold was Kathy, the last person she would have expected to see.

Never one to stand on ceremony, Kathy barged past Ella with, "Hi, Ella. Hello there, Shug, nice to see you. I can bunk down with you for a few days, Ella, can't I? I need to lay low. Nice flat. Spare room this way?" She headed off down the hallway, leaving Ella behind with an open mouth.

"I guess we're stuck with her," said Ella, looking at Shug. She had no problem admitting that Kathy did intimidate her, just a tiny bit. She sat back down. "So, where were we?"

"Ah, aye, well," said Shug, still standing, his body almost vibrating from nerves. He felt too self-conscious to sit back down and continue where they'd left off. The moment had passed. He shrugged. "Ah think ah'll head off now. If ye need any help with her nibs," he indicated the hallway, "just give me a shout."

Shug had automatically extended his hand just as he realised that they were beyond a formal handshake. He retracted it but then wasn't sure if he should give her a hug or a peck on the cheek and ended up waving at her awkwardly and leaving before Ella had even got up from the sofa to see him out.

48

Ella dragged herself out of bed and slumped to the kitchen where she could hear Kathy clattering about. As she walked in, she found Kathy seated at the kitchen table eating a pot of fruits of the forest yoghurt, her body tense and her left leg twitching so fast it was practically a blur. Turning around, she gave Ella a big Cheshire-cat grin.

"Good mornin', sunshine."

"How much coffee have you had?" asked Ella. An empty packet of breakfast cereal lay on its back on the table, sugar was scattered around, and four pots of chocolate mousse that Ella had just bought yesterday had been consumed. "How hungry were you?"

"Oh, yes." Kathy looked at the devastation on the table. "I ate all your stuff. Pretty much everything, sorry. Today's the day of my second revenge. It's brilliant. The plan is to make the man believe he's being publicly humiliated. After all, that's what he did to me. How could he have done that to me? *To me!*"

"So, who's this guy then? What did he do to you?"

"His name's Dan. Dan Stewart."

Ella interjected, "Dr Dan Stewart? Would he be the gynaecologist? Great guy. I can't imagine him doing anything bad to anyone."

"Do you know everyone in Glasgow?" Kathy couldn't believe it.

"I'm a barmaid. Of course I know everyone." Ella opened the fridge door looking for any scraps that Kathy had left behind that she could call breakfast.

Kathy ignored her as her eyes drifted towards the window and focused on the tree outside, its branches waving in the morning breeze. Her body became absolutely still and her voice softened. "When I met Dan, I could feel the gentleness in him. He couldn't have been more different from Jack. He was extremely sensitive and treated me like a china doll."

Ella's search for breakfast had come up empty so she poured herself a coffee and sat down, a willing ear to Kathy's confession.

Kathy continued quietly. "He was caring and gentle. Our relationship was the most profound I'd ever experienced. He seemed to truly care for me and I gave myself up to him. I thought he was the one." Kathy bowed her head as her eyes welled up. "One day, completely out of the blue, he dumped me." Kathy drew a ragged breath, her voice fraying at the edges. Ella put a hand over Kathy's, but Kathy withdrew it. Her pain her own.

"We had met for coffee. He was unusually quiet and subdued, playing with the packets of sugar until one burst open and sugar spilt all over the table. I remember laughing, and then he told me it was over."

Ella put her hand over Kathy's hand again. This time she didn't resist. "He couldn't tell me what had gone wrong. All he said was that it felt wrong and he didn't want to deceive me. That he was going through a difficult time and needed to be alone. Then he left me there, sitting with the sugar everywhere, my heart shattered into just as many grains spread across the table."

"I'm sorry, Kathy." Ella spoke gently. "It's really hard when you've invested a lot in a relationship. We've all been through it."

Kathy yanked her hand from underneath Ella's, stood up and paced the tiny kitchen.

"Well, I'll bet this has never happened to you! A couple of weeks later, I was at a party I'd forced myself to go to, determined to move on, when I heard the whispers. That's where I discovered that Dan had come out. I was his last girlfriend. Can you imagine the humiliation?" Kathy's voice rose. Ella felt for the neighbours and waved her hand to indicate that she should lower her voice.

"Don't you shush me! I was devastated and humiliated. Do you know how that feels? I'll bet you don't! Was I such an awful girlfriend, that he thought he'd be better off with men? Did he do it to spite me?"

"I really don't think that's how it works," ventured Ella.

Kathy ignored her. "Maybe he'd planned it! Go out with me, dump me and then come out!"

"I'm really sorry for how you felt. Are feeling," Ella added hastily at Kathy's thunderous expression. "But I'm sure Dan didn't do it deliberately and I'm sure you didn't turn him gay. I imagine he was struggling with his own identity and, sadly, you got caught up in it."

"Well, you can imagine all you like but that doesn't help me! He has to suffer the consequences of his actions!" The upstairs neighbour banged on the floor and Kathy shouted, "Fuck off!" at the ceiling before continuing. "I'm going to give him a taste of his own medicine. He may be out to his friends but not to his family and his work colleagues. Today he'll feel how I did. Humiliated."

Kathy sat down, then jumped up, then sat down again. "Shit, I've got nothing to do." She got up again and started pacing. "Fiona the traffic warden has her revenge today too. Think I'll go and see what's going on. It should be entertaining if they manage to pull it off. Can't trust people to do anything properly if I'm not there."

49

Dan was whistling as he entered Sheena's kitchen looking for the devil's brew in the coffee pot. He hated cooking of any sort and preferred, whenever possible, to live out of Sheena's kitchen. As did The Wee Besom. Sheena was seated at the kitchen table tucking into a plate of bacon, eggs, sausage, fried bread and tomato. The ensemble was completed by a cup of tea and a slice of buttered bread.

"Why on earth are you eating that heart-attack stuff? It'll kill you, you know."

"I'm eating it because I can," responded Sheena, waving a deliciously smelling slice of bacon under his nose. "So, you have a hot date tonight."

"How did you know that?" Dan was convinced he'd kept this one to himself.

"Because you whistle when you have a hot date. Always. Everyone knows that. Even The Wee Besom. Don't you, sweetie? Wag your tail if Dan has a hot date tonight."

The Wee Besom, always happy to be the centre of attention, wagged her tail obligingly.

"OK, you've got me. No one you know. Nothing to tell. I've got to run. Got a busy day ahead." He swiped Sheena's buttered bread and three slices of bacon from her plate, made a sandwich and left the room whistling with his mouth full. The Wee Besom chose to stay, hoping a bit of sausage might come her way.

The staff of the health centre where Dan worked had arrived and were busy hanging up raincoats, shaking umbrellas and arranging them on the floor to dry out. As he sat down at his desk he saw, within the bundle of mail waiting for his attention, an A4 brown envelope, identical to one he'd noticed on each of the desks as he passed through the main admin area.

Curious, he opened it first, and pulled out a letter accompanied by a photo. He sat back, shocked. When he realised that he was holding his breath, he forced himself to draw air into his lungs to allow him to think. He looked through the open door to the office and could see people at their desks opening the same envelope. Dan got up and closed the door. Once again seated, he studied the photo that lay on the desk in front of him. His hands were shaking. It had been Photoshopped, but to the outside world who didn't know better, it would look authentic. The photo was S&M. Dan's head had been put onto a body that wore black leathers with a hole cut in the buttocks, and a mesh vest covered with chains. This figure was on his hands and knees looking up at another man holding a leash which was attached to this, now Dan, person via a studded collar fastened round the neck. It was sleazy and serious. Dan could barely drag his eyes from it to read the accompanying letter. It read:

> *Dan, Dan you are the man.*
> *It's about time. I wonder if you expected this?*
> *I very much doubt it. Yes, it's been a long time,*
> *but you know what they say, actions have*

consequences. Each action provokes an equal and opposite reaction, and this, my dear Dan, is it. This is it.

You didn't, couldn't, have hurt anyone as much as you hurt me. You must know that. After all, what you did to me was special. Now, I want you to feel the humiliation you made me feel.

I know you are out to your friends but not to your family or colleagues. I hope you like the photo. So far, it's only your colleagues who have received it. I may, or may not, send it to your family. It depends on you now. Keep quiet and don't say a word to anyone. Not yet, I'll let you know when.

It's my time now, you've had yours. Have fun – not!

K

Struggling for composure, he focused on the names of all the guys he'd dated that began with the letter 'K'. He'd been no angel when he was younger, still wasn't, and that made imagining who might have written this letter and doctored this photo difficult. Being outed was one thing but this image would ruin his reputation. As for his family, he dreaded to think.

A brief knock on the door and, before he could say a word, Joanna came into Dan's office with the file for his first patient of the day. Dan managed to hide the photo and letter underneath the rest of the mail as she approached his desk. He was pale and trembling. Joanna turned her head away from him as an involuntary smile lit up her face.

Joanna turned back. "Dr Stewart," she said reverentially, in her polite English accent, "you don't look well. Can I get something for you?"

"No, no, I'm fine, I'm fine." Dan's voice shook. "Please send Mrs Cochrane in." In the intervening moments of quiet before the next patient, Dan prayed to whoever, or whatever, to help him regain his composure and focus. By the time Mrs Cochrane walked in he was still pale but he managed a smile.

Joanna was a proud member of GIVE! After moving from England only to be dumped by the fucker she'd mistakenly thought loved her and wanted her to live with him, Joanna had joined a nursing agency and was in the perfect position to wangle the temp job at the practice Dan worked at.

She'd arrived at work early and had left an A4 brown envelope on each desk, containing a letter and photo, and a separate identical-looking envelope for Dan. She then left for a breakfast coffee before returning at her usual starting time.

As she walked in, she could hear the buzz of excitement. Her colleagues had opened their envelopes.

The letter explained that a surprise tenth work anniversary party had been organised for Dan and that it'd be fun to make oblique references to the photo to pique his interest but not let on about the party. The theme was fancy dress and as an example, the photo showed Dan and two of his mates, James and Jack, dressed as ABBA at a party held the previous year.

Helen, with her large bosom and coiffed hair, was fussing over what she'd wear.

"If Helen of Troy's face could launch a thousand ships, I'll bet your bosom could launch a million down the Clyde. Dress as one of those figureheads on a ship," suggested June, proud of her historical knowledge even though it came from her teenage son who was currently studying for his history exam.

"It's on the same day as my birthday. I wonder if we could have a joint party?" Senga was practically jumping with excitement. The chorus of "No!" put her rapidly in her place.

"I was considering retiring but I think I'll hold on for the party," said Agnes. "Haven't been to a fancy-dress party since the millennium."

"What's the millennium?" asked Ashley, the millennial.

"Shh! Here he comes!" Joanna hissed. As he walked past his colleagues, Dan felt all eyes following him and heard the odd suppressed giggle. A wave of humiliation blew over him. He needed fresh air. As the outside door closed, he heard an upsurge of chatter and laughter. His shoulders slumped. He was a laughing stock. His career was in ruins. He'd have to leave Glasgow.

Operation 'Up Yours' was well under way. Joanna knew that Kathy would be pleased.

50

~~

Kathy arrived at the scene of Fiona's revenge. 'Clamp City', she'd called it. She walked towards Sonia who, due to the slightly inclement weather, had every button of her emerald cape fastened and, undoubtedly, underneath, her cardigan tightly tied. Her umbrella was up and, just as Kathy approached, caught a gust. Kathy swore that Sonia levitated a few inches off the ground. Her theory that Sonia was a reincarnation of Mary Poppins looked like it was about to be verified. Looking around, sure enough, Sanjit had found a bench to sit on while he waited. Kathy detected a note of resignation, even from that distance.

Fiona, in the middle of her revenge, was grinning from ear to ear, her victim raging in front of her. Fiona had borrowed a couple of uniforms for Stuart and Dougie, hoping her 'bodyguards' would keep her safe. Stuart was enjoying himself hugely and could not have made his uniform more camp if he'd tried. He wasn't going to be much use if punches were thrown. Dougie was too tall for his uniform, white socks clearly visible at the ankles, and he kept pulling the sleeves down which rounded his shoulders, making him look like the Traffic Warden version of Notre Dame.

That said, it didn't really matter. Their victim's car had been clamped on all four wheels. It hadn't taken much to convince the tow truck driver to do it. Anything to fill his quota early and knock off for breakfast. Four parking tickets were neatly tucked under the windscreen wiper. Fiona had just finished explaining that, to release the car, he had to pay one ticket at a time, not online but at the pound, and it served him right for his foul attitude and really, really bad parking. The tow truck would come and release one wheel clamp and only come back when he'd paid the second ticket, for the second wheel clamp, and so on. Fiona had made sure that he'd waste an entire day trying to free his car.

The man was shouting at Fiona. Stuart and Dougie, flanking Fiona, couldn't stop giggling. Their obvious enjoyment of his predicament only served to enrage him further. All three then walked off, the man shaking his fist at them. Stuart and Dougie exchanged a glance then, simultaneously, mooned the man before running off giggling like two schoolgirls.

51

Kathy wandered about for a while, at a loose end. With an understanding that all she was doing was delaying the inevitable and, more importantly, if she was close to Jack she could keep an eye on him, she decided to go to work and face the music after all. She went back to Ella's place and, using the key that she'd practically had to prise out of Ella's fingers, picked up her bag and went straight to the clinic. The minute she arrived, Jack dragged her, literally by the ear, into his office.

"What the fuck, fuck, fuck did you think you were doing, leaving me alone with Ella?" Jack paced his office, fingers twitching, as if all they wanted to do was put them around Kathy's throat and throttle her.

"Why?" said Kathy in the coolest, mildest tone of voice she could muster.

Jack hesitated. Of course, he couldn't tell her. "Because it's extremely unprofessional. Anything could have happened!"

"Oh. You're friends. I really didn't think much of it. I'm sorry, I won't do it again," Kathy added, managing surprised, contrite and sorry-not-sorry in the same facial expression.

Jack, thwarted of his ambition to give Kathy the ear bashing she deserved, could feel the acid rising in his stomach. An ulcer was only days away.

***

Kathy's day took a surprising turn when an eminent surgeon and valued drinking companion of the boys arrived in reception. He was the ugliest plastic surgeon she'd ever seen but his extraordinary talent meant that no one cared that he'd not gone under the knife himself.

While he waited for the boys, he casually mentioned to Kathy that his wife was out of town, nod, wink, and would she like to accompany him to the surgeons' dinner on Saturday? Thinking of Jack, and keeping that eye on him, it took Kathy about a millisecond to see the opportunity for what it was and accept the invitation.

52

James and Jack had lunch together. For a man with a famously large appetite, Jack barely ate. He worried at the small childhood scar above his right eye which always signalled he was upset. James recognised the sign but knew better than to ask. He'd pestered Jack all morning to no avail but Jack wasn't letting on.

"So, how's it going? Have you decided about Lizzie? Are you going to ask her to the dinner?" Jack waved a fork in James's face.

James sighed. "Yes, I'm going to ask her but I'm really not that sure it's a good idea. The charity dinner might not be her thing. But, we'd stay the whole weekend, which would be fun. I'll talk to her about it tonight. I've got a bottle of her favourite wine and flowers, just in case it goes tits up."

Back in the office he tried to complete the day's patient files but couldn't concentrate, so he went home early to get ready. He took his time getting changed, searching for the right casual-smart, cool look. The wine was in an ice bucket, crisps in a bowl, and the flowers and an envelope were next to the wine glasses. Lizzie arrived, bedraggled, due to the lashing rain outside. Cursing.

"Just as well it's summer," she said, dripping on the carpet.

"Oh, come on, it's not that bad. Anyway," he continued with a slight case of nervous verbal diarrhoea, "summer was last week, on Wednesday, I think. No, that's not right. It was two weeks last Wednesday. I may even have noted it in my diary. It was between 12.30 and 1 p.m. I remember thinking that I was stuck in a consult when I could have been outside on a pavement terrace drinking cappuccino like normal Europeans do. But, really, the UK doesn't qualify as normal European, not least and not only, because of its crap weather. When you think about the political, social, cultural and economic differences, not to mention Brexit—"

"Jeez, James, I just commented on the weather."

James took a breath. "Have a glass of wine. I have a present for you." They chinked glasses with a solemn "*Slainte*", and he gave Lizzie the flowers and the envelope, and held his breath.

Lizzie let out a squeal of delight when she opened the envelope and read the invitation. "A weekend in Edinburgh in a posh hotel! Thank you so much! No one has ever whisked me away for a romantic weekend before. That's brilliant! Dead, braw brilliant 'n' 'at, no?" She laughed and hugged James while trying to do a jig at the same time.

"Eh, well, it's not exactly the two of us. It's, um, about a hundred and fifty really. It's the Scottish Plastic Surgeons' charity dinner on Saturday night at the hotel. Jack will be there too and I wanted to take you as my partner. Lots of people will be taking their other halves. It'll be fun."

Lizzie sat down heavily on the sofa. Her shoulders slumped and her face took on an expression that James had never seen before, but found unnerving. Then her expression changed, then changed again, her face went red and crumpled as a tear trickled down her cheek. He took a big gulp of wine and waited nervously as Lizzie chose her words carefully, in between sniffs.

"You want me to be like them. You want me to dress like them and talk like them. I can't do it because I'm not like them!" The last words came out strangled as she tried to choke back a sob. "I don't want to lose you but I'm not enough for you, am I? I'm trying, but I can't be like them."

While Lizzie was talking, James's brain sent out supplications to the powers that be. *Please, please don't do this to me. Please don't do this to me.*

"That's it." Lizzie's voice took on a hardened tone. "You did it to make me feel bad."

James's brain stalled. "What?" He stared at her.

"You want to show me up. I can't go. What would I wear? What would I say to all these fancy women? I have nothing in common with them. Can you see me at a posh charity dinner discussing cuts of meat?"

"Well, we are plastic surgeons. That's all we'll be talking about. Haha." James's feeble attempt at a joke fell on barren ground. His next thought was, *I'll kill Jack when I get my hands on him. I knew it! I'm never listening to him again!* He tried to pull his mind back to the matter at hand and get himself out of the pickle he'd just landed himself in.

Lizzie looked at him for a moment, indignantly, then dissolved into tears.

Oh God, oh God, oh God streamed through James's mind, occupying all the mental space required to think about how to manage the situation and find the right words.

Lizzie turned towards him and he looked into her beautiful eyes as the tears welled up. That shocked him out of his inertia.

"I really, really want you to come. I don't expect you to be shallow and plastic and fake like the wives. God only knows I've had enough of them. You are my authentic Lizzie and I want it to stay that way. Come, please come. I won't leave your side and when you want to, we can sneak off and have some fun. Please?"

Lizzie looked at James for a long moment. "But I don't have anything to wear!" she wailed.

"By Jove, I've got it!" he said pompously. "Sheena's lost her job and is at a loose end. She lives to shop. She'll help you out with clothes and the whole weekend, including your wardrobe, is on me. How does that sound?"

"So, I'm your Lizzie Doolittle then." Lizzie giggled.

"That's the spirit!"

Lizzie blew her nose, leaned over and gave James a kiss on the cheek. James loved his Lizzie. She was coming to Edinburgh with him. All was right in the world.

53

Shug couldn't stop thinking about Ella. She had awakened in him the deeply buried romantic soul that was the real Shug. It was a side of him that he never showed in public and, as the years went by, it had become buried under the hard layers of life experience. But now, just by being near Ella, it was gradually working its way through those layers, like a free diver knowing when the time is right to return to the surface. He almost didn't dare to think about it but he knew, in his heart, that he and Ella were soulmates.

Loada nonsense. Shug admonished himself. *She's out ma league. Nothing more than a serious case of needin' a shag. Haven't had ma leg over in ages*, he thought. *Ma brain's addled.* And on that note, he set off for the pub where Ella worked in the hope of a decent pint and a chat.

As he entered the pub he saw her there, behind the bar, a halo around her head. He paused in wonder then, with an internal *I need glasses* reminder, sat on a stool at the bar and casually, he imagined, nodded in her direction. What Ella saw was a puppy wagging its tail madly, tongue lolling, desperate for attention. She smiled at him.

"What'll you have, Shug?"

"A pint of yer best, hen." Shug suddenly realised that he was maybe being a bit over-keen. "I, ahem, am here in an official capacity to check out the situation and to see whit we can do about the problem yer havin' wi' the punters."

"So, you didn't come to see me, then?" Ella smiled, teasing.

"No, no, no, well yes, but no, but …" Shug couldn't keep up with the female psyche. His shoulders slumped.

"Oi! You!" Ella shouted. Shug jumped. "Not you, you numpty." She smiled at Shug then turned to continue shouting at two punters who had squared off. "You two! Stop that right now or I'll have you barred! Sit down and behave!" Ella had crowd control rights and the punters respected that. She also had the voice of a foghorn.

She turned her attention back to Shug and patted him on the arm. "It's good to see you, Shug."

Shug's smile was Cheshire-cat wide.

"See that man over there? The balding one with the beer belly?"

Shug looked round. At least ten punters met that description.

"The one sitting just over there, about ten feet away from you, leering at me."

As far as Shug was concerned, that narrowed it down to five.

Ella huffed in exasperation. "The one with the ginger hair sticking out his ears!"

That got the total down to three. Shug looked at Kathy helplessly. "Gies another clue."

"Oi, Hamish!"

Four men turned round but only one that was ten feet away with ginger hair sticking out his ears.

"Oh, him. Whit about him?"

"He's disgusting. The worst of the lot. He leers at me all the time and pinches my bum every chance he gets. My boss thinks it's funny. I'm sick to death of it. I've barred him umpteen times but the boss just lets him back in. That man needs to learn a lesson in respecting a woman."

"Right." Shug stared at the rows of bottles behind Ella for a solid five minutes while Ella served drinks. Pensively, he walked outside to make a phone call.

On returning to the pub he found Ella taking another punter to task. "Mr McGowan, didn't you say you had to amputate a toe in the morning? I'm not going to serve you another whisky chaser! What if it were my toe? Would I want my surgeon out on the razz the night before? No. That's my final word!" She extended an arm, pointing at the door. Mr McGowan nodded meekly and left.

Twenty minutes later, Fiona walked into the pub, and, on Shug's indication, walked up to Hamish, pinched him on the bum and walked out again.

The man jumped, startled, and then he and his mates burst into laughter.

"She fancies ye, mate!"

"You'd better get off after her. You'll no' have many women chasin' after ye these days!"

The man got up and looked out of the window. "She's gone."

"You'll have to be quicker off the mark than that! You'll never get a woman if you don't shift that fat arse of yours!"

"Looks like it's ma fat arse that she's after. Maybe she'll come back." He sat back down, keeping an eye on the door just in case.

Ella looked at Shug like he'd lost his marbles. "Is that it? Is that the best you can come up with?"

"Patience, hen, patience." He looked smug. "I have tae go. I have tae see a man about a cow." And with a wave, he left.

54

Sheena answered the door to James and Lizzie with a flourish. She was sporting an oversized gentleman's smoking jacket in deep burgundy, pale pink silk scarf, original Madonna cone bra visible under the half-open jacket, hair tied tightly back in Eva Peron bun, tight black trousers, extraordinarily high black Jimmy Choos, a glass of cava in one hand and a cigarette in a black holder in the other, completing the slightly outlandish look.

James's eyes involuntarily went heavenward. Lizzie was fascinated.

"I've been what the Americans call 'antiquing' and found these brilliant clothes. Aren't they cool?" Lizzie's eyes followed the outfit to floor level and widened as they arrived at the Jimmy Choos. Her jaw dropped. She knew good shoes when she saw them even if she could never afford to buy them.

"Yep, they're the real deal. Trouble is, they cost a fortune and I daren't wear them outside. You're getting a rare treat seeing them." Sheena took a bite out of the chocolate cigarette in the holder. "So, guys, what can I do you for?"

"We're here to ask you a favour," said James, dragging

his eyes back to her from as he'd become transfixed by a spider as it spun its web on a corner by the ceiling. He gave her the once-over. "Although I'm beginning to think it wasn't such a good idea after all."

Lizzie nudged him in the ribs. "Yes, it is. I need your help. I need clothes for the Plastic Surgeons' charity dinner thingy in Edinburgh this weekend. James is taking me and I don't know what to wear. He's offered to pay for the wardrobe and thought you would be the perfect person to help me." She stretched up and gave James a loving kiss.

Sheena looked away, slightly stung by the gesture, realising that James wasn't likely to be hers any time soon. But, never one to bear grudges, and with the prospect of a shopping spree with a blank cheque in sight, she quickly recovered.

"Fabulous. Come in to my chambers, my dear Lizzie, and let's discuss your shopping needs." She put an arm around Lizzie and led her into the living room, leaving James in the hall.

"I'll be off then," he muttered to their backs as they left him without so much as a goodbye. The Wee Besom wandered out of Sheena's bedroom yawning and stretching her legs then went mad at the unexpected pleasure of seeing James. After giving her the attention she needed from him – *good girl!* at least three times, a variety of pats on the head and a full minute's worth of a bottom scratch – she wandered off to see what else was going on, leaving James on his own again. He headed out into the pouring rain.

55

The next morning, Sheena bounced happily into the kitchen, thoughts of a major shopping expedition providing its own high, only to be hit by a wall of bitter burnt coffee as she opened the kitchen door. Dan was slumped in a chair, head in hands, a mug of coffee spilt over the kitchen table. She rushed over to him calling his name. The grunt and stale alcohol belch in reply calmed her. Just a bad hangover. As her worry dissipated, she dumped the burnt coffee and tried to make a fresh pot without burning herself. She cleared the mess on the table and presented a fresh mug to Dan, sat down and began the interrogation.

"So, what happened to the hot date? What was he like? Did something good happen? Bad happen? What'd he look like? Will you see him again? When did you get in?" She finished the interrogation with: "You look like shit."

Dan's brain hurt, his eyes hurt and now his ears hurt. He tried to get up, couldn't quite manage equilibrium, and slumped back down again.

"You're in no fit state to go to work." Sheena picked up the phone.

Chapter 55

At that, Dan made what seemed like a superhuman effort, leaped up and grabbed the phone out of Sheena's hand, stumbling on The Wee Besom who was slumbering in her favourite position at his feet. She yelped, shot out from under the table and hovered by the doorway like an earthquake victim hoping the doorframe would save her as her world crashed down around her ears.

Now Sheena was really worried. She grabbed the phone back from Dan, noting that he'd turned even paler, if it were possible.

"Sit!" she commanded. The Wee Besom obediently plonked her bottom on the floor and looked expectantly at Sheena. "Not you!" Sheena continued, exasperated. "You, Dan. Sit down. You've got some explaining to do."

Dan wobbled but regained his stability by clutching the kitchen table. "No, I won't. I'm going to work. I can't not go to work. They'll all know why. I can't let them win. I have to go to work."

He continued to mumble to himself and, ignoring Sheena, took the mug of coffee and carefully walked out of the kitchen, one hand held out for balance. Gripping the banister for dear life, he went upstairs to take a shower. Sheena stayed at the kitchen table, an idea forming in her mind.

Decision made, her next thought was on breakfast. Bacon and eggs or plain toast? The Wee Besom's face made up her mind: bacon and eggs it would be.

56

Sheena took her role as personal shopper seriously. The blank cheque offered additional motivation, but most of all she was dying to interrogate Lizzie. Considering that the girl seemed like a genuine, down-to-earth type of person and completely different from the girls that James usually dated, Sheena's curiosity was well and truly piqued.

They arranged to meet at 1 p.m. at John Lewis. Lizzie texted that she'd be late.

"You're late!" exclaimed Sheena who'd spent the last half hour pacing back and forth past the window displays. "My feet hurt and we haven't even started yet!"

"I'm really sorry. There was a lunchtime rush at the butcher's. We had a half-price burger promotion on and I couldn't just abandon my dad." Lizzie looked down at her well-worn trainers and compared them with Sheena's over-the-top high-heeled sandals. "Why are you wearing high heels for shopping?"

"Because you have to shop how you want to look and look how you want to shop." Sheena looked at Lizzie as if she were mad for not knowing this.

Sheena marched Lizzie into the store as Lizzie held back

like a dog at the vet's, reconsidering what she had thought would be a fun outing, and worrying that it could potentially be a painful experience. "Come on! First stop's coffee."

"But ..." exclaimed Lizzie.

"But nothing," said Sheena. "I'm in charge here. We have to figure out what we want to buy before we go and do it. Planning. Shopping is all about planning. Now, mine's a cappuccino and a slice of carrot cake. Off you pop." Sheena sat down, diva in the making.

"But didn't we do that yesterday?"

With a wave of a hand and a "Shoo!" from Sheena, Lizzie gave in and went to the counter to make the order. Once seated with their coffees and cake, the thinly disguised interrogation began.

"Now, clothes have to fit not only the figure but also the personality and thus lift both up a level. Do you understand?" Sheena looked intently at Lizzie.

Lizzie chose to nod quietly. A retort was only a nanosecond away from breaking free of her lips but she thought better of it and kept quiet.

"To that end, I have to know everything about you."

"Everything?" Lizzie was startled.

"Well, we don't have time for everything today. Give me the basics. How did you meet James?"

"What's that got to do with buying clothes?"

Sheena shrugged. "More than you know."

Lizzie looked at Sheena, incredulous. "OK. He's a regular at the butcher's and one day he just asked me out. That's it. Now, can we please shop?" Lizzie finished her cappuccino in one go and sat with her arms crossed. Mouth closed in a firm straight line.

The girl's got character, thought Sheena. "OK. Tell me what you need for the weekend."

"A dress for the dinner, that's all."

"Lizzie, Lizzie, Lizzie, you have a lot to learn. You're going to the Balmoral Hotel. You can't turn up looking like that!" Sheena waved her arm up and down the full length of Lizzie.

"That's it! I'm not going. I'm sick to death of people criticising my clothes, my appearance. I'm going home!"

Sheena put a restraining hand on Lizzie's arm. "I'm sorry, but I'm responsible for getting you the outfits you need for a weekend in Edinburgh and we're going to do just that. Now listen and learn."

Lizzie glared at Sheena. Sheena ignored it and carried on. "You'll need the right outfit for your arrival at the hotel because there'll be a lot of money walking around and you need to look like money even if you're broke. It's half the battle. OK?"

Lizzie added a quiet, "OK."

"You'll need a dress for the dinner and smart but casual for the following day and informal for going home. Remember, James is paying. We might as well make the most of it. Got it?"

"This isn't a wedding. I don't need to get changed every five minutes."

"I know, but you have to fit in. It'll just make everything easier, honestly. Now, we have to attend to the first rule of shopping which is you can't try on clothes unless you're wearing the right bra. First stop is the lingerie department. You need to look a bit perkier in that department."

Lizzie looked down at her chest and had to admit that Sheena was right. Three matching sets of bra and pants later, two of the bras had gone in a bag while the third graced Lizzie's boobs, her old bra deposited in the bin at the cash desk. As they left the lingerie department the sales assistant carefully picked out the discarded item and, holding it at arm's length took it to the bin in the back where it wouldn't offend her sensibilities.

Lizzie, however, was definitely feeling perkier. "I never shop in department stores. The choice is just overwhelming. I have no idea what will suit me and what won't." Lizzie gazed at the racks and racks of clothes that stretched away as far as the eye could see.

"That's where I come in. I can look along a rack of clothes and know instantly what will work for you. Here." Sheena grabbed a white shirt from the rack. "The classics are always the best."

Sheena darted in and out of the clothes rails, travelling from one designer to another like a dog sniffing out truffles, handing clothes to Lizzie until she was almost invisible under the pile.

"This is a selection of classics that you can wear any time and in any combination. We can accessorise later. Go and try them on and I'll be over in a tick."

As Lizzie walked into the changing room, she noticed an employee of the store looking at her curiously.

"May I be of assistance?" The woman smiled at Lizzie.

"Well, maybe we can check the sizes?" offered Lizzie who didn't want to offend the woman.

Sheena breezed over. "No need, I can tell a person's size just by looking at them. They'll be a perfect fit." She practically shoved the woman out of the way as she followed Lizzie into the changing room.

Ten minutes later, a delighted Lizzie walked out laden down with more clothes than she actually needed, but didn't care. All she needed now was the all-important cocktail dress.

As they worked their way around the dress rails, Lizzie whispered to Sheena, "I think that woman's following us."

Sheena ignored her, pulled out a cocktail dress then put it back. Seemingly indecisive, Sheena's hand surfed over the top of the dresses, feeling the fabric, without picking any out. Trying to look casual, Sheena tried a second line of questioning. "I've known James for a long time. What's it like going out with him?" she asked casually, like it wasn't important, then whipped out two fabulous little black numbers and waved them in front of Lizzie.

Sheena twirled them round to get a better look. "Hmm, I think you're more Marilyn Monroe than *Breakfast at Tiffany's*." She put back one of the dresses and held the other in front of her. "So, what's it like? With James, I mean."

Distracted, Lizzie started talking. "Do you know what it's like when you lean in to someone? When you just fold yourself into them? Within minutes of our first date, I felt like that. I felt enveloped, wrapped up, cuddled in a warm blanket. It was a lovely feeling. He made me feel really special and, with a few missteps, he's shaping up nicely!" Lizzie smiled.

Sheena turned away, pretending to look for dresses as the tears stung her eyes. She was simultaneously jealous and happy for Lizzie. She cleared her throat and turned back. "I'm happy for you. It sounds like he's the one!" Her voice turned into a loud squeak as she tried to cover for her emotions. "Here, try this one on too but I think the Marilyn dress is the one."

As they wove their way in and out of the rails, the woman reappeared.

"Sheena, she's making me nervous."

"Don't worry. She's probably just security thinking we're going to do a runner." Sheena laughed.

"I can barely walk, never mind run, with this lot."

As they walked into the changing room the woman approached Sheena and said, "Excuse me, but I'd like a word with you."

Sheena nodded, unconcerned, and left with the woman. Five minutes later, she was back in the changing room with a business card in her hand.

"That woman's offered me a job. She's head of personal shopping and she said that she's never seen anyone work as efficiently and confidently with a client. She said that I could join them anytime. Getting paid for shopping. What's not to like?" She looked at Lizzie. "That cocktail dress is even more amazing on you than I imagined."

It was Lizzie's turn to have tears in her eyes. "I love it. I really do," she whispered.

"Great! So, now we have to accessorise and then I have some shopping of my own to do. Chop, chop! We haven't got all day!"

57

⌫

Fully energised from the afternoon's shopping, Sheena breezed into Dan's clinic. Lizzie trailed in her wake, arms leaden from carrying the bags of clothes and shoes, and totally exhausted. She wasn't trained for marathon shopping. She collapsed on the sofa in reception and weakly waved Sheena on. Sheena relieved Lizzie of two bags of clothes that she'd bought for herself.

"I'll wait for you here."

As Sheena strode purposefully through reception towards Dan's office, Kathy's spy, Joanna, waylaid her. "Hi, Sheena. Come to visit Dan, I'm guessing?"

Sheena was a regular visitor. She liked to show off any new purchases to Dan as soon as she bought them. Waiting for an appropriate moment, such as at home at the end of the day, never crossed her mind.

"Yep. I've got some really cool stuff to show him." She lifted her shopping bags for Joanna to have a peek. "And he looked hellish this morning. I thought I'd come and see how he is now."

"He really does look awful, and is he actually wearing make-up?" said a nurse as she walked past, giggling.

Sheena overheard the remark and grabbed Dan by the

elbow as he was making his way back to his office with a cup of tea. She dragged him into the room and slammed the door behind her.

"Sit!" she commanded for the second time that day.

"Jeez, Sheena," he complained, brushing spilt tea off his lab coat, only managing to blend it in further.

Sheena ran a finger down his cheek. She showed it to him. "Are you wearing my blusher?"

"I borrowed a tiny spot this morning to give me a bit of colour. I looked so washed out I thought it would help. Is it that obvious?"

"Absolutely. And not only to me. One of the nurses commented on it. What were you thinking? This isn't normal behaviour, not even normal hangover behaviour."

Dan scrubbed at his face, turning his cheeks a brighter shade of red. He let out what sounded suspiciously like a sob, slumped into his chair and hung his head. Sheena was taken aback. Jack, now Dan. Was Mercury in retrograde? Sheena sat down opposite him and put a comforting hand on his arm, waiting for him to regain his composure. After a few minutes he sat up straight, took an envelope out of his desk drawer and handed it to Sheena.

She took one look at the photo and knew it wasn't real. She knew Dan inside and out and this was not part of his life. She read the letter carefully. None of it made any sense. She looked up, appalled. "What's this?"

"I wish I knew. Please, please keep this to yourself. I'm trying to figure it out. Last night I wrote a list of every single person, at least as far as I can remember, I've ever gone out with whose name starts with the letter 'K', but they were all nice guys and we parted amicably. At least that's what I thought. But," he hesitated, "there have been one or two one-night stands."

Sheena raised an eyebrow at the understatement but kept her counsel.

Dan continued. "At the end of the day there aren't that many people whose names begin with 'K'. I came up with Keith and Kevin and Ken and Keegan if we include surnames and that's probably about it. I remember a few boys from on holiday with names I could barely pronounce never mind spell. That's it, honest. Nice lads the lot of them." He added, "The entire office has seen the photo. It's killing me hearing them laugh behind my back, but I have to be here for my patients."

Sheena stood up. "I have to think. Give me a minute." She lay down on Dan's consulting table, her legs swinging between the stirrups.

"Sheena, I have a client waiting outside. Can't you go and do this elsewhere?"

Sheena didn't even look at him. She stretched out her arm, palm facing him, silencing him. "Shhhh."

It wasn't worth trying to interrupt Sheena when she was thinking. It was a rare enough occurrence, so Dan left her to her own devices.

For the following thirty minutes, Sheena talked to herself, considered the facts, imagined all the possibilities. Lying on her back gave her a clear head. Her colleagues had never understood that when they found her on her office floor. She sat bolt upright, leapt off the examining table and, on opening the door, had a quick look at the desks of some of the staff. She saw what she was after and called Lizzie who was now, impatiently, waiting under the pile of bags.

"Psssssssst. Lizzie! Come here!" Sheena's hoarse whisper attracted everyone's attention. Once inside Dan's office, with the door firmly closed, Sheena whispered in Lizzie's ear so quietly that she could hardly hear. "I need your help. See this envelope?" Sheena indicated the offending envelope sitting on Dan's desk. "Dan's secretary has one just like it on her desk. I need you to get it for me without her realising."

"What? Me? Why?" Lizzie gulped. "What's this all about?"

Sheena ignored her. "Just dump all your shopping bags onto her desk, show her your purchases and surreptitiously put the envelope in a bag and bring it in here."

"But why?"

"It's for Dan. He needs our help. You want to help Dan, don't you?" Sheena glared at Lizzie. Lizzie took an involuntary step back.

"But I don't even know him. I've only met him once, briefly, and you want me to steal for him? Why don't you do it?"

"Because I'm thinking."

"What do you mean 'you're thinking'? Can't you steal stuff and think at the same time?"

"No, when I'm thinking that's all I can do."

"But—"

"Go! You can do it. I helped you out shopping, didn't I?"

And on that note of emotional blackmail, Lizzie left the office to do as asked before she could change her mind. The secretary was a bit surprised by this complete stranger wanting to share her shopping with her but was happy to *ooh* and *aah* over her new outfits. Lizzie managed to get her hands on the envelope and went back into the office where she found Sheena lying back on the consulting table, 'thinking', but the gentle snore emanating from her said otherwise.

After a nudge from Lizzie, Sheena woke with a start and jumped off the table. "Right, let's see what you've got."

Sheena took the envelope from Lizzie, pulled the paper and photo from it and proceeded to hum and haw.

"Right. Lizzie, come to my house in the morning for some more accessories. Bye."

And on that note Sheena left Dan's office, both envelopes in her handbag.

58

↶

Two hours later, Shug walked into the pub where Ella worked, made himself comfortable on a bar stool and waited. Ella was surprised to see him.

"For the love of God, Jock, that's your tenth packet of pork scratchings. These things will kill you." Ella was busy keeping the punters in order. "Hi, Shug, what are you doing back here?"

"Shhhh," was all he said.

At that moment, another of Kathy's group walked into the bar and, indicated by Shug, walked up to the man who pestered Ella, pinched him on the bum and walked out. The man jumped up, his pint of lager flying, spraying his companions at the table.

Ella supressed a smile.

Shug gave her a thumbs-up, got up, and left.

59

⬿

Shug's soon-to-be-ex-wife was extraordinarily proud of her tiny patch of garden at the front of the council house that had been the marital home until the incident with the milkman. She kept the grass immaculate and had filled the border with colourful flowers. Mrs McNally was partial to a pink dahlia or two, purple primulas, peonies and a variety of long-forgotten-the-name-of flowers.

After a tiring day selling sausage rolls and sandwiches in Greggs, Mrs McNally's only thought as she rounded the corner by her house was a lovely cup of tea. The sight that greeted her was a man in wellies sitting on the wall kicking his heels against it. The 'Oi, you!' had barely left her mouth when she noticed what was standing in her garden behind him.

"Hello there. Mrs McNally, I presume?" And, without waiting for confirmation, the man continued: "Meet Meg. She's a fine Friesian cow. They're well known for their excellent milk production. Your husband said you make your own yoghurt, butter and cheese! I'm impressed, I have tae say. A regular little dairy ye must have inside that wee hoose. I cannae think of a better present than yer own coo!

Chapter 59

You'll save plenty money although ye'll need to find her a better place to live. Not much nourishment in peonies, I'm tellin' ye." Meg lifted her head and mooed in agreement.

Mrs McNally had never been so speechless in her life. She looked over her wall just in time to see the last tiny patch of green go under Meg's hefty hoof and return as brown mud. A worm wriggled on top of the pile before being squashed into the quagmire. The last purple primula poked out of Meg's mouth.

Swirling and blending into the mud was creamy white milk. She saw it squirting from each of the cow's teats. Mrs McNally's stomach turned. A townie, she'd never seen such a sight. Milk grew in bottles, didn't it?

"Now, she has to be milked. She's an hour overdue. I didn't expect ye this late. Have you ever milked a cow before? It's easy."

The farmer produced two tin buckets, turned one upside down, took Mrs McNally by the hand as she looked like she needed help, guided her to the bucket and let her sink down onto it. The bucket wobbled and Mrs McNally instinctively put her hands out to steady herself, accidentally pushing into Meg's side. Meg shuffled and lowed.

"There, there, Meg, you'll be fine." He positioned a bucket under Meg's udder. "Here now, this is how you do it." He guided Mrs McNally's hand to one teat. "Grasp firmly at the top. Close all fingers from top to bottom squeezing as you go. That's it! Well ..."

Mrs McNally looked up at him, her face covered in warm, fresh milk. She turned her head and retched. Sonia appeared out of nowhere and looked over the wall, ready to offer assistance. Meg mooed, briefly under the impression that the green cape was a pile of fresh grass for her delectation.

"What are you lookin' at?" Mrs McNally snapped at her, finally recovering the power of speech.

Sonia backed off. "I'm just over here if you need me," she said, waving her medicine bag at Mrs McNally and then returning to her vantage point. She glanced over at Sanjit who was waiting patiently for her from a safe distance.

"Don't you worry, you'll get used to milking. It's trial and error until ye get the hang of it." The farmer tentatively patted Mrs McNally on the head.

"The idea is to aim the teat into the bucket. Now, you cannae leave her udder full of milk. She has to be milked twice a day at 6 a.m. and 4 p.m. I hope you're an early riser. Welcome to the farmer's life!" He chuckled.

Mrs McNally looked nauseous. Meg shifted, uncomfortable, and knocked over the bucket. The one solitary drop of milk that had miraculously made it in there, slowly rolled towards the edge, marking time with the tear that rolled down Mrs McNally's cheek.

60

Kathy was up early, and by 8.25 a.m. had found a convenient tree to hide behind on the corner near David's flat. Kathy had considered excluding him from the roster of revenge as, technically speaking, he was the one who woke her up, finally, to take action in her life, and she should probably be grateful, but, hey.

His beloved car was parked outside his flat. Kathy's first instinct had been to slash the tyre on that left-hand front wheel that he'd gifted her, or take it with her, but, after some thought, decided to rise above it.

Just at that moment a red car arrived and double-parked, blocking in David's car. The driver got out, locked the car and walked away. Kathy looked around for a traffic warden and saw one disappearing round the corner. Fiona, the traffic warden in the group, had arranged for her colleague to turn a blind eye.

Kathy spotted Sonia just as she flew around the corner, emerald cape floating behind her for all the world as if she'd just made an elegant landing out of sight. She put down her medicine bag and smoothed her sari then stood, alert, hands folded in front of her.

After a quick scan of the area, Kathy saw Sanjit standing across the street, arms crossed. She thought she could see a hint of frustration on his usually impassive features. *Maybe Sonia's right*, thought Kathy. *Maybe patience works.*

At the strike of 8.30 a.m., David walked out and saw his car blocked in.

"What the fuck!!!" He walked round the red car looking in the windows, then spun round with his arms wide and high. "What the fuck!!!"

And I thought I was the drama queen, thought Kathy.

David kicked the tyres of the red car as if that was going to have an effect, then paced up and down the road. "Oi! You with the red car! Where are you? Shift that pile of shit right now!" His face was puce, his fists clenched and his neck bulged.

Net curtains twitched.

After another two minutes of pacing and insulting a litter bin, a broken branch, a random pigeon and a passer-by who happened to be in the wrong place at the wrong time, David looked at his watch. He was going to be late for work. He shook his fist in the air.

"If I ever catch you, I'll, I'll ..." He banged his fist on the car bonnet and started to sprint down the road. Kathy shrank behind the tree.

As he receded into the distance, his strangled cursing gradually fading away, Kathy heard one final "fucking hell" as he was forced to wait at the pedestrian crossing, bouncing on both feet. Music to her ears.

61

At that very same moment, Sheena was admiring herself in the mirror, particularly pleased with her choice of attire. The fourth Doctor Who, played by Tom Baker, a personal favourite. A deep red velvet jacket with matching cravat, a waistcoat in various autumn shades, grey trousers and an extraordinarily long (even for Doctor Who) striped scarf wrapped twice around her neck. The ensemble was finished off with a floppy, brown felt hat. Satisfied but sweating slightly, she opened the door with a flourish to Lizzie, who was punctual this time. Lizzie stared at Sheena and chose not to comment.

Sheena was high on excitement and caffeine. She hopped, skipped and practically jumped into the spare bedroom/box room/office/multi-purpose throw-whatever-you-can't-find-a-place-for in there, colloquially known as the room of doom. Lizzie followed behind at a more leisurely pace. Once they'd squeezed in and around the overflowing boxes of clothes, the stationery bike, a set of skis, two random golf clubs, a stack of board games and an old computer, Lizzie found a bit of floor space to stand on.

Sheena stood proudly by her work of art and proclaimed, "Ta dah!"

On the wall she'd stuck Jack's photo on the left and Dan's in the centre. Next to that on the right she'd drawn question marks on sheets of paper in the place of photos. Below Dan's picture Sheena had placed the photos from the envelopes, the letter that had accompanied each photo and below that, a large letter 'K'.

She had stuck a picture of Ella below Jack's photo. Jack had given Sheena her name and, after a quick online search she'd found her Facebook profile photo. It dawned on her that she'd been the startled woman who Shug had dragged out of the pub. And so, Shug's photo was stuck below Ella's. There had to be a connection. It couldn't just be a coincidence. Next to Shug's photo was Mr Dun. She'd got his picture from the company website just before they changed it. She didn't really think that he was involved but the connection had to be registered. Sheena considered herself a professional. No stone could be left unturned.

She looked over at Lizzie like a proud mother. "So, what do you think?"

It was too early for Lizzie. "I don't know. What do you want me to think?"

"That a nasty individual is trying to ruin my friends' lives and I'm doing something about it, don't you see?"

"Why's Jack on the board, then?"

"Because this woman, Ella, has accused him of sexual assault."

Lizzie took a step back in shock and her booted foot landed on top of The Wee Besom's paw. The dog let out a painful squeal and ran out to hover by the door, a safe distance away.

"I don't know Jack well but it doesn't seem like the sort of thing he would do."

"He wouldn't. That's the point."

"OK. So, you think there's a connection between these two events?"

"No shit, Sherlock."

Lizzie threw her arms up. "What do you want from me? I'm not a detective."

"Well, if you're no use, let's see if Annie's still at home."

Lizzie bristled at the slight.

The Wee Besom bounced up and down with excitement. She was enjoying her time with Sheena. She normally spent the day at the doggy park with her sitter but Sheena was much more fun. Never a dull moment.

"Annie!" Sheena bawled up the stairs. "Annnnnnie!!!!"

A door crashed and Annie's face appeared over the banister. "What the fuck do you want? I was meditating!"

"Keep yer wig on! We need you down here now. It's a matter of State."

"There'd better be coffee involved."

Sheena ran into the kitchen, poured a cup and had it ready to hand to her as she walked in.

Annie grrrumphed. "So, what is it?" Two minutes later she was wiping the tears from her eyes. "How could ...? But who? How can ...? Why?" The 'why' was plaintive. "This is devastating. Isn't it just a weird coincidence?"

"It's no coincidence. It's one person and it's obvious who. Just look at the evidence." Sheena waved her hand across the wall. "It's all there!" she insisted.

Lizzie and Annie studied the wall intently and shook their heads.

"It's Ella, you numpties!"

"Ella? How do you know that?" Lizzie was perplexed.

"I can't see the link either." Annie was equally perplexed.

The Wee Besom looked at the wall, head on one side, then looked at Sheena, just as perplexed.

"Because Ella's surname is Kay! Look, the letter's on the letter to Dan. That's the link!"

"Well, if you'd actually fucking told us that, then we might fucking well have worked it fucking out!" What was left of Annie's equilibrium flew straight out the window.

"OK. Calm down." Sheena drew a deep breath. "Does this help?" Sheena had her patient voice on. She wrote 'ELLA KAY' on a sheet of paper and pinned it to the wall.

Lizzie nodded and Annie said, "Immensely."

"What do you think Ella might have against Dan? There are plenty of names beginning with 'K', after all," Lizzie pondered.

"I don't know, but I intend to find out."

"Who do you think you are, Columbo?" Annie had run out of patience.

Sheena looked down at her outfit, not ideal for the weather, and started dreaming of raincoats.

"Oh, for the love of God, you really are forty going on twelve." Annie turned to leave but something caught her attention. She looked back at the wall. "Hang on. You're going about this completely the wrong way." She pointed at the two photos of Dan's set-up. "Why are we talking about their lives being ruined? You have proof that there was never any intention to ruin Dan's life. As far as we know, Dan was the only one to get that horrible photo. What does Dan say about it? He must have felt hugely relieved at the news."

"Oh." Sheena looked guiltily up at the ceiling, Dan's floor.

"You didn't tell him? You've let him suffer all night? How could you do that!"

"I, eh, I got caught up in the investigation." Sheena hung her head. "Anyway, he's not here."

"Give me your phone." Annie sent Dan a WhatsApp telling him to get his arse on the line as soon as possible.

"And does this mean that Jack's accusation of sexual assault was a set-up too?"

"Ooooh." Sheena and Lizzie breathed out in unison.

Meanwhile, Lizzie had been ruminating. "You think there might be more victims?" she pointed at the question marks. "Who do you think they might be?"

"I don't know, but I need you, Lizzie, to find out at the Plastic Surgeons' charity dinner,' Sheena said. 'I want you to do a bit of sleuthing. Maybe there are surgeons with a similar problem. We also can't ignore the fact that, as we know two of her victims, we might know more. It's just that she hasn't struck yet."

"Who, you mean like James?" Lizzie was horrified. "I hardly think that the surgeons will be wandering around slapping each other on the back and discussing sexual assault cases against them, real or otherwise."

"Just keep your nose to the ground. Hang around conversations. You never know."

Lizzie sighed.

"And William," added Annie.

"And William," confirmed Sheena. "It could be any of the boys, anyone else, or even us. Have you thought it might be one of us?"

They exchanged glances. There were no words.

"Do you now understand the gravity of the situation? Off you go now, Annie, I may need you later. Lizzie, you need to investigate and report back." She handed Lizzie a bag. "Here's your accessories. Now, off you pop. I need to think."

Sheena literally shoved the pair of them through her front door.

62

Dan finally returned Sheena's WhatsApp. She arranged to meet him in his office during the afternoon. She swanned in wearing a dirty mac and holding a cigar.

"You look like a pervert, Sheena, what's up?"

"I'm Detective Columbo and I'm here to investigate." She threw the two photos onto his desk with a flourish.

"What's this?" Dan picked up the party photo.

"This, my dear Dan, is a set-up. The rest of the staff has the party photo. At least, I'm pretty sure they do. Anyway," she continued, "it seems that someone's trying to manipulate you, make you feel bad, but not actually do you real damage."

Dan sat down with a thump. He didn't know what to think. Sheena jumped onto the consulting table and sat with her legs swinging.

"Tell me, when did you see Ella Kay last?"

"Ella Kay? About six months ago, I think. I can check her file if it's important. And maybe once in the pub she works at."

"She's a patient of yours? Did you ever go out with her?"

"Nope. That's a definite no."

"So, all she is, is a patient of yours. Hmmm, that's interesting. I'll add that to the wall. Did you know she went out with Jack about twenty years ago?"

"Really? I don't remember that. At that age Jack had a new girlfriend practically every week. It was hard to keep up. 'Research', he'd say whenever I saw him with a girl who didn't look his type."

"She's the one who set you up. She's set Jack up too and her surname is Kay. K. A. Y. It has to be the same person."

"Jack? What's happened to Jack?" Dan looked alarmed.

Considering Sheena had been sworn to secrecy, she was now breaking that promise for the third time.

Once Dan had got over the shock, he said, "That makes precisely no sense, Sheena. Your Columbo outfit isn't working. Now grow up and start looking for a proper job." Dan started shuffling the papers on his desk.

"I may still be in touch with my inner child, unlike you, but I know I'm right, or, at least, partially right anyway. Who knows who might be next. James maybe, or William, or even me!"

Dan's eyes grew wide. "You are joking, aren't you?"

"Nope, I absolutely am not. One more thing. I need a staff list including the temps you've had in the last few weeks. There's a connection between Ella and the person who distributed these envelopes. There's no stamp on them. It had to be an inside job."

Satisfied that her inner Columbo had not deserted her, Sheena waltzed out of Dan's office.

63

෯

Lizzie walked confidently, hand in hand with James, into the Balmoral Hotel in Edinburgh. She was happy to admit that a fancy set of underwear did, indeed, give her a spring in her step and that the shopping trip had gone brilliantly, even taking into account how insufferable Sheena was at times. Lizzie's carefully chosen arrival-at-the-hotel outfit by Sheena involved distressed jeans, a tight white shirt open at the collar showing off a narrow black velvet choker, and an oversized watch on her wrist surrounded by a variety of leather bracelets. Her hair was tied back in a high ponytail. Lizzie felt trendy, sophisticated, rich and worldly-wise, even though it was nothing more than smoke and mirrors.

The hotel lobby was impressive, and intimidating, and full of plastic surgeons and their Botoxed, lifted, shaped, tightened-and-tucked wives wearing Dior, Chanel, Versace and Prada, amongst the this-year's-fashion-to-be-seen-in designers. Lizzie's hand slipped out of James's as she slowed and slid in behind him, keeping in time with his footsteps and hoping for invisibility. James turned to see where she'd gone and she crashed into him like a startled pickpocket.

"Lizzie, what the ...?"

Lizzie started walking backwards, trying to get out of the front door before she was too committed to the lobby. Her eyes were down, and she was trying to look inconspicuous, but it served only to attract the exact attention that she didn't want.

"I've kind of changed my mind." Lizzie laughed nervously, still walking backwards. "I don't think I'm made for this world. I like my old clothes and my wrinkles."

"Me too." James smiled. He grabbed hold of her, swung her around and, holding her in front of him, frogmarched her to the desk. The immaculately dressed receptionist's polite "Good afternoon, how may I help you?" only served to strike Lizzie dumb. She closed her eyes, wishing the entire world would just disappear. Which it did. Because her eyes were closed.

"We're attending the charity dinner tonight and I have a room booked," James said over Lizzie's head.

As they checked in, neither of them was aware that Kathy, partially hidden by the bulk that was her date, was staring at them intently from the opposite end of the lobby.

64

James had his arm affectionately round Lizzie as they walked towards the lift, room key in hand. Lizzie was perfectly aware that it was more designed to stop her from bolting than from affection, but being tucked in under his arm was lovely and, she thought, she caught a couple of jealous glances as they walked by.

James had pushed the boat out and booked them into a deluxe room with a view of the castle. While he hung up his suit and laid out his shirt, Lizzie walked around the room letting her hand drift over the luxurious soft furnishings. She started to spin, arms outstretched. She could barely swing a cat in her own bedroom. Here, if she could have lifted it, she could have swung an entire horse. Each and every thoughtful detail of that elegant room added to the harmony and tranquillity. Everything matched, but not in a couples-wearing-the-same, aren't-we-cute kind of match. The tones were cool greys and beiges. The sofa at the end of the bed was covered in a pale cream and blue Harris Tweed and the bed cover, soft shades of grey paisley pattern.

Feeling slightly dizzy from the spinning, she steadied herself by the window and looked out over the filigree of the

Scott Monument just a little further along Princes Street with Edinburgh castle in all its glory rising behind it. It was a gorgeous view, and a sunny day to boot.

Turning her back to the windows, she saw fresh, pale yellow flowers in a vase next to one of the numerous standard and table lamps. She started fiddling with the lights, testing out different combinations of romantic moods and jumped when James put his arms round her.

"I've drawn you a lovely hot bath and poured in every bubbly bath foam I could find. It smells delicious in there. Go and have a nice long soak and, if you're lucky, I might join you." He winked at Lizzie.

Lizzie sprinted into the bathroom shedding her clothes as she went. She practically dived into the massive bath full of bubbles and, on surfacing, smiled at James as he undressed and carefully folded his clothes and put them in drawers. *We are so different*, she thought. James slowly slid into the bath, trying to avoid making a mess, as if that would make any difference to the pool of water and bubbles that Lizzie had created on her exuberant entrance. Once in the bath, his free-diving breathing practice at the local pool came into its own, although not, perhaps, for the original intent, but he could stay under water long enough for Lizzie's smile to be replaced by a giant smug grin. She slid further down in the water as he resurfaced and took a deep breath.

"Now, if I'd known about that particular talent, I'd have had you rip out the shower in your flat and have a bath installed." She smiled and ran her hand down his soapy back as he got out of the bath.

65

Lizzie's only regret after the bath was that she'd got her hair wet. She shooed James out of the bathroom, found the hairdryer and set about trying to create the style she wanted. That done, she tipped her make-up onto the counter and started applying. Happy with the result, she opened the bathroom door, shooed James in, closed the door and told him to wait there while she got dressed.

Sheena, Lizzie had to admit, really did have an eye for clothes. She'd got it completely right. As long as Lizzie could get into the bra. The dress had one-inch-wide straps and a deep V neckline that required a special bra and detailed instruction from Sheena to attain invisibility, immobility and support. Convinced that the bra was a greater feat of engineering than the Eiffel Tower, Lizzie grabbed hold of its sides and, with one final yank, pulled it into place.

The dress was Marilyn Monroe-inspired and accentuated Lizzie's curves. Glad that she'd resisted Sheena's suggestion to dye her hair platinum blonde to complete the look, Lizzie wriggled into the dress. It was black, of course, slightly above knee length and body-hugging, and it clung to her curvaceous backside. Her boobs were framed by a long, revealing slice of neckline outlined with sparkling stones. A pair of discreet earrings and carefully applied come-to-bed eyes finished off the look.

She pulled on the stiletto heels, higher than Lizzie was comfortable with, and, as they sank into the plush carpet, her attempt at a sophisticated sashay turned into a tottering headlong trip that almost pitched her out the window. Gathering herself together, she picked up a tiny matching evening bag and called James out of the bathroom.

One look at Lizzie's little black number elicited a wolf whistle.

Lizzie's self-confidence lasted the ride in the lift and as far as the door to the bar where the pre-dinner cocktail drinks were being served. She took hold of James's hand and gripped it tightly. To shake all the hands that required shaking, James had to prise her hand off his right hand, finger by finger, and let it latch on to his left, limpet-like.

William appeared out of the crowd with a glamorous woman clinging to his arm. James raised an eyebrow. She didn't look his type.

"James!" William grinned at James. "This is Jane, who's anything but plain." He smiled at his own joke and pecked Jane on the cheek. She looked far too serious for his frivolity. "And, Lizzie, isn't it? We met briefly at Sheena's birthday party. Lizzie, Jane."

If Lizzie hadn't been intimidated before, she certainly was now. The woman had sky-high legs, was model-thin and clearly treated food with extreme caution. James wanted to take William aside and interrogate him about the model, but Lizzie's face told him that leaving her alone was not an option, and, anyway, he'd lost all feeling in his left arm.

They filed into the restaurant. Classic tartan, traditional elegance, walls of expensive whiskies, the staff immaculate and beyond efficient. The tables were dressed with the crispest, whitest linen Lizzie had ever seen. Delicate bone china, silver silverware, Edinburgh Crystal glasses and a beautiful posy of white heather decorated each table. Lizzie noted that each fork was probably worth an entire month's wages.

Once they'd all sat down to dinner, Jack appeared and took his place next to them. An empty seat beside him spoke volumes. He looked drawn.

"Are you all right, mate? You don't look great. No girl hanging off your arm, and hanging on every word? Is that the problem? Finally lost your mojo?" James covered his genuine concern with teasing. Jack really did look terrible.

"No, I'm fine." The tone of his voice was flat and he shifted in his seat, uncomfortable, looking around as if expecting the police to come and arrest him there and then.

Lizzie, stressed to the eyeballs about the whole posh social event, had completely forgotten about the Jack and Dan situation, until Jack turned up. She couldn't look him in the eye, even when he addressed her directly. Every time he looked over, or said something, or James said something or anyone said anything, Lizzie took another slug of wine to try and cover her nerves. At one point she filled her glass up herself rather than wait the two milliseconds that the attentive waiters would have taken to do it for her, raising a few eyebrows.

"Are you OK?" James looked at her, concerned.

Lizzie made to get up. "Um, fine. I just need to go to the Ladies'." She burped. "Oops." An attack of the giggles burped up with it and she slumped back into her chair.

Jane gave Lizzie a disapproving look and whisked William off to talk to friends of hers and to get away from the scene.

"I'm really sorry. I laugh when I'm nervous. And drunk."

"I'm really sorry I insisted you come, Lizzie. I didn't appreciate that this would be so stressful."

"It's not that. It's Jack." Her pointed finger waved roughly in Jack's direction. Jack stiffened. "Sheena swore me to secrecy and told me, or rather, instructed me to investigate but how can I when I'm rubbish at subterfuge?" She waved her arm around indicating the room full of plastic surgeons. "How am I supposed to find out which surgeons have been accused of sexual assault by Ella Kay, too? Tell me, how am I supposed to do that? Go up to each one and ask them? Make an announcement? Or stick my nose in every conversation in the hope that a surgeon just happened, by pure coincidence, at that precise moment, to be saying that Ella Kay had accused him too? Or," she continued after a large glug of wine, "was it just Jack? Fuck me, Sheena should have come and done it herself." Lizzie wobbled, suddenly feeling sick. She gulped back rising, wine-infused bile and stood up unsteadily. "Excuse me."

As James looked on, concerned, Lizzie wiggled, as fast as she could, towards the bathroom. The stilettos, none too steady on the plush carpet, tilted dangerously to the sides threatening to take her ankles and the rest of her with them. Even though it would probably have been quicker to kick off her heels and run for the bathroom, Lizzie kept going, her eyes glued to the door with the standard female symbol stuck on it, ready to projectile vomit into the first available stall. She knew from vast experience that she could projectile vomit a good six feet into a toilet bowl, assuming the stall door was open and she had a line of sight. Subconsciously, this was factored into her calculations.

She slammed open the bathroom door, the vomit rising into her mouth, only to hit what anyone in dire need most fears. The anteroom, the powder room – elegantly decorated with two comfortable chairs, a large mirror and counter to facilitate hair and make-up retouching. This added six uncalculated feet to the real entrance and the toilet stalls. Lizzie didn't know if she could make it.

66

As Lizzie wobbled out of sight, James turned his attention back to his friend.

"I don't know what to say, Jack. Did this really happen? What the hell?"

Jack looked distraught. "The accusation, yes, but not the assault." He glanced around and got up. "Let's talk about this outside."

They left the hotel and started pacing back and forth outside the hotel entrance, heads together.

Kathy had watched events from a discreet distance, totally ignoring her date, and left the table to follow Jack and James outside. She couldn't find decent cover so she tried to make herself invisible behind a pillar. With the sound of the traffic, she could barely hear their low voices, and only snippets drifted to her ears.

As they neared the corner and turned back, Jack insisted, "I didn't do anything. Ella Kay is just a girl I went out with for a while years ago. We got on well together and once we realised that there was no real chemistry between us, we parted as friends. She arrived for the consult and looked genuinely surprised to see me. I swear, she has absolutely no motive to set me up." They turned from the hotel entrance back toward the corner again as Kathy shrunk further into the shadows. "It sounds like it has to be more complicated than that. It can't be that simple. I mean, how many Jack Trainers are there in Glasgow? Maybe it was deliberate after all. Is she in financial difficulties? Could that be it?"

"There has to be a simpler way of getting money than accusing a plastic surgeon of malpractice and going through the stress of a court case without any guarantee of winning. It doesn't sound plausible to me," responded James. "Let me get William out here. He should know too. He might have some ideas."

"No! Please, no. I'm humiliated enough as it is."

"He's a partner, Jack."

"I know. Just give me a few days. William will go mad if he thinks the practice is threatened. Let's leave Sheena to get on with her investigations for the time being."

"You're leaving your life, potentially your career and the reputation of the clinic in Sheena's hands. Really? I mean, really?"

"Well, when you put it like that. Look, let's enjoy tonight and we can check in with Sheena when we get back. How does that sound? OK?"

"OK, I guess. I don't think Sheena can do too much harm on her own." James was not entirely convinced of his own words.

"I'm glad you know now, James. I feel better. Now, I'm going to get bevvied and see if I can find someone to chat up."

"OK. I need to find Lizzie and get her out of there before she gets into trouble."

"You're a lucky man, James. Lizzie's a great girl and

233

she clearly tried her best. Sheena shouldn't have put her in that position. And, I'll tell you something for nothing, she wouldn't have put up with Sheena and her mad idea if you weren't important to her. Go and look after her and don't mess it up."

James smiled. "You're right. I thought she'd got drunk because she hated being here but, really, it's Sheena's fault."

Jack gave James a friendly slap on the back. "She's a lovely girl. It's not easy going out with you."

As they walked past Kathy into the hotel, she turned away, hoping they wouldn't spot her. She hadn't learned anything of importance while eavesdropping but those last words that had drifted her way had given her an idea. She now knew exactly how she was going to get even with James.

67

Having watched Lizzie's speedy exit to the bathroom, Kathy walked back into the hotel and went to see how she was faring. She found her splayed out, zonked out, on a chair in the powder room. She looked like her batteries had died. Her hair was stringy, damp, and flopped over her face. One shoe lay nearby. The other was nowhere in sight. Kathy walked into the main toilet area and saw Lizzie's shoe poking out of a stall. She looked in. It looked like someone had thrown a bowl of Russian salad at the wall. She didn't recall diced carrots on her dinner plate but that was the funny thing about vomit. Diced carrots. Kathy held her breath, averted her eyes, leaned in and picked up the shoe.

She pushed Lizzie's legs up, bending the knees, and put her shoes on, then straightened her dress. She gently pushed the strands of hair away from Lizzie's eyes and tucked them behind her ears. Then punched her arm, hard. No reaction. She punched harder, in the same spot. Lizzie's eyes dragged open halfway like a creaky winter shutter. She looked vaguely at Kathy.

"What ... who ... you?" Complete sentences were beyond her.

"I'm Kathy. I work for James. We met at Sheena's party."

The shutters creaked up further as Lizzie tried to focus on Kathy's face. "Oh."

Kathy pulled over the other chair and sat down facing Lizzie. She took make-up from her evening bag, laid it on the counter, pinched and lifted up Lizzie's chin and started to repair the damage done during the act of revisiting her dinner.

"Now, tell me. What's up? What happened? Is it something between you and James? Or Jack?" Kathy tried to be conversational as she dabbed Lizzie's cheeks with blusher.

Lizzie started to round and looked at Kathy suspiciously. Kathy back-pedalled.

"I only mentioned it because James talks about you all the time in the office."

"He does?"

"Yes." Her voice lowered to a quiet, whispered, hypnotic tone. "James loves you. You have to do whatever you can to make him the happiest man on earth. He'll love you all the more for it. Lizzie, you are madly in love with James, aren't you?" Kathy was sowing the seeds for her plan against James.

Lizzie was surprised at the question. "Well, yes. I've never met anyone like him before."

Kathy stood up to admire her work. "You're ready now." Her voice was louder, bossier. "Up you get. Go to him!"

With a helping hand from Kathy, Lizzie stood up and, with an effort, managed to stand tall on her stilettos and walk out of the bathroom, straight into James's arms.

68

Shug sat at the bar. Ella was Saturday-night busy and only had the time to give Shug a passing nod. Not too busy, though, to miss another member of Kathy's group walk in, sneak up behind the same punter, pinch him on the bum and walk out. The punter looked annoyed. His friends were laughing at him and his face reddened with humiliation. Ella smiled and gave Shug a thumbs-up. Shug smiled back, blushed and left.

Little did either of them realise that, at that very moment, Sheena was in the pub watching them. She was dressed like a French burglar. Black trousers, black-and-white horizontal-striped top, black beret with her hair tucked in and large black-framed sunglasses. Sometimes, she reasoned to herself, the best way to blend in was to stand out.

Simple detective work had directed her to the pub. Not only had she confirmed that Ella worked there, but she'd witnessed the bottom-pinching episode and Ella's thumbs-up to Shug. She needed a drink, and a good think, somewhere discreet.

A G&T in hand in the pub next door, Sheena got out her

phone and clicked onto Facebook. She found Ella's profile and saw Shug on her friends list. She was surprised that he even had a Facebook account. He didn't look the type. Whatever that was. She went to his page. It was pretty empty, not a man who Facebooked much. Running her eye down his short friends list, she found Ella's photo and then one of the woman who'd pinched the punter's bum. Interesting. She took a swig of G&T and practically choked on it when she saw another photo that she recognised. Kathy. Shug and Kathy were Facebook friends. If there was ever a moment to feel discombobulated, this was it. Sheena stared at the screen. *Shug and Kathy are Facebook friends. Shug and Kathy are Facebook friends.* Absent-mindedly, Sheena got up and ordered another double G&T at the bar. By the time she'd sat down again, it had sunk in. Shug and Kathy were, indeed, Facebook friends. Two minutes later, Sheena had established that Ella and Kathy and that other woman were Facebook friends too. They were all Facebook friends. Sheena's brain began to overheat. She asked for more ice.

She took screenshots of the Facebook pages and connections and carefully put the phone in her handbag, afraid that the evidence might disappear once her phone was out of sight. She went home on automatic pilot, barely aware of her surroundings, changed into her pyjamas and lay on her bed, staring at the ceiling. When her eyes finally closed, she dreamed of Ella, Shug and Kathy.

69

Sunday morning was quiet. Sheena needed help and wasn't afraid to shout for it, even though it was only 7.30 a.m. Lacking a response, she banged on Dan's door. The Wee Besom stood at her side, tail wagging, keen to see her master who, frankly, hadn't been around much lately. No answer. *Still out on the razz,* Sheena thought. *I don't blame him after all that stress.*

She walked up another flight of stairs. The Wee Besom didn't mind, she could just as happily lick Annie's face. Bleary eyed, Annie peered around the crack of the door. "What?"

"I need your help."

"What, now?"

"Yes, now."

Annie sighed. "Can I get dressed first?"

"What are you wearing?"

"Pyjamas."

"No, you're fine as you are."

Annie sighed again.

Sheena waited with arms crossed while Annie got her dressing gown. The Wee Besom did a joyful figure of eight around and between Annie's legs. She thought that was clever and looked up at Annie for a pat on the head. All she got was an aggravated "Get out of the way, ya big lump!"

Once seated and caffeinated in Sheena's kitchen, with The Wee Besom enjoying the square of sun that shone through the glass doors, Sheena declared: "Kathy did it."

"Did what?"

"All of it. She put Ella up to it, I'm sure. And the 'K' on Dan's letter is actually 'K' for Kathy." Sheena could be succinct when she needed to be.

Annie was shocked completely awake. "No! What? No! No, I mean, that doesn't make any sense!"

The Wee Besom jumped at the sudden change of tone and Annie called her over to give her a hug. She needed to hold on to something.

"It makes absolute sense," Sheena said. "Believe me, it does. I have proof. Well, circumstantial proof for now, but proof nonetheless."

Annie waited, all ears.

"Kathy's the common denominator. She wasn't in the room when Jack was with a client which is what brought the police out."

Annie shrugged, disappointed. "Yes, Sheena, we knew that."

"Yes, Annie, I know we knew that." Sheena glared at her. "Patience, Annie, patience, I'm building my case. This is what I was trained for."

If Annie's eyes had rolled any higher, they'd have been visible from the International Space Station.

"She's the 'K' that might want revenge on Dan. She's an ex whose name starts with the letter 'K'."

Annie looked startled. "Kathy's Dan's ex?"

"Kathy was Dan's last girlfriend before he officially came out."

"Oh, OK, I never knew that. But *might* – you said she *might* want revenge, which means that you don't know. What you do know is a supposition. Not that I'm a lawyer, of course. Not like you." Annie and The Wee Besom exchanged a knowing glance. "You're the expert, after all, of course, whatever." The Wee Besom raised her eyebrows at Annie. Annie raised hers in acknowledgment. Sheena chose to ignore the exchange.

"If I may continue ..." Annie nodded. "If she was really into him and he suddenly left her for a man, I can imagine it would have come as a massive shock. I've tried to put myself in Kathy's shoes, or boots, I should say. Imagine how you'd feel? Especially that long ago. For a young woman, she might have struggled to manage it emotionally. Do you think that maybe she thought people were laughing at her? Or, in her young mind she thought that she was so awful that she turned him gay? Would she have thought that? I don't know. That could certainly mess with a sensitive girl's head twenty-odd years ago." She paused. "Dan did go out with a few girls in his teens and it ended with Kathy. What do you think?"

"I imagine Kathy has never been the most stable of individuals. Even at that tender age she could have come up with all sorts in that head of hers." Annie looked at Sheena. "You really, honestly, truly believe that Kathy's behind it?"

"The more I think about it, the surer I am. She went out with Jack too. It was a long time ago, but then Dan too ..."

"It does seem to be a rather elaborate way to get revenge, you have to admit," said Annie.

Sheena started to prepare another pot of coffee. They were going to need it. "I'm trying to find a thread that runs through all the evidence I've found to date, to figure out who might be her next victim."

Annie looked alarmed. "I was hoping that the possibility of more victims was one of your flights of fancy. You're convinced there are more?"

"Kathy has got through her fair share of heartbreaks over the years. Let's go and look at the wall again and try to join the dots. Here, have a doughnut. You look like you need a sugar hit."

Sheena had tidied up the spare room, that is, she'd shoved stuff further into corners and piled other stuff on top of whatever appeared stable enough to hold it, leaving more space to move around. The Wee Besom had got bored of the conversation and was dozing off in the warm comfort of a puddle of sun in the kitchen.

Sheena and Annie stood in front of the wall and looked at Jack and Dan's pictures. Sheena added a photo of Kathy next to Ella and with a red marker carefully drew connecting lines between them and up to Jack and Dan. She then moved Shug's picture up beside them and put a Facebook profile photo of the woman from the pub below him. Shug and the woman were the only ones who didn't appear to have any connection with either Jack or Dan.

"There are two problems here," said Annie. "Who delivered the envelope to Dan? There's a missing link there. And who are these people?" She looked at Sheena. "It seems way too elaborate. Assuming you're right and it is Kathy, it's not as if she's wandering around with nothing better to do than exact elaborate revenge on people, is she?" Annie looked pointedly at Sheena who clearly had plenty of time on her own hands.

Sheena ignored the implication. "I've asked Dan for a staff list including any temps working for them. We may find the connection there." She continued. "We all know Kathy's temper and ability to hold a grudge. I mean, I think she's held a grudge against me for years, or maybe she just doesn't like me, but I've often wondered if it had anything to do with Dan. Maybe she thinks I should have warned her off. If all this is about revenge then I may be a target too." Sheena looked at Annie, eyes wide. The Wee Besom's eyebrows furrowed. "The only thing is, I don't have a reputation to ruin so she'll be well and truly barking up the wrong tree."

Annie was staring at the board. "Maybe the trees are different?"

"Eh?"

Annie pointed at Jack's photo. "What was Jack like as a boyfriend at that time?"

"Well, I can't really tell. He had a stream of girlfriends. Every single one was completely different. But he was young. I won't say that he's settled down but he does seem to have finally found his type."

"Hmmmmmm. OK. Hmmmmmm." hmmmed Annie.

"Care to elaborate?"

"I'm just wondering. Her experiences with Dan and Jack would have been completely different. This revenge stuff, if you're right," she added, "is indeed elaborate. She's not working alone. I wonder if there's a whole series being carried out?"

"Oh my God, oh my God! That makes absolute sense!" Sheena was beside herself with joy. "That confirms it!"

"It does? How?"

"Last night I went to the pub Ella works at." She pointed to Ella's picture. "And Shug was there." She indicated his picture. "Then this woman came in." She pointed at the picture of the woman. "She pinched a man's bum and walked out again. Ella gave Shug the thumbs-up and he left."

"So?"

"It must be a kind of tit for tat! Tell me, what's one of the most annoying things about a drunken punter in a pub?"

"Getting your bum pinched. Tit for tat. I think you're right. Whatever the crime, the punishment is tailor-made. High five." They high-fived.

"I need to have a think." Annie was silent while Sheena thought, muttering to herself. Her thinking lasted so long that Annie had excused herself, gone to the toilet, made another cup of coffee, drunk it, petted The Wee Besom and made herself comfortable on the spare bed before she'd finished. Very quietly, she started speaking. Annie and The Wee Besom leaned in to hear her.

"This is what I think is happening. Kathy must have felt used by Jack. That makes sense, doesn't it?" Annie nodded. "Dan told me how some of the girlfriends Jack had were 'research'. Maybe Kathy felt like that, that he didn't appreciate her as a whole human being. So ... she wants to make him feel how she felt. What do you think?"

"If that's how Jack treated her, then, honestly, he deserves what he gets. But is Kathy really that bitter, that devious? I mean, it fits, but it does seem a bit of a stretch, all the same." Annie continued. "Right now, I think we need to figure out if the policemen who visited Jack were real or whether it was all a set-up, like Dan's."

"Fair point. We have to figure that out and then we have to get our own back on behalf of the boys." Sheena's smile was guileless.

"What! Why don't we just confront her?"

"Because," said Sheena, grinning, "that would be boring. She needs to learn her own lesson. We need access to her computer. I want to know how she did it and who with, because she's not doing this alone, that's for sure. Kathy wants revenge? Well, so do I."

She paused then added, "She dated James too."
Sheena was now officially on the warpath.
Annie gulped.

70

Shug walked into the pub. Neither the punter nor Ella were there. Assuming that they hadn't left together, God forbid, it had to be Ella's night off. He was on the point of calling the group member assigned to bum-pinching duty to tell her not to bother, when the phone rang. It was Ella.

"That bloody milkman's left me curdled milk!"

"I'll have the wee toerag!" shouted Shug.

Half the punters in the pub left, hurriedly.

There was a pause. Then gales of laughter came down the phone line before Ella cut the connection. Shug took a deep breath and smiled to himself. No one else could have teased him like that and lived. But Ella could.

71

As Sheena no longer had anywhere to go on a Monday morning, she'd taken her time deciding which outfit to wear at what she considered her new job. She'd chosen to revisit Doctor Who as the weather had cooled, and she was surveying the information on the wall of the spare room with an intense expression on her face when the doorbell rang.

Lizzie was bang on time for the 9.30 a.m. meeting that Sheena had summoned her to the night before, and Annie came downstairs just as Sheena let Lizzie in. As they stood in the kitchen waiting for the coffee to brew, Lizzie found herself under interrogation. Although not unexpected, she was none too happy about it. She'd not touched a drop since Saturday night but still had a hellish hangover and was thoroughly ashamed of her behaviour at the dinner. Amazingly, James had been really nice about it. She really didn't know what she'd done to deserve him. At least she hadn't humiliated him in public and made a complete arse of herself by throwing up all over the dinner table. She was thankful for that, at least. She sat down heavily and Sheena stood over her.

"Right! Time for your debrief. What did you find out at the weekend?"

"Can I have a coffee first?" Lizzie implored. A mug was plonked in front of her. To put off the inevitable, she got up, found some kitchen roll and then meticulously cleaned up the coffee that had slopped on the table, in ever-decreasing concentric circles. Sheena and Annie watched her, their eyes almost going round in circles following the hand movements.

Finally, Sheena removed the sodden kitchen roll from Lizzie's hand and insisted, "Well?"

"Well, I found out basically nothing because I'm useless at this sort of thing. I told you. Anyway, James now knows about the sexual assault. I kind of blurted it out. I'm useless at secrets and was a few sheets to the wind ... and well, that's about it." Lizzie's voice petered out.

"About it? So what's the rest?" Sheena got her phone and activated the torchlight, ready to shine it in Lizzie's eyes until she gave everything she had.

"When I said *about it*, I really meant just *it*. I mean, the about part was just a figure of speech. That's it. Full stop. End of story."

"That's all? That's the best you could do?"

"Yep. Told you I was rubbish at this kind of thing."

"And William?" added Annie.

"Oh, I don't know. I don't think he has a clue." She kept her eyes on the coffee and slowly raised the mug to her lips, holding it with both hands.

"Useless, absolutely useless. So we're no further forward on that front," exclaimed Sheena, pacing the kitchen.

"But you had a good time, didn't you?" Annie was kinder. "What did James say when he found out?"

"Well, he was shocked at the time but he said that later

he and Jack had a good talk and they would talk to Sheena when they got back to see how the investigation was going."

"Talking of the investigation, come this way." Sheena whipped her scarf around her neck and marched to the recently designated war room while Annie and Lizzie followed behind her trying not to stand on the ends of the scarf. On seeing the updated war room wall, along with Sheena's explanation, Lizzie let out a series of ooh and aaahh and "Bloody hell, what are you going to do about it?"

"What *we* are going to do about it," clarified Sheena, "is that we are going to go into Kathy's studio and find evidence. Once we know what she's up to, we can act accordingly."

In unison, Annie and Lizzie took several steps back, out of the door and into the hallway.

"Any criminal activity that you wish to engage in, Sheena, is all yours, have at it." said Annie.

"I've suddenly remembered that I have some giblets that need attending to," blurted Lizzie, halfway to the front door.

"Stop!" shouted Sheena.

"In the name of love," sang Annie.

"Before you break my heart," continued Lizzie.

"Think it oooover," they sang in unison as they danced backwards towards the front door.

"Ha bloody ha." Sheena was suffering a sense of humour bypass. "To work. Nobody's going anywhere except upstairs to Kathy's flat. I have a box with all the spare keys in it."

A quick phone call confirmed that Kathy was at work and at her desk. The box had at least thirty random keys in it. Squashed together on the tiny landing in front of Kathy's door for a total of ten valuable minutes, Sheena tried key after key until she heard a satisfying click and the door opened. The tension could have been cut with a sharp-edged object as the three of them stood on the threshold looking in. The Wee Besom, never far away when something interesting was going on, made a dash for it, but Lizzie grabbed her firmly by the collar to keep her and her shedding coat out of Kathy's studio. She shooed her downstairs and shut her in the living room.

As they stepped into the studio, they heaved a collective sigh of relief. Knowing Kathy, the presence of a tripwire or exploding door handle would have come as no surprise. Their first glimpse of Kathy's private life was not at all what they would have expected, if they'd thought about it.

"I really had no idea," commented Sheena.

"Who'd have thought?" said Annie.

The studio looked as if it had been ransacked over and over again. And then one more time, just to be on the safe side. More clothes were strewn on the chairs and floor than in the wardrobe, and the laundry basket had clothes hanging off the outer sides. Kathy seemed to have an infinite number of bras of every shape and colour. They were everywhere. Several plates with the congealed remnants of poached egg on toast were littered around the room along with bowls of leftover concrete porridge in the bottom.

"Ah, so this is where the breakfast bowls go to die. I wondered where they'd disappeared to," commented Sheena.

Candles of every colour sat on every surface.

"Bloody fire hazard," said the ever safety-conscious Annie.

"Wow," said Lizzie, standing by the half full trunk of Barbara Cartland books. "That's a lot of romance."

"Have you seen this?" Sheena pulled at the frou-frou dress in the wardrobe. A bag fell out and the Barbara Cartland wig tumbled onto the floor. They all jumped.

"And this." Lizzie pointed to the Barbara Cartland dolls.

"This is seriously creepy." She noticed the vision board. "I think we've found our culprit."

Sheena looked at the board. "Woah. OK! High five, ladies! That's it confirmed." She pointed at the word 'Vengeance'. "Couldn't be clearer than that. What we need to know now is how and why Ella and Shug are involved. Is it organised? Like a criminal ring? It must be. Keep looking."

All eyes turned to Kathy's computer on her desk by the window. The screensaver of Loch Lomond shone in the dim light. They gathered round it.

"Now what?" breathed Annie. "I don't suppose you happen to have a box of spare passwords lying around as well, do you?"

Sheena pressed the space bar, the picture of Loch Lomond disappeared and the desktop screen appeared. No password required.

"What? No password? She locks her door but not her computer?" Annie, always the prudent one.

"I don't have one," said Lizzie.

"Me neither," added Sheena.

Annie looked at them as if the world had truly gone mad.

"Right," said Sheena, cracking her knuckles. "Let's get to work."

Kathy's job didn't involve any after-hours work. All the files on her computer were personal and there weren't many. The largest they found was a folder with the title 'Barbara'. Sheena clicked on it and her eyes widened.

"Wow, look at this! There are literally thousands of articles, all written by Kathy, by the looks of it. It refers to a blog. She's obsessed with Barbara Cartland. She must live in a dream world." Sheena looked up at Annie as the medical professional of the group. "That can't be healthy, can it?"

Chapter 72

"Who'd have thought it?" responded Annie. "Kathy looks more goth than romance. She only wears black."

"But have you noticed that she always wears a wee touch of colour? Could it be a subtle reference to a secret life? A reminder? I mean, even if she were obsessed with Barbara Cartland, and it certainly looks like she is, she's not daft enough to go out in that." Sheena indicated the dress in the wardrobe. "So, maybe she chose the opposite."

Sheena clicked onto the internet and found the blog along with Instagram and Twitter accounts under a pseudonym which could only be Kathy.

"She has hundreds of thousands of followers!" Annie looked jealous.

They weren't quite sure how to relate this to what they knew of Kathy.

"Does this make her a psychopath?" Lizzie chimed in.

"Eh, what?" Sheena and Annie looked at Lizzie.

Lizzie blushed. "I don't know. I mean, it makes her something, doesn't it?"

"Weird is what it makes her," muttered Annie.

"An incurable romantic. Well, well, we're not so different, after all," mused Sheena.

The only other folder of any importance on Kathy's computer had the title GIVE! As Sheena clicked on it, she realised what she had just found.

"This is the motherlode!" Sheena could barely contain herself. "Annie, I need a pen drive. Now! Quick!"

Annie jumped up and skidded on the rug as she ran out of the room, banging her head on the doorknob as she went. She was still rubbing her forehead as she climbed the stairs back to Kathy's studio with the required item. Sheena copied the file onto the pen drive and the three left the studio. One glance round confirmed, what with all the mess, that it was impossible to tell that anyone else had been there.

"I need to study these. I'll call you later." Sheena distractedly waved Lizzie and Annie out.

73

Sheena stuck the pen drive in her computer, said a little prayer to the universe and opened the folder GIVE! Three sub-folders popped up. The top folder was called 'Finances', the second 'Revenge', and a third 'Grand Reveal'.

The mere thought of finances plunged Sheena into a state of depression. She hated numbers, mainly because that tiny little minus symbol seemed to sit permanently in front of each number on her bank statements. She never understood it. She opened the folder and the Excel sheet she found there. The list of names and numbers on it didn't make any sense on its own.

Sheena found the website link, clicked on it and discovered exactly how Kathy was raising money for her venture. She couldn't believe her eyes. She scrolled up and down the main webpage, studied how the concept worked, clicked through each page covering the details of each charity that GIVE! purportedly supported for their clients, read the testimonials which were presumably bogus, and finally came across the payment page. Impressed by Kathy's ingenuity and the level of deviousness involved to come up with and then execute the idea, Sheena knew that this, nevertheless, had to be fraud.

Sheena's thoughts, as they always did, processed out loud. "It's fraud, for definite. In fact, it's criminal. Do you know what I mean?" As she paced the room, Sheena looked at The Wee Besom who returned her gaze with the canine equivalent of a shrug of the shoulders.

Sheena continued. "I mean, even I know it's fraud. I should report her to some kind of internet authorities, whoever that might be, or the police." She stopped to look out at the grey sky. "But how could I? I mean, I don't like her very much but she still ... and William. I couldn't do that to William. But then she has to be stopped. And if I don't report it, I'm breaking the law too, aren't I? Guilty by association. I'll have to think about that. Maybe it's a crime of passion? But what she's done so far is one step, well, maybe two or three steps away from murder. But, would it, could it, come to that?" She resumed her pacing wishing she had her Columbo gear on. It would help her think. "If I don't stop her in time then I'll have that on my conscience. But maybe it's not that bad. Just get Kathy to take down the webpage and say no more about it? Is that right, though, what about the money she's stolen? Would she give it back? Would these people report her? Would I end up in jail too?"

Her brain reached saturation point, her breath shortened and, only one step away from full-blown hyperventilation, she grabbed the ever-handy paper bag and breathed into it. After a few breaths she felt better but needed to lie down, which she did, in the middle of the living-room floor, arms and legs wide like a starfish. The Wee Besom looked shattered from listening to Sheena. She did, however, lick her face in consolation.

74

After a brief siesta with The Wee Besom snuggled up next to her, Sheena felt refreshed. She couldn't believe how her life had changed in such a short space of time. In a matter of a few days, she'd gone from bored lawyer to detective extraordinaire. From her point of view, as she lay there looking at the ceiling, life was certainly looking up. She chose to worry about how she would actually earn a living later.

Back on her feet and with another coffee and biscuit to hand, Sheena turned her attention to the 'Grand Reveal' folder, but it was empty. She decided not to worry about it and clicked on the 'Revenge' folder. She stared at it for a few moments, not sure that she wanted to see what she thought she was about to see. Within the folder were more folders, each one with a name on it. Amazed by the extent of the operation, Sheena scrolled down until three folders with familiar names appeared on the screen: Jack, Dan and James. All the other names included surnames, except one, David. *Logic*, thought Sheena, *says that each name on a folder is a target for revenge and these four are Kathy's personal targets.*

Who's David? Have I met him? No surname. An ex? Recent or old? If he was, then he must have dumped her. I never saw him round here.

Putting aside the question about David for the moment, Sheena's finger clicked on the folder titled 'Jack'. A Word document gave a brief description of the objective of the revenge. In Jack's case it was all about treating her as body parts, not as a whole human being; therefore the revenge would be focused on one body part.

An Excel sheet described the actual revenge with a timeline, down to the minute, and places, down to the square metre, for each individual involved. Shug and Charles had posed as police officers. "That's it! This lets Jack off the hook. The whole sexual assault case was an invention! We should celebrate." Sheena jumped up, and she and The Wee Besom danced around the living room.

The brief description in Dan's file told her that, in his case, Kathy wanted to avenge the humiliation she felt when he came out. She wanted him to feel the same. The punishment fits the crime. Sheena now understood Kathy's *modus operandi*.

Scanning Dan's Excel sheet, her eyes landed on the name Joanna. Sheena had met her a few times recently and now knew that she had delivered the envelopes.

She opened the folder with the name 'James' on it. It was empty.

Several hours engrossed in the documents she'd taken off Kathy's computer resulted in large sheets of paper stuck to the wall of the war room where she added notes, times, dates, names and plans. She added photos of the intended victims. After two hours of intense concentration, she took a step back and looked at the filled-in sheets on her walls.

Chapter 74

She was stunned at both the size of the operation and the issue of Kathy's mental health.

"Do you know something, Besom? I don't give a flying fuck about Kathy's mental health. She's going to learn the mother of all lessons."

75

↶

Sheena spent an entertaining hour making almost imperceptible amendments to the plans, just enough to mess up their timing. She crossed fingers that the group members would be connected to the Google Drive folders and would see the revised timings too.

She extracted the pen drive and left a baleful Besom shut in the living room and sneaked back upstairs to Kathy's studio. The sneaking was technically unnecessary as the house was empty, but she considered it appropriate under the circumstances and Sheena always needed to make an impression, even if she was on her own.

She unlocked Kathy's door and went flying, literally. A rug rucked at the edges caused the pen drive to fly in one direction and Sheena in another. The swan dive, almost Olympian in form and function but perhaps lacking style, ended with a sweep of Sheena's arm across the desk the computer was on, and as Sheena landed, somehow, on her back, the computer teetered off the desk and landed with a thump on her stomach. She clutched at it reflexively as her head hit the hard floor with a resounding crack.

Chapter 75

Sheena lay there, dazed. The next thing she knew, a shadow fell over her.

"What the hell?" Kathy. Then, "Are you OK?" Kathy took the computer out of Sheena's hands and helped her up, a concerned look on her face.

Once Sheena was seated at Kathy's table, slightly shaky but obviously in no mortal danger, Kathy let rip.

"Right now! I want to know right now! What are you doing here? You're snooping around. Why? How did you get in? Did you break in? Do you have a key?" She stomped back and forth across the room, fists clenching and unclenching in time to her steps.

Sheena needed a moment to think. "Can I have a glass of water, please?"

Kathy got the water and then sat down opposite Sheena, waiting, tapping her foot.

Sheena avoided Kathy's eyes. "We've got mice. You know these tiny, little field mice? I saw one in my kitchen this morning. I was checking each flat to see if they'd got in to all the kitchens. I was just going to check for droppings under the sink. I'm sorry. I'm bored and no one else was home and I should have asked first. I have all the spare flat keys together and just went ahead without thinking."

Kathy softened a fraction. Sheena let out a long, silent breath of relief.

"Why were you holding my computer?" Kathy's look bored into Sheena. It wasn't over after all.

"Well, I slipped on the rug and my arm hit the table – look, there's the bruise coming up – and the computer went flying and I managed to catch it. It was difficult as I had to twist and reach out while I was falling and that's why I hit my head. I couldn't save myself so I saved your computer."

Sheena smiled, trying to look innocent, until she realised that the pen drive was missing. "Eh, can I have a top-up, please?" She gulped down the water in a oner and handed the glass to Kathy.

While Kathy's back was turned, Sheena scanned the floor. There it was, peeking out from under the edge of the trunk. So close and yet so far. With Kathy there, it would be impossible to retrieve, so she went over to the trunk and kicked the pen drive out of sight.

Mission unaccomplished, Sheena left. She was going to have to go back to recover the pen drive as soon as possible, though, just in case Kathy took a notion to tidy up, unlikely though that may be.

Shug walked into the pub and sat at the bar on what was now his usual stool. Ella nodded hello. She raised an eyebrow when Stuart walked in. Shug nodded at the punter and Stuart walked, or rather, minced over to the man, pinched him on the bum and skipped off. Literally. Skipped.

The roar and the crashing of the table and glasses to the floor stopped all conversation. The punter leapt up and made to chase after Stuart who had stayed by the door, hopping from foot to foot with excitement, waiting to see what would happen next.

Shug got up, stretched himself up to his full five feet two inches and, as the punter weaved his way between the tables in pursuit, stepped in front of him with a confident swagger and put a firm hand on the man's chest. At a height and weight disadvantage, Shug had a Plan B. He could see the shadow of Charles's large frame blocking the light from the window just outside. Shug wanted to be Ella's white knight, but, outclassed by this big lump, he'd instructed Charles to be available but to stay well out of sight.

"STOP!" roared Shug in the man's face, spittle spraying his cheeks.

"In the name of lov—" Ella's words trailed off as Shug turned to look at her.

"You! You're behind this. Sittin' on that stool every night. Chattin' up the barmaid!" The punter bawled back with at least the same amount of spittle.

Ella raised her hand. "Ella, my name's Ella." Shug turned back to look at her. "Just saying, that's all." She picked up a clean glass and absent-mindedly started polishing it.

"And you!" roared Shug, unnecessarily, as the man's ear was still only six inches away from his mouth. "You! And all of youse!" Shug's arm swept the room. "Youse better respect that woman." He pointed at Ella.

"Ella," whispered Ella.

"That woman, Ella," continued Shug. "Enough is enough. There'll be no more pinchin' her bum. Got me? No more starin', either! That woman has a brain and is much mair than boobs and bum. DO YOUSE UNDERSTAND?" Shug glared at each and every punter. Heads dropped. Pints of beer were minutely studied. Ella was gratified to hear the embarrassed shuffling of feet, clearing of throats and quiet yesses and OKs.

The punter planted in front of Shug stayed put. Glaring.

"What dae ye want? Are ye deef?" shouted Shug, pointing at his ears. "Do you need mair information? An instruction manual on how not to pinch a woman's bum? A drawing showing where her heid is in relation to her chest? Is that it?" His chin pushed out in a challenge. His hands were in fists, and he bounced on the balls of his feet. He hadn't boxed for years but he still had the moves.

The man feinted forward then went to punch Shug but lost his balance. Too drunk to be in complete control of his movements, he landed with a crash on the floor. Shug hadn't even touched him but wasn't about to let that minor detail take away from his victory. Shug stood tall as if he'd won a great battle.

Sonia materialised out of thin air and began administering first aid to the punter practically before his head hit the ground.

Ella, the veritable rescued damsel in distress, rushed out from behind the bar, stepped over the punter and kissed Shug on the forehead.

"Thank you, Shug! You're a great friend. I don't think anyone will bother me now. You don't have to come round every night now."

Shug froze. Ella had kissed him. This was the first time her lips had met a part of his body but the shock and despair he felt went deep. A kiss on the forehead could only mean one thing: he'd entered the dreaded Friend Zone. A place where dreams go to die. And, to avoid any doubt, she'd used the word 'friend'. And, the cherry on the cake, she didn't want him round the pub every night any more, now that he'd solved her problem. Shug was stung and upset. His eyes filled up. He had to get out of there.

Ella went back behind the bar, and when she turned to talk to Shug, his unfinished pint was there but he was nowhere to be seen. She turned her back, her own eyes filling up, surprised at her reaction. He'd left. The rejection. He mattered. For once, it was someone who mattered. Anger rose, accompanied by its good friend, dejection. She slammed her hand on the counter and the glass she was holding smashed, cutting her hand. Her tears flowed as she cleared up the mess and watched her blood mix with the beer from the smashed glass.

Outside, Shug gave one final look back through a corner of the stained-glass window at Ella. Her back was turned and it looked like she was working away as if nothing had happened. Thrown away like a used rag. She didn't need him now. Rejected. Dejected. His shoulders slumped and he walked away, dragging his feet. Charles followed a short distance behind, a large shadow reflecting Shug's posture.

The following morning, The Wee Besom found herself shut in the living room again. She wanted her dog sitter back. At least she'd be out in the doggy park having fun, not stuck indoors on a rare sunny day. She did, nevertheless, have a box of toys to choose from. The lucky girl had a different box of toys in each flat, except Kathy's, of course. After rummaging around sniffing each toy in turn, she carefully pulled out her much-repaired favourite teddy and proceeded to rip it to shreds, shaking it from side to side until she was dizzy, and yanking the stuffing out with her teeth. Once it was only a shadow of its former self, and The Wee Besom was satisfied that the stuffing was evenly spread around the living room, she picked out a bone and settled down for a good chew.

Sheena sneaked up to Kathy's studio. This time mindful of the rug, she got down on her hands and knees and fished the pen drive out from under the trunk, leaving behind various unidentified objects which could have been old chewed sweets or dead spiders. She sat in front of Kathy's computer. A little surprised that Kathy hadn't added a password after yesterday's events, Sheena went straight onto the internet and opened Google Drive. Every member of the group was indeed connected. Sheena allowed herself a smug moment or two. A loud ping drew her attention to the desktop WhatsApp. Top of the list was a group chat called GIVE!

"Hallelujah, Hallelujah, hallelujaaaaaah!" Sheena sang. "That's it. I'm giving up law. I'm going to become a detective. This is brilliant."

A new message from Kathy herself popped up: "Planning meeting tonight. 10 p.m. at the chess club as soon as the ballroom dance class finishes. BE PUNCTUAL! NO EXCEPTIONS! YOU KNOW WHO YOU ARE!" Sheena forgot everything else, whipped out the pen drive, shut down the computer and rushed downstairs. She opened the door to the living room and, before she could see the devastation, The Wee Besom rushed out and stood by the front door with crossed legs and a strained expression on her face. Feeling guilty for abandoning her, Sheena took her out for a brief walk. The Wee Besom dragged Sheena to the doggy park where she had a ball, both literally and figuratively.

While waiting for The Wee Besom to get bored, which was never going to happen, Sheena sent messages to Annie and Lizzie: 'Meeting in the Beaver's Butt at 7 p.m. to discuss strategy. Lizzie, keep your evening clear. Dress ballroomy.'

78

The Beaver's Butt was a haven for hipsters and was, as such, discreet, because no self-respecting Glaswegian would be seen dead in there, which meant no Kathy. Sheena, Annie and Lizzie were huddled round a tiny table with their G&Ts. They felt conspicuous by their lack of beards. That is, until Sheena noticed Jack chatting to someone at the bar. She caught his eye. As he recognised her, his expression changed to horror. Clearly, he'd thought that his choice of pub was a guarantee of discretion too.

Sheena beckoned him over and Jack reluctantly went over to say hello.

"Hi, Jack. And you are ...?" Sheena smiled at the stranger who'd followed him.

"Hi, I'm Matthew. Matt to my friends. Terribly pleased to meet you." His rounded, plummy English accent was a pleasant change from broad Glasgow.

Jack looked extremely anxious. "Matt's a colleague from another practice, you know, a plastic surgeon." He stared at Sheena, willing her to keep her mouth shut.

"So, Matt," said Sheena blithely, "has Jack told you about his recent upset? It must be helpful to get objective advice and support from another professional in the field."

Matt looked at Sheena, confused, and then at Jack. If looks could kill, Sheena would have burned to a crisp and her ashes pushing up daisies in no time.

"Sheena, please!" he implored.

"Don't worry yourself into an early grave, Jack. The situation will shortly be under control. It was a set-up."

He sat down with a thump. "What?"

"Yes. I found out yesterday when I was—"

Jack shouted, "You knew *yesterday*? A whole day ago and it didn't occur to you to tell me?"

The bar went quiet. A sea of beards whipped round to stare at the scene, bringing with it a waft of Slow Explosions. Jack rubbed the scar above his eye and brushed his hair off his forehead. "I can't believe you didn't tell me! Have you any idea how I've been suffering?"

Sheena tried to look contrite. "I'm sorry, but I was busy investigating with the sole purpose of figuring this out for you. So shut up and listen ... Kathy got Ella to go to your office. She couldn't have known that you knew her of old. Then she left you alone with her, and later on two members of her merry band pretended to be the polis to scare you."

"They certainly managed that," stuttered Jack. "Are you sure?"

"Do you recognise this man?" Sheena handed Jack a photo of Shug in her most detective-like officious fashion.

"That's him! That's the policeman."

"Well, there you go. He's no policeman. He's part of Kathy's gang. That's proof enough for me." She paused and looked, one by one, at Jack, Lizzie, Annie and, finally, Matt. She loved being centre stage. Her eyes lingered on Matt. "I had a plan but," she gave Matt an appreciative once-over, "I now have another idea."

Jack's body fell in on itself and he let out a huge wail of

relief. Matt looked alarmed at the visible display of emotion. *Not very manly*, he thought, squaring his shoulders.

"Jack," said Sheena, "Kathy wanted to get her own back on you for treating her like a collection of body parts rather than a whole human being, and then dumping her."

Matt looked a little shocked. "Not very gentlemanly," he muttered.

"She set this whole thing up just to get back at me? And got three other people involved? Its a bit over the top, isn't?"

"That's the least of it. I'll fill you in later but I have plans to make. Just keep on looking miserable any time you see Kathy," insisted Sheena.

"You mean as opposed to launching myself at her and strangling her with my bare hands?"

"Exactly." She turned to Matt. "Could I have your phone number?" she smiled flirtatiously.

Matt seemed to sense that resistance would be futile. He keyed his number into Sheena's mobile.

"Thank you," she said. "I'll call you later."

"Bit forward," muttered Matt.

Sheena dismissed the boys with a "Shoo, we've got work to do! And three more G&Ts, if you don't mind. Call it payment for my services." She turned her attention to Lizzie and Annie. Jack and Matt went back to the bar and Matt settled down to ask Jack a thousand questions about what on earth was going on.

***

"Kathy has set-ups planned out with military precision," said Sheena after giving Annie and Lizzie a thorough briefing of what she'd found. "And that military precision is her Achilles heel."

Lizzie didn't care. "What did you find out about James?"

"Nothing, nothing at all, but Kathy has organised a

271

meeting tonight at the ballroom dance chess club and I'll bet you anything that's what the meeting's about. It's the only plan that she hasn't set up yet and you, my dear Lizzie, are going to find out."

"I knew you were up to something." Lizzie smoothed out the folds in her flowing A-line dress. "You know I'm hopeless at this stuff. Can't you get Annie to pitch in for a change? I'm too much of a scaredy-cat to do anything that isn't a hundred per cent kosher."

"No fucking way, I've got a reputation to keep," said Annie.

"What, and I don't? Who do you think you are?" Lizzie bristled.

"Have you ever played hide-and-seek?" Sheena said, trying to distract Lizzie who was glaring at Annie.

"Of course."

"Well, now's your chance to play again. You go to the ballroom dance class and then when it's over, you hide in a cupboard and listen to what's said by Kathy and her gang. Easy peasy lemon squeezy."

"You've got to be joking," said Lizzie.

"Lizzie, my dear." Sheena put on her adult-talking-to-toddler voice. "It's all in a good cause. You're doing it for James, after all. You can't abandon him, can you? Who knows what could happen to him?" Sheena managed to cajole, patronise and manipulate all at the same time.

Annie, who, even if she was physically the most flexible of the three, had no intention of hiding in a cupboard, added, "No, you can't abandon him," which earned her a look that made her sit back.

Sheena added, "It won't be hard. No one will see you."

"Just make sure you go to the toilet before hiding.

Nothing worse than needing the loo when you can't do anything about it," offered Annie.

"And then all you have to do when everyone leaves is walk out after them." Sheena shrugged her shoulders. "Easy."

Lizzie was not remotely happy at this turn of events. She took a swig of her G&T then looked at Sheena and then at Annie. They waited. Patient. "OK. I'll do it. But you don't know where it is, so the point's moot." Lizzie thought that was the end of it.

"Of course we do," said Sheena smugly. "How many chess clubs in Glasgow do you think also run ballroom dancing classes? One. That's all. Just one. Here's the address, Lizzie. It starts at 8 p.m. You'd better leave now." Sheena picked up Lizzie's G&T and drained it for her. "Go!"

79

Lizzie walked into the ballroom dancing class and saw a sea of faces and colourful dresses. She was surprised at the wide range of ages and happy to note a few potential male partners in amongst them. Then she remembered James and that she was here for him. Still, if it all went west, she now knew she could ballroom her way into a new relationship.

First, though, she had to get past the moment she hated the most: arriving in a new place where she didn't know anyone and having to take courage in both hands by walking up to someone and hoping they would talk to her. She looked around for a friendly face. Fortunately, the teacher, all too happy to see a new face, approached.

"Welcome! Welcome!" He was slight and lithe and his movements were fluid as if music permanently played in his head. He looked at Lizzie's concerned face. "We're very pleased to have you amongst us tonight." He waved his arm across the group, eliciting various friendly 'hi', 'great' and 'welcome!'. "Now, do you have rhythm? Can you sashay? Have you ever salsa-ed? What about your Paso Doble?"

"My what? Was I meant to bring something?"

One look at Lizzie's face told him everything he needed to know. "Don't worry, tonight's for beginners. All you have to do is relax and enjoy yourself. Come. John can be your partner for now."

Lizzie chose to make the best of it, and, to her surprise, really enjoyed herself. She thought she might actually join the group and learn to dance.

At the coffee break, Lizzie remembered that she was there with a purpose that had nothing to do with the quick step. The tension pulled her shoulders up round her ears and her heart started to race. She surreptitiously opened a large cupboard at the far end of the room, and peered in to see if she'd fit.

"What are you looking for, love?" called the teacher.

Lizzie jumped as if she'd been caught smoking. "Nothing, really. Just some biscuits. I'm starving after all this exercise."

"There's a box of Jaffa Cakes right here next to the coffee pot," chirped the teacher. "Help yourself, the sugar hit will keep you going."

It did, but it took two Jaffa Cakes to calm her down and another two to perk her up again. As the dance class drew to a close, Lizzie started to stress and her shoulders crept up towards her ears again. She wasn't sure how she was going to pull this off.

As they all packed up and left, Lizzie said her goodbyes and went and hid in the toilet. She'd always had a nervous stomach and didn't have to fake it when one of the other women came in to check that no one was there.

"You go ahead. I'll be out in a minute." Lizzie clutched her stomach, doubled over and groaned. "I'm fine, honest."

A few minutes later, Lizzie started to feel better. She stuck her nose out of the bathroom door and looked down the corridor. The coast was clear. She crept into the main room and went straight to the large cupboard knowing that she had only a matter of minutes to find her hiding space. Once inside, the stale sweat that impregnated the mess of old gym equipment smelled like it had been thrown in there back in the seventies forced Lizzie to focus on her gag reflex before she could move the stuff around to make room. No sooner had she squeezed herself into a space under the bottom shelf and was pulling a tennis racket from underneath her that had got stuck in an awkward spot, than she heard people arriving, chatting, excited. Lizzie held her breath. The cupboard door was partially open and she didn't dare pull it closed in case anyone was watching. Very slowly, very carefully, inch by inch, she piled a stack of gym equipment into a pile in front of her and a towel over her head. She could barely breathe. The stench of stale sweat, and God knows what that towel had been used for, was revolting. On every breath inhaled she cursed Sheena and, on every exhale, Annie.

Lizzie tried to figure out how many people were in the group. She guessed about a dozen. A few voices came close enough for her to imagine that they were just outside the cupboard. She gulped her nerves back and willed them not to look in.

"Order!" shouted Kathy.

After general shuffling and scraping of chairs, the group settled down and looked at Kathy expectantly.

"Let's get on with it. I don't think there's any need to review the activities of the past week. I'd only like to say congratulations to you all and the detailed planning and immaculate execution that ensured such success. You should all be proud."

Stuart stood up and led a round of applause. Shug sat as

far away from Ella as he could manage. This was awkward in a circle, the furthest point being directly across from her. He sat side-saddle on the chair with his arms and legs crossed. Ella was a mirror image on the other side. They were so busy not looking at each other that they didn't realise that the other was just as offended. *A lover's tiff*, thought Kathy. *Knew it wouldn't last.*

She continued. "Is everyone clear on their role in the next few days' activities?"

There was a general murmur, and nods and thumbs-up went round the group.

"OK, then that leaves us with only one to sort out. My very own ex, James."

On hearing James's name, Lizzie sat bolt upright and banged her head on the shelf above.

"What was that?" gasped one of the girls, hands clasped to her chest.

"Probably someone upstairs. No need to be so sensitive." Kathy paused for a second to gather her thoughts. "Now, I knew James a long time ago, a time perhaps few of you could imagine. A time when not everyone could afford a mobile. Calls were expensive to make and the internet wasn't accessible on your phone and WhatsApp didn't exist."

A gasp went around the room. "What?" exclaimed the youngest of the group. "How did people manage?"

"Aye," said Shug, the irrepressible romantic. "It was way mair romantic then. Ye called a lass and she'd be sittin' by the landline at home waitin' to hear from ye. Ye'd arrange to meet the next week and there would be so much mair to talk about because ye hadn't spoken for days." He looked wistful.

"A *week*? I go into a state of panic if I don't hear back

within ten minutes." The youngest was appalled at what life must have been like in those ancient times.

"Shug," continued Kathy, "I'm not talking that far back. But, anyway, I lived in a student flat which didn't have a landline and I couldn't afford a mobile so James and I used to prearrange to meet. The last time was in a pub in the West End. I arrived on time and waited. And waited. And waited. Finally, a bloke came up to me and handed me his mobile. James was on the other end. And he dumped me. Just. Like. That. Before I could react, he hung up. I tried to call him back but he'd switched off his phone. His mate took his mobile back and left." Kathy paused, gathering herself. There was absolute silence. "There I was, in the middle of a heaving West End pub on a Saturday night, devastated, and I couldn't talk to him about it. I didn't even know why!" Kathy's eyes filled to the brim as she remembered not only her broken heart, but the added humiliation of being dumped publicly and unable to talk to respond. She needed closure.

"That bastard!" exclaimed Shug. "Ah'll have him. Ah'll string him up, cut his baws off and feed them tae the dugs." His fists came up, ready.

Lizzie, sitting uncomfortably in her dark cupboard, was of the same opinion. No wonder Kathy wanted revenge.

"So," Kathy continued, "Lizzie, James's current girlfriend is going to dump him."

Lizzie, startled, bumped her head again. Everyone looked up at the ceiling. Shug shook his fist at it.

"Excuse me," said Charles politely. "But I don't understand. How are you going to convince Lizzie to dump him?"

She just did, thought Lizzie.

Kathy stared intently at Charles for a brief moment.

"I don't mean that Lizzie will dump James herself, you numpty." Charles looked hurt.

Shug put a hand on Charles's arm. "She didnae mean it, she's a bit ..." He put a finger on the side of his forehead and twirled it.

"Oi! Stop that!" Kathy continued in a calmer tone of voice. "Lizzie won't dump James herself."

Are you sure? mused Lizzie to herself in the cupboard.

"He'll be dumped by proxy."

A general confused murmur went round the group.

"Jeez. If you lot had two brain cells to rub together, you'd be dangerous. I meant that one of us would do it. And by that, I mean Shug," said Kathy.

Shug looked surprised and then proud of the honour of yet another leading role in one of Kathy's schemes. He glanced over at Ella to see if she appreciated his vital role in the group's affairs, but she was staring grimly out the window.

Kathy continued. "On Saturday morning you have to steal Lizzie's phone and switch it off, or put it out of commission. Then, on Saturday afternoon you go to James's flat and break the news."

At that point a huge deep sigh emanated from Charles. The only visible confirmation was the slump in his shoulders as the rumble left his body. Everyone stared.

"Shug, can you come up with a plan and run it by me tomorrow?"

"Aye, OK."

"In that case, it's meeting over." Once everyone had packed up and left, Shug had a quick look round to make sure they'd gone, and pushed closed the cupboard door. Lizzie struggled to withhold a gasp as she heard the click of the door locking. Shug continued round the room, put the milk in the tiny fridge, ate the last Jaffa Cake, switched off the lights and left, turning the key in the lock and putting it in his pocket as he walked off.

Lizzie heard the main door close and lock. She had better plans than to spend the night in this cupboard. She shoved the smelly clothes and towels out of the way, wriggled round and put her feet against the door and pushed with all her might. It didn't give but she realised that the middle panel was starting to crack. With one final almighty kick, the panel broke and, not entirely sure that she could get through the small space, Lizzie was, nevertheless, going to try. She managed to get her upper body out and was trying to force her hips through, when she heard a noise. She looked up to see Shug's shadow through the window by the door. She panicked. She wanted to be rescued but not by any friend of Kathy. She heard a rattle and saw the key plop through the letterbox onto the floor.

As she lay there, suspended half in and half out, she took a moment to reflect on the good news–bad news situation. The good news was that Shug had left the key. However, the bad news was that she was stuck in the cupboard, and she needed a pee.

It took Lizzie a full half hour and a tennis racket to complete the destruction of the cupboard door from the inside. She rushed to the loo and then, as she bent over to pick up the key from the floor by the front door, a movement caught her eye. She shrank back then lifted her head slightly to peer out of the window. She saw a shadowy figure wearing some kind of cloak run across her line of sight. Just before it disappeared around the corner, the figure ran under a street lamp and Lizzie caught a flash of green. She slumped down onto the floor with her back against the door, terrified, and stared at the key in her hand.

80

It took Lizzie a while to gather her wits and make a run for it. Safely home, she called Sheena, who proved to be singularly disinterested in her adventure and only wanted the relevant facts. She instructed Lizzie to meet her for lunch at Dolly Roger's Diner the following day.

After a long, long shower and a good sleep, Lizzie perked up and arrived at the diner, punctual, as usual. As she walked in, she was startled to see James, Dan and Jack as well as Annie and Sheena.

Annie looked around at the decor. "What is this place? Where do you find them, Sheena?"

"I don't really know. They sort of find me, really."

The decor shouted sixties acid trip. The over-the-top-over-decorated cafe included tasselled lampshades and three functioning lava lamps.

"I need sunglasses." Dan shielded his eyes.

Lizzie plonked herself onto a seat and scowled at James. Nonplussed, he gingerly sat down next to her, careful not to touch her, wondering what he'd done now.

William rushed in late and, pulling a seat in to the already crowded table, squeezed himself in beside Sheena.

The owner handed out the menus. Her long, wildly plaited grey hair and bright colourful clothes were testament to her role as architect of the cafe's decoration. Her clothes sometimes blended and seemed to swirl into the background, and she almost disappeared. At other times, the contrast was so dramatic that it was like looking directly at the sun. She nodded to Sheena.

"Hi, Dolly, how are you? How's Roger?"

"Oh, he's fine. His hip's bothering him. We're not the young things we once were." Dolly shook her head in resignation. "I have to do most of the work nowadays. It's all getting a bit much. If I don't get decent help soon, we may have to close."

Jack elbowed Sheena. "You need a job. Maybe you could work here." He grinned at her.

Sheena ignored him and gathered the menus out of the group's hands before they had time to open them. She handed them back to Dolly and ordered for them all: "Seven bacon rolls and seven teas, please."

"But," said Dan, waving, trying to attract Dolly's attention.

"Dan, we've no time to waste looking at the menu or complicating orders. We need to get on with it," said Sheena.

"Wow! You sound just like Kathy!" said Lizzie.

"When did you meet K—?"

A look from Lizzie that would have curdled milk effectively stopped James in his tracks.

"Dan!"

Dan jumped. He'd been trying to telepathically cancel his tea and order a strong expresso from Dolly. She nodded. Message received.

"Sheena!" He acknowledged Sheena equally loudly.

"Where have you been? I haven't seen you in days," asked Sheena.

"Celebrating. And keeping my head down."

"But I didn't tell you everything. There's stuff you should know."

"That Kathy set me up was enough for me. But I did follow instructions. I'm looking miserable around the clinic."

"She set you up too?" asked Jack, surprised.

William looked shocked. "Who's being set up?" He looked at everyone. "What on earth is going on?"

"Jack, you were first. You start. In ten words or less, tell the others exactly what happened. Go!" Sheena said.

Jack stuttered for a moment but a dig in the ribs from Annie shocked him out of his brain fart. "An old girlfriend appeared out of the blue for a consult. Kathy left the room just as I was starting the exam. Then, before the consult was finished, she upped and left without a word but seemingly unhappy. It was weird. A few hours later, what I honestly thought were two policemen arrived and accused me of sexual assault."

William's eyes looked like he was on his own acid trip, but not a pleasant one. He was literally speechless.

"Dan, let's see if you can do better on the word count. Ten words or less. Go!" Sheena looked at Dan.

"I received an envelope with an awful Photoshopped photo and a letter saying that this person was outing me. The entire staff at work had the same envelope delivered to their desks. Turns out they had a totally innocent photo in it. It was a set-up, we believe, by Kathy."

"Kathy? My sister, Kathy?" It was William's turn to stutter.

Sheena nodded. "Now, start again. Jack, why did Kathy do this to you? Five words or less. Go!"

Jack's voice lowered to a confessional whisper. They all leaned in. "Because I treated her like an anatomy experiment rather than a whole human being." Jack hung his head in shame and picked at the Formica.

"Dan?"

"Well, I could have been a little more sensitive to Kathy's needs as I was really only double-checking my own sexuality."

Before anyone could speak, Sheena added, "And youth is no excuse." Pointing fingers at each of the boys.

"But still, we can't just let this pass," said Dan.

"And we won't." Sheena smiled. "I have a plan. We will avenge you, Jack, and you, Dan, and by we, I mean all of us. We are the Avengers!" She cheered, looking way too happy about the whole situation.

"I can't believe that I'm the last one to hear about this, especially as you're all implicating my sister," said William.

His flow of thought was interrupted as the tea and bacon rolls arrived. Dan gave a big thumbs-up to Dolly when he received his coffee. James suddenly sneezed all over the table. It was his first contribution to the proceedings.

"Aww, gross!" was the general consensus.

Lizzie said, "I mean, seriously? You couldn't use your hand to cover your mouth? Didn't they teach that at posh school?" Her tone was glacial. Everyone was taken aback at the strength of her reaction. James sat in silence, shame-faced.

William continued. "Look, Kathy was never easy, not even as a little girl. She's extremely sensitive and doesn't handle the challenges life throws at her very well." He raised his hand to halt the outraged chorus of "You're not fucking kidding!".

"And if this is all true," Sheena nodded her head vigorously, "the question is what happened to bring it all up? I can't imagine what that is. Does anyone know?"

Murmurs of *no* went round the table.

"Has anyone even bothered to ask her?" said William.

Sheena blurted, "Of course not!"

"Why not?"

"Well, where's the fun in that?" Sheena looked a little guilty and continued before William could get another word in. "That reminds me, has anyone heard of a David? Maybe a boyfriend of Kathy's by any chance?"

"Yes, she's been going out with him for a few months now. Spends time at his place, I think, so you may not have bumped into him," said Jack.

"He's on the list."

"There! Maybe that's the catalysing factor! I'll talk to her," insisted William.

Sheena didn't want anyone talking to Kathy. She hadn't done all this investigating just to have the best part taken away from her. She tried to sound reasonable.

"I don't think it would make any difference. She has a whole group of people who are wreaking revenge on their exes and anyone else who's pissed them off in one way or another. This has become bigger than just Kathy. I think the best way to stop her is to make her, and her group, learn the lesson. Make them feel the impact of their actions." Sheena paused for a moment to gather her thoughts. "I honestly don't think that Kathy would even listen to a rational argument. There's too much at stake. She's way beyond the rational if you ask me." She looked at William. "Seriously, we're beyond talking. The whole thing's completely out of hand. Look, just so you know, as an example, a traffic warden in her group had someone get all four tyres clamped at the same time."

"I saw that on the local news. That was quite funny. Sounds like he deserved it," admitted William.

"She's had a farmer put a cow in an ex's garden because she slept with the milkman," she added.

"That one was really quite inspired, when you think about it, Sheena." Annie grinned. She'd seen the photos on Sheena's wall.

"And had a punter in a pub tormented for days by having his bum pinched, which was actually quite a hoot," Sheena admitted. "And, James, don't get too comfortable. You're next."

All eyes swivelled in his direction. James gulped.

"How could you!" Lizzie slapped him on the arm. He was lucky it wasn't his face. "I heard all about it, and that was the meanest way you could imagine to dump someone. No wonder Kathy wants her own back. I'm amazed she lasted this long. If it'd been me … if it were me," she turned to James and looked him cold in the eye, "I have butchery skills that no plastic surgery could fix."

James, contrite and not a little scared said, "I know. I was young and selfish, and she was persistent. I didn't know what to do. I just wanted to make sure that she wouldn't pester me again."

With his head hung low, and at Sheena's insistence and Lizzie's egging on, James sheepishly explained. "I arranged to meet Kathy in a pub and sent a mate to hand her the phone so I could dump her and hang up."

A collective intake of breath let James know that even for the boys this was beyond the pale.

Sheena looked from James, to Jack, to Dan. "You do realise that through your idiotic, immature actions, you've created the monster that is Kathy today?"

They all looked down and intently studied their untouched bacon rolls.

"So," Sheena continued, "when this is all over, I expect you to make amends. No matter what evil Kathy has done, you three started the chain of events. You need to apologise and support her and help her to get back on an even keel. Her actions, based on her hate for you three, only came from the love she originally felt for you all, and which was thrown back in her face. Remember that."

Neither James nor Jack nor Dan dared to raise their eyes and look at Sheena. In any case, she was right.

"In the meantime, the plan is to give her a taste of her own medicine." Sheena rubbed her hands together. "This is going to be fun!"

"You're enjoying this way too much," commented Dan.

"So, William, are ye with us or agin us?" asked Sheena.

William nodded. "Well, if there's any chance of seeing James suffer, then I'm up for it. So, yes, I'll hold judgement until after we've seen how James fares."

"Excellent," said Sheena. "Just to bring you up to date, we broke into Kathy's computer."

Before anyone could react, Annie commented, "It didn't have a password so you can't really say that we broke into it and you have a key to her studio so you technically didn't break into it either." Annie liked clarity.

"Yes, anyway, I have all the documents from a group Google Drive detailing every set-up. If I change the timings here and there by a few minutes it will truly fuck up everything that's in place. I'll do that around six tonight as I know Kathy won't be at home. In fact, I know where she'll be and who she'll be with." Sheena smiled. "It's a surprise. At least, it will be for her. Thank you for introducing me to Matt, Jack; he's the perfect one to exact revenge."

Jack was surprised but knew better than to interrupt.

"Lizzie, tell James what's going to happen to him." At that, content at having spoken her piece, she took a big bite out of her bacon roll and sat back.

All eyes turned to Lizzie. Suddenly nervous she started to explain. "The reason I know how James dumped Lizzie is that I hid in a cupboard during their group meeting last night and heard everything. Then I got locked in the cupboard and had to break out, otherwise I'd still be in there. But that's another story."

James looked at her with new respect.

"They plan for me to dump you." She looked directly at James. "After what I heard last night, honestly, I could easily do it myself, right here, right now."

"No, no, no, no." James's brain was misfiring under the stress of the situation. This was becoming a habit. "Please don't. I really love you and I'd never hurt you and if I have to embarrass myself by saying it in front of everyone then I will."

"You just have." Lizzie laughed and the tension eased. James's face went as red as a freshly boiled lobster, but he felt that, at least, he appeared to have extracted himself from trouble. For the time being.

"Their plan is to steal my mobile tomorrow morning to make sure that you can't contact me when you want to, then go to your place and tell you that I've dumped you. Ring a bell? It's almost exactly how you dumped Kathy. A man called Shug will do it, but they didn't mention timings or any details other than it would happen during the afternoon."

"I'll check the folder while I'm there this evening and

see if there's an update on James's file and I'll let you both know," Sheena said. "Now, when Shug dumps you on behalf of Lizzie, you need to come over all devastated and shocked but leave the impression that not everything is quite right. That should throw Kathy off kilter. With luck she'll actually be there, watching. If not, then you need to make some kind of comment that Shug will report to Kathy. I don't really know what you should do but do you know what I mean?"

"Let Lizzie and me put our heads together and see what we can come up with," said James. "If she'll let me, that is."

Lizzie nodded.

81

Every Friday, early evening, Kathy went back to the pub she had frequented as a student. They had a type of beer that she liked so she'd have a pint and sit by the window contemplating her life. Today was different. She couldn't stop smiling. The regulars didn't know what to do with this newly friendly Kathy, so they smiled back and left her in peace, as usual. She didn't even notice, absorbed as she was in her self-congratulation. She could feel the weight lifting off her shoulders. She looked at her reflection in the window to see if her worry lines had reduced. With the notable exception of Shug and Ella who looked miserable, the morose group that she had gathered together was now a much happier bunch. Some arrived at their meetings with a spring in their step, others with a big smile on their faces. The prospect of the 'Grand Reveal' party had created such a level of excitement that they were donating whatever they could to add to the measly amount of money the website was generating. It would be a huge event and, hopefully, a huge success.

While Kathy was occupied planning the party in her head, Matt was seated at the bar surreptitiously checking a photo that Sheena had sent him to confirm that it was her sitting by the window.

Matt had been delighted to get involved in the payback. He was disgusted at Kathy's actions and was more than happy to scare the living daylights out of her on Jack's behalf. And that was exactly what he planned to do as he picked up his pint and walked over to her table.

"Excuse me, em, hello. I, eh, hope you don't mind if I join you? I saw you sitting on your own over here and you looked so happy that I wanted to sit next to you to see if it would rub off on me." Matt's smile was disarming. But then he appeared to change his mind and backed off. "I'm awfully sorry. I'm being terribly forward. I really shouldn't disturb ..."

Kathy was startled out of her contemplations and intrigued by the English accent. "No, no, you're fine. Have a seat. You're a long way from home, aren't you?"

"Ha, ha, no, I mean, yes, you're right but I live around the corner. Can't get a touch of the English accent past you!"

"A touch?" Incredulous. "A tad more than a touch methinks."

"So sorry, I haven't introduced myself. My name is Matthew but I'm generally called Matt. The curse of having a long name. Ha, ha."

"And mine's Kathy, short for Katherine, so we're even."

"Indeed. So, what brings you to this," he waved his arms around, "establishment?"

"I used to come here as a student. I've kept the habit. I'm here most weeks for a pint."

"Ah, and what did you study, if I may be so bold?"

"Nursing."

"A noble profession. I'm in the same field but have sort

of sold out, you might say. I'm a career doctor rather than a vocational doctor."

"Oh, what kind of doctoring do you do?" Kathy enquired.

"I'm a plastic surgeon. Practically nothing but Botox and boobs but it's a growing, ahem, industry in Glasgow."

Kathy was taken aback for a moment. "Oh! I assist in a plastic surgeon's office in the West End. Do you know Jack, James and William by any chance?"

Matt put on his best pensive face. "Can't say I do, I'm afraid. Being from south of the border I don't really know the local surgeons yet. Just my colleagues. Are they worth getting to know? It would be nice to have more professional contacts in Glasgow."

They carried on talking for a while. Kathy thought that she was being chatted up and was enjoying it all while Matt was desperately trying to find an opening into the conversation Sheena had instructed him to have with Kathy. It wasn't as easy as he had thought. He went to the bar and got another round of beers while figuring out his next move. When he sat down again, he found an opening and managed to turn the conversation in the right direction.

"What I really hate is how careful you have to be with patients these days. They'll sue you at the drop of a hat."

"Really?" said Kathy, a bit uncomfortable. "Isn't that an American thing? Suing, I mean."

"It used to be but it's caught on here now, so we have to be ultra-careful. I've had friends find themselves in the most awful trouble. And you have to be careful too."

"Me?" Kathy sat up. He had her attention now.

"I'm afraid so. Just last week a colleague of mine in London lost his licence. The patient claimed that she'd been left alone with the doctor 'at her own risk'. Said she feared for her life."

"And what did that have to do with the assisting nurse?" Kathy had a queasy feeling in her stomach.

"The nurse had left the doctor's surgery for literally a second at the request of the patient who'd asked her to get her glasses from her coat pocket which she'd left in reception."

"So?" Kathy felt bile rise into her throat.

"Well, the patient sued the doctor. Absolutely ridiculous! She was clearly looking for an excuse to make money, but he lost his licence for malpractice, even though he didn't do anything wrong. The problem is that no one could corroborate his version of the story and the jury chose to believe the patient. She was the vulnerable woman. That's why there always has to be a nurse present." Matt looked intently at Kathy, who avoided his gaze by staring out the window and fixating on the traffic lights on the corner. "Anyway, as the doctor's career was over and he had nothing left to lose, he sued the nurse for negligence and failure to fulfil her duties."

Kathy's eyes whipped back to meet Matt's. "Oh my God! What happened?"

"Well, she lost her job and her licence too."

Kathy thought she was going to throw up.

Matt leaned towards her, alarmed at the change of colour in her face. She'd gone grey.

Unconsciously, Kathy pushed the palm of her hand into his face and held it there. Her mind felt like a hamster running in its wheel. Going at great speed but going exactly nowhere. For a moment she believed the story that she'd created. She believed that she could lose her licence. She believed that Jack could lose his. *Oh Lord, what have I done?* she thought. She took her hand from Matt's face and, without a word or a glance in his direction, got up and walked out of the bar in a complete daze.

Mission accomplished, thought Matt. *Maybe too accomplished.*

82

Kathy woke up with what felt like a terrible hangover even though she hadn't drunk much. The vivid dreams had lasted all night, and seemed to presage a horrible future for her. She was too shattered for action, or even to consider a plan of action. With all that had already happened or been set in motion, it was too late to back out now. The show must go on.

*****

The previous evening, while Matt was keeping Kathy entertained, Sheena had revisited Kathy's computer, made a few tweaks to the files, and found the information she needed to pass on to her colleagues-in-crime. Kathy's plan involved stealing Lizzie's phone while she was serving a customer at around 10 a.m. Lizzie promised to be 'careless' at 10 a.m. and hope that the right person pinched it at the right time. She'd backed up her phone in readiness and made James buy her the latest iPhone to replace her steam-driven Nokia when it was taken. It wasn't exactly a fair deal but he didn't mind. If it helped him get back on Lizzie's good side then it was worth every penny.

The next detail that Sheena had found in the folder confirmed that Shug and Charles would be the perpetrators of the 'crime'. She sent Lizzie their photos.

The plan worked perfectly on all sides. At 10 a.m. Shug and Charles walked into the butcher's shop. Lizzie spotted them immediately. While Charles ordered a pound of link sausages, Shug looked around none too optimistically for Lizzie's phone. This part of the plan left a lot to chance, but, if necessary, they'd have to follow her when she left at lunchtime and find an opportunity to pinch it then. Fortunately, the shop was busy, and both Lizzie and her dad had their hands full serving people. He spied Lizzie's mobile next to her on the counter, eminently nickable.

Lizzie watched Shug's hand creep across and slide her phone away like a dog stealing a pork chop. Her dad finished serving Charles and, as soon as they left the shop, Lizzie sent a quick thumbs-up to the Re-Avengers group on her brand-new iPhone, then tucked it firmly into her jeans pocket.

Shug had sent his own message to Kathy on his not quite so new phone.

83

A few hours later, on the dot of 3 p.m., the team was in place. Sheena and Annie loitered a bit further up the road to see the show, even if they couldn't hear anything. They were fascinated to find out how Shug planned to dump James by proxy. Kathy walked round the corner towards them then crossed the road and positioned herself at the bus stop opposite James's flat. Sheena and Annie had to dive between two cars and stay low to avoid being spotted. Just then, Mr Dun walked past and stopped in his tracks when he recognised Sheena crouched down, peering round a bumper.

"Oh, hello, Mr Dun. How are you? How's retirement?" said Sheena, twisting her head up and around but away from Kathy. "I'm afraid my friend has stomach flu and isn't well."

She grabbed Annie's head and twisted it towards the ground. Getting the picture, Annie retched. Mr Dun recoiled and walked briskly away.

Sheena sent James a text telling him to ham it up on the doorstep as Kathy had arrived.

Kathy, dressed in a hat and dark glasses, was trying to look inconspicuous. She felt hellish. She hadn't slept a wink all night and the anxiety had given her severe heartburn.

Nevertheless, in spite of her feelings regarding her revenge on Jack, she still felt that this one on James was totally justified. And, although she wouldn't hear what was being said, she wanted to see his face when Shug told him that Lizzie had dumped him. "And serve him right too!" she whispered out loud.

As had become her habit, she looked around to see if Sonia was nearby. It took a moment to find her. She was standing next to a tree, the bright green leaves merging with her emerald cape, part tree, part force of nature, medical kit to hand, as ever. Sanjit marched up to Sonia and took hold of her arm. Startled, Sonia twisted away. Kathy couldn't hear but she could tell that Sanjit was talking intently and Sonia turned back to listen. Sanjit opened his arms, Sonia paused for a moment and then leaned in and hugged Sanjit. He put his arm around her and they turned to walk away. Sonia gave Kathy a big thumbs-up behind Sanjit's back. Her patience had clearly paid off. Another tick on the list of GIVE! successes. It helped to renew Kathy's faith in the entire operation.

She turned back to the front door of James's ground-floor flat on Hyndland Road. It had its own front entrance with six steps leading up to the door. With a critical eye Kathy took note of the untidy squares of shrubbery and the desperately-needing-a-lick-of-paint steps.

At 3 p.m. on the dot, Shug stepped up to James's front door, cracked his knuckles and rang the doorbell. As the ding-dong faded, Shug heard footsteps approaching the door. *Game on.* He bounced on his feet like a boxer warming up for a bout.

James opened the door and Shug started his spiel even before James could take in all of Shug's features, never mind ask him what he wanted.

"*Guten Morgen*, Herr Trainer. My name iss Kurt and I am from ze Rent-a-German agency und—"

"The rent-a-what agency? Sorry, I'm having trouble with your accent."

"German, German!" Shug was not to be deterred. "I haff been asked to deliver you a message. It is like a strippergram but not in a goot way." He cleared his throat. "Lizzie does not loff you any more. You are a piece of shite and you will liff to regret your actions. You! You betrayed her! You vill hear nothing more from her. You will not contact her. You understand? You vile man!" Shug tried to look intimidating while German.

James reacted dramatically. "No! I don't believe you!" He wailed loudly, putting his face in his hands. He sat down heavily on the top step in full view of Kathy, head down and shoulders heaving.

Sheena was impressed.

"So," said James quietly without lifting his head. "You're from Germany?"

Shug sat down beside him.

Kathy silently shouted at Shug. "Leave! It's time to leave!" She pulled at her hair in frustration.

"*Ich bin ein Berliner.*" Shug had heard that somewhere.

"Really? I know Berlin very well. I have friends there. Which part?"

Shug blushed. Caught out. "Zat is not important. Iss important that you leef Leezie alone. You no goot!" He stabbed a finger at James.

"Do you know what it's like to be heartbroken? Do you have no heart?" whispered James, in quiet anguish.

Shug sniffed, caught up in the emotion of the moment.

James turned his head towards Shug. "I love Lizzie. I can't believe that she could do this to me. Only last night she told me she loved me. What did I do wrong? What did I do wrong?" He wailed, eyes searching the heavens for answers.

Sheena thought the hamming up may have been overly hammed up.

"Please, tell me what she said! Tell me how I can make amends! You must have a heart. You look like a good man, deep down. Have you never had this happen to you?" James grabbed hold of Shug's lapels and shook them vigorously.

"Aye, ah was cheated on. And, recently, ah lost whit ah thought could be ma one true love." All semblance of a German accent gone, forgotten.

"I'm so sorry. Would you like to talk about it? Shall I make us a cup of tea? A misery shared is a misery halved, they say, I think," said James.

Shug, wanting to have someone to share his misery with, said, "Aye, all right."

They both got up and turned to walk into the house. As they did so, James put a consolatory arm around Shug's shoulders as.

Kathy was apoplectic. *What the hell?*

They walked into the living room with its pale, cream, modern furnishings and James motioned for Shug to sit at the blonde wood dining table which he'd positioned by the bay window earlier just in case Kathy turned up. James sneaked a look outside and saw Kathy peering over. He couldn't exactly describe how she looked, but she certainly wasn't happy. Nonchalantly, he sat down next to Shug.

William walked into the living room and set a tray down on the table with three mugs, a pot of tea and a plate of Rich Tea biscuits.

"I hope you don't mind my friend William joining us. As it happens, he's very good with affairs of the heart."

Shug and William shook hands.

Kathy didn't know where to put herself. This was all wrong. And to see her own brother there too was the worst of all. She felt the life punched out of her. She was too tired to think. She hailed the bus that was approaching, not caring where it went, and climbed aboard.

In the meantime, Lizzie, who'd arrived at lunchtime, had hidden behind the front door and listened to the conversation outside. She'd then scuttled into the bedroom when Shug came in, and then back into the hallway to listen in on the conversation in the living room and await her cue.

84

Lying in bed, restless, the much-needed siesta was not forthcoming. Kathy's mind kept flashing back to the image of James's arm around Shug. She hated it when she wasn't in control of a situation. What had got into Shug? Had he been found out? Even worse, did they know about her? These questions, and hundreds of others swirled around in her head. She called an impromptu group meeting for 6 p.m. to get an update on the day's set-ups and get some answers from Shug.

Due to lack of inspiration, she told the group to meet her in their usual pub. They squeezed into the snug pretending that personal space wasn't an issue, and with a few elbows nudged and shins kicked, they settled down. All they had to do now was breathe in sync. Charles blocked the doorway to put off anyone optimistic enough to think that they could get in.

"Settled? Then let's begin," said Kathy.

You could almost hear the ding of the round one bell. A series of arguments erupted.

Fiona was pointing her finger accusingly at Ian. "You were late!"

Chapter 84

"I wisnae! I arrived on the dot."

"Then your watch is wrong!"

"It is not. It's Swiss engineered, accurate to a nanosecond."

"Then why were you late?"

"I WISANE!"

Ian knocked over a pint of beer as he gesticulated, which managed to splash every single person in the snug. A general clamour of aggravated voices ensued.

"Shut up! Shut up all of you!" shouted Kathy. The entire pub was silent for a moment. As chatter returned in the general area of the pub, Kathy rubbed her tired eyes and looked at everyone. "What. Is. Going. On?" she enunciated each word through gritted teeth. "The instructions were clear enough. What happened? Did you synchronise your watches?"

"No need. We checked at the last meeting and they were fine," said Ian.

"Then why were you late?" Kathy insisted.

"For the love of Mike. I wisnae late!"

"OK. Check your watches, the two of you."

"It's 6.15 p.m. and thirty seconds," said Ian.

"Agreed," said Fiona.

"I arrived at the designated point, stood where I was meant to stand, adopted the effing attitude I was meant to adopt and waited. It was 5.56 p.m., bang on, as per the effing instructions," said Ian, through gritted teeth.

"No, you're wrong. I arrived at 5.48 p.m. and you had to be there by 5.52 p.m. otherwise we'd miss our chance. Which we did." Fiona was furious at the missed opportunity.

"No, I had to be there at 5.56 p.m. It's written as clear as day in the document. 5.56 p.m.," insisted Ian.

"5.52 p.m.," argued Fiona. "It's there in the document.

I downloaded it days ago after our last meeting. 5.52 p.m. You read it wrong, idiot."

"I did not. The file must have been updated since then because I downloaded it this morning to double-check. Because I'm like that. Because I like to do things properly. You shouldn't have downloaded an old file," Ian persisted, glaring at Fiona.

"Kathy, you should warn us if you change the details after we've gone over them," said Fiona.

"I haven't touched that document since we went over it. Ian, you read the time wrong. Simple as that."

"I DID NOT!"

Kathy held her hand up. "Stop it. Now, where's Shug?" Everyone looked around. "Charles, where's Shug? Is he at the bar?"

"No, I haven't seen him all day." He shook his head. "Not like him to miss a meeting."

Kathy's entire body started to shake. She didn't know what it was. Fear?

85

$\backsim\!\!\circlearrowright$

What had followed in James's flat changed Shug's perspective on the immediate future.

Both James and William watched Kathy get on a bus and leave. After a moment, William sat down next to James, both of them across from Shug. William was deeply concerned. It was only actually seeing Kathy and experiencing the set-up that he really took in what they'd told him. He took his time pouring tea into each mug and silently passed one to James and another to Shug.

James understood that William was in a state of shock, much like his own, but at least it wasn't his sister behind it all.

"Milk?' William offered politely.

Shug declined. He'd gone completely off dairy.

"Biscuit?"

Shug again declined, feeling a little nervous.

James dunked a biscuit in his tea, took a bite and began. From that moment, all pretence was dropped. He spoke quietly. "I know your name isn't Kurt and your German is atrocious. I honestly wouldn't ever advise trying that again, if I were you."

Shug looked embarrassed. "Ma name's Shug."

"I know, Shug," said James. "I also know that the whole thing was a set-up and that Lizzie hasn't left me. Do you know how I know that? Here, Lizzie, tell Shug if you've dumped me."

Lizzie walked into the living room with her own mug of tea and stood in front of Shug. "Hi, I'm Lizzie and I haven't dumped James ... yet ..."

Shug sat back in his chair with shock. He looked around nervously and briefly considered throwing himself out the window. He was wiry but, unfortunately, surrounded. Lizzie looked like no walk in the park either if he tried to fight his way out. Shug took the Nokia out of his pocket and, with his head hung low, handed it to Lizzie.

"Ah'm sorry. Ah was only following instructions. Ah meant no harm."

"Keep it. I have a brand new one now." Lizzie looked at James while stroking her iPhone with rather more affection than she'd been offering him lately. He looked a little jealous.

"Thank you. Ah'll give it tae ma pal, Charles. He works with underprivileged kids. Ah'm sure it can be put to good use." He looked at James and William. "Whit are ye goin' to do with me? Beat me up?" He readied his fists, just in case. "Call the polis?"

"No, Shug, at least not for the time being. William is Kathy's brother. He, we, all know what's going on. What we don't know is how long it's going to go on for and how, if ever, it will all end. We have to know." He looked intently at Shug. "Have you any idea how dangerous this is? Revenge is one thing, but these goings-on are messing with people's mental health, like making them believe that they've been accused of sexual assault. We don't even know the half of it, I'm sure."

Shug looked out the window to gather his thoughts. He wished that Charles was with him. He looked back. "You may no' believe this but Kathy has helped us all. Ah know that our methods have no' been ideal, but it has meant that we can move on with oor lives. And ah've met a woman, well, ah don't know whit's goin' tae happen now. Ah'm no' sure if she likes me any mair."

Shug looked so sad that Lizzie sat down next to him and put a consoling hand on his arm.

"Any road, once we got started, we all egged each other on. It's been a bright spot in our lives. Cleared the decks. Closure, ah think the trick cyclists call it." He paused. "But you dinnae need tae worry. We're no' goin' to leave people hangin'. We're goin' to tell them. It's for everyone's benefit, if you see whit ah mean."

"No, Shug," said William. "I don't see what you mean."

At that point the doorbell rang. Sheena and Annie stood on the doorstep in a high state of excitement, desperate to join them. Sheena barged past Lizzie and stuck her nose round the living-room door. James saw her and warned her away with a shake of the head. The situation was complicated enough without adding the wild card that was Sheena into the mix. Reluctantly, Sheena walked back to the front door and with a "Tell James to phone me the second he's finished", she and Annie left to go back home and wait.

Shug continued. "The thing is, the point is, eh, Kathy told us that these people needed to learn a lesson. And she's right and that's whit we've been doin'. And when they've suffered a bit ... like we've suffered!" Shug went to stand up, his nervous energy needing an outlet. James stretched out his arm and indicated that Shug sit back down and calm down. Shug sat down with a thump and wriggled in his chair. "When they've suffered for a while, we will tell them it was all a big mistake. They have tae learn their lesson!"

Annie stared at James. "You know, I don't totally disagree with it, James. I don't think you've suffered enough yet."

James looked alarmed and then looked at William, not sure how to proceed with Shug. Winning Lizzie over again would have to wait.

William got up and paced the living room. "Shug, this has to stop now. Even if the set-ups aren't real, you're still doing real damage."

"And real damage wisnae done tae us? We're no' allowed our own back?"

"You've had your own back, Shug. It's time to stop before this gets out of hand. Will you help us? I'm really worried about Kathy. The situation might escalate and she could end up in prison." William looked distressed. "And I don't think any of us want that. What do you think? Will you help us, please?"

Shug was silent for a few moments then exhaled slowly. "Ah see what ye mean. Ah knew someone like Kathy once. Started off as a mean wee shite, for a girl. Ended up killin' her mother." Lizzie's hand flew to her chest in shock. "But me? Whit can ah dae? Ah'm just a pawn. Ah do whit Kathy says and that's it. Anyways, it'll all be over by Friday. We're nearly done."

"What's happening on Friday, Shug?" Lizzie intervened. "The Grand Reveal we've heard of? What is it, exactly?"

"How did youse know about that? Never mind, it's a big party, fancy dress, the whole works. We wanted a big posh ball but we're a bit short of the readies. So, we're goin' to hold it in the place where we have our meetin's."

"Why fancy dress?" William asked, surprised.

"Because we want tae have a bit o' fun. We'll all be in disguise and no one will recognise us until we decide tae take aff the masks, that's the Grand Reveal part o' it, and tell them whit we've done. Then they'll be repentant, promise not tae dae it again and it'll all be fine. That's whit Kathy said."

"You do realise that they're not going to take it well," William added.

"Ah tend tae agree with ye but Kathy was adamant that it'd all be a good laugh and we'd all end up pals. Somethin' to laugh over in the future."

James threw his hands up in the air. "You're all delusional. You can't do this. You'll all end up in hospital, or jail or both."

"Like ah said, ah'm just a pawn. In ma case it's no' so serious. Ma wife's spittin' but she'll get over it. She knows it wiz me."

"I'm not concerned about you, or anyone else. I'm concerned about my sister," said William. He looked at James and Lizzie. "I'm really worried. As the chief instigator Kathy's fired from her job; I'll fire her myself. But she may be sued by someone, maybe even Jack, or reported to the police. What can we do?"

"I'm not sure there's anything we can do. It's too late," said James.

"I guess not," said William, "but there's still time for damage control. Listen, Shug, that's it, you're going to help us. I'm not giving you a choice. OK?"

"Aye, OK. Ah'm no' that bothered to be honest."

"Can you keep our meeting secret? You realise that we're trying to stop a potential tragedy? Can you keep out of Kathy's way until we get back in touch?"

"Aye, ah can do that. No skin off ma nose."

86

Kathy had spent Sunday planning the Grand Reveal. She thought it would cheer her up, but it didn't quite work out that way. She couldn't have the party she wanted for lack of funds and planning an elaborate, over-the-top glamorous event with no money required more brain power and imagination than she had the energy for. She gave up on glamorous and went for basic.

She considered a really fancy fancy dress would make up for it but was stuck for ideas. She looked longingly at the Barbara Cartland outfit hanging in her wardrobe. It would be so easy, but her penchant for wearing Barbara was her secret and she didn't want it out there in the world.

She turned to the design of the invites, in particular the tone and the images needed to create a powerful and intriguing element of mystery. The invitees had to accept an invitation from an unknown party and be prepared to spend money on fancy dress. It would take a lot of creative writing to stop its inevitable journey to the bin. The increasing pile of paper balls that littered her room was testament to the difficulty of the task.

Chapter 86

She wished she'd stayed in bed. She was losing control of GIVE! and a sense of foreboding told her that things were about to get worse.

87

Kathy stepped into the office on Monday morning, listless and planning to keep her head down. Be quiet, be compliant and get the hell out of there at the stroke of 5 p.m.

A figure approached her desk. "Ahem, excuse me."

Kathy looked up from her computer and practically fell off her seat.

"Oh, hello, it's you, Kathy. How are you? You looked terribly pale when you left the pub on Friday. I wondered if you were coming down with something."

Kathy stared.

Matt continued, polite and solicitous. "You mentioned the names of the partners at this practice so I thought I'd get in touch. I made an appointment with a Jack Trainer ..." Kathy had gone almost as pale as when she'd left him on Friday night. "Would you mind letting him know that I'm here?"

Before Kathy could gather her wits, Jack's office door opened and Jack himself appeared. "Ah, you must be Matt. Come into my office. Kathy, could you ask William and James to join us, please?"

Kathy didn't know what to think. It *seemed* innocent enough but she smelled a rat. She called James and William and they practically sprinted out of their respective offices rubbing their hands in glee. Their high spirits lasted as far as Kathy's desk. They paused, glared at her, then carried on, laughing, into Jack's office. That rat was getting smellier by the second. She looked at Jack's closed door and wondered what was really going on in there. She had a thought. What had Shug told James and William? Why had it all started going wrong? Matt suddenly appearing out of nowhere. She didn't recall giving him any more details than the boys' first names and yet, here he was, in the office, with no record of an appointment in the office calendar. Something was very, very smelly.

A roar of laughter emanated from Jack's office. Kathy stared at the door. What did they know? How did they know it? Shug, it had to be Shug. He must have spilled the beans, the little sissy. Then she remembered the complaints about the timings of the plans. She never, ever, changed them after the planning meeting to prevent exactly what had happened from happening. She turned back to her computer and pulled up Saturday's plans. She saw that the files had been updated at 6.34 p.m. on Friday evening. Kathy stared at the screen. A client who wanted to make another appointment got a "The server's down. You'll need to call back later", and was shooed away.

She had been in the pub talking to Matt at 6.34 p.m. on Friday night. Kathy had not ceded admin privileges to anyone else. Someone had accessed her files. In her mind's eye she saw Sheena lying on the floor of her studio clutching her computer.

"That little bitch!" Kathy blurted out, startling those waiting for their appointments.

Jack's door opened and he stuck his head out. "Everything all right, Kathy?"

Butter wouldn't melt, she thought. "Yes, fine, just closed the drawer on my finger. Ouch." Kathy held her finger up, the middle one.

88

Monday night gossip night had taken on a whole different dimension. Sheena, Dan, Annie, Jack, William, James, Lizzie and The Wee Besom were all in Sheena's living room. Matt was an honorary guest. All doors and windows had been closed and they spoke at barely above a whisper.

"Kathy looked like she was about to have a heart attack. I suspect she knows we know." Jack looked at Sheena.

"So, she knows. That's not a bad thing." Sheena grinned, holding up her glass of wine in cheers. The others followed suit. "It must be driving her up the wall. Let's figure out our next steps."

"It might not only blow up in Kathy and her gang's faces, but ours too, if we're not careful." Dan was extremely concerned.

"Listen," said William, "the only way this won't blow up in anyone's face is if we take charge of this mess. We have to pre-empt their Grand Reveal with one of our own."

"Interesting." Sheena nodded. She was in her Sherlock Homes outfit, deerstalker included, and she tapped her pipe on the side of her cheek. "Do you have something in mind?"

"Yes, I do. I've spent the entire weekend worrying over

this. She is my sister, after all." William looked round. Everyone was focused on him except The Wee Besom who was watching Sheena closely and inching, an imperceptible millimetre at a time closer to her. "I think we should contact each person on Kathy's dumped list and talk to them. Take the sting out of the whole thing and then organise a fancy-dress party for Thursday night and invite Kathy and her group. The tables are turned and the Grand Reveal will be on them. It's basic damage control and a little bit of revenge on Kathy for the sleepless nights I've had since I heard about her shenanigans." William managed a smile through his worry.

Lizzie could see holes in the plan. "That's all very well but how on earth are we going to get them all to the party without giving the game away? And where are we going to hold it?"

William was silent for a moment. "I didn't say I had a whole plan. I have the makings of a plan. Ideas, anyone?"

James interjected. "Shug, we'll get Shug to do it. We can say that it's the Scottish Melders' Association annual party and—"

"What's a melder?" asked Lizzie.

"I don't know. Whatever. We can make invitations specially and say it's fancy dress with masks because it's their centenary and they want to push the boat out. Shug could suggest that, as they'll already have fancy-dress costumes for their own version of the Grand Reveal, it makes sense to use them both nights. I'm sure he'll persuade them to go. He clearly enjoys a challenge."

"Makes sense." Jack agreed and Matt nodded, not quite sure what to make of it all. Life in Scotland was certainly different from Oxford.

"Excellent idea." Sheena looked in the bowl of her pipe

and picked out a red Smartie. "There's a backgammon club a couple of streets away. I'm sure we could hire the space for an evening for next to nothing. It would be the ideal setting for our melders, or meddlers or whatever they are. I'll design the invitations."

Sheena sucked on the Smartie then stuck out her tongue to see if the colour had come off. The Wee Besom tensed. The naked white Smartie rolled off her tongue and The Wee Besom shot across the room and snatched it out of thin air.

"James, I'll have them ready for pick-up tomorrow at lunchtime. I'll get cracking this evening."

"Sounds good." James got up to leave. "Come on, Lizzie. Fancy a curry?"

"Wait. Before you go," said Sheena. "There's so much to organise. Who's going to talk to the people that Kathy's group have avenged?"

Everyone got up and prepared to leave. "You," they said in unison.

"Oh, come on! Why do I have to do everything round here?" she shouted after them until she found herself alone. Even The Wee Besom had left.

89

↪

While Sheena and her cohorts were plotting downstairs, Kathy was already in her studio, oblivious to the conversations taking place in Sheena's living room but focused on Sheena herself.

Kathy took her time showering. It was a cleansing ritual. She washed her hair, stuck her fingers in her ears to make sure that they were especially clean, and scrubbed her nails. She rubbed scented lotion all over her body, moisturised her face, roughly dried her hair and pinned it up. She dug out her not-used-as-often-as-she-would-like special occasion underwear, dragged on a pair of tights and then, very carefully, unhooked the Barbara Cartland frou-frou frock from its hanger on the wardrobe. Once on, it took five minutes of twisting one way then the other, right arm up and over her shoulder while the left hand held the fabric from below, then swapping over, until the zip finally slotted into its little garage at the top. By that time, Kathy was red-faced and flustered, her hair a haystack. She took a calming breath and put her hair back up to put on the wig. The earrings and necklace kept in the evening bag were clipped on, and a giant ring shoved, with a bit of an effort, onto her ring finger. She then stood in front of the bathroom mirror, opened the little cosmetic boxes that she kept exclusively for this occasion, took out the brushes and carefully smudged a vast quantity of white highlighter on her eyelids and up to the eyebrow. The eyeliner then plastered on was thick and black. The false eyelashes were fiddly and took too long to put on, but Kathy persevered. She refused to shortcut any part of the process. With lashings of mascara and a ton of blusher, Kathy was fully made up. Shoes on, Kathy opened the wardrobe door to look at herself in the full-length mirror.

"If anyone sees me like this, I'll be locked up for sure. Talking of locking up ..." Kathy turned the key in the studio door. Her housemates had the nasty habit of banging and entering without waiting for a response. This was not the moment.

She sat back down as regally as she could. The wig itched. She lit a candle, stared into the flame and incanted: "Barbara, Barbara, Barbara." She stood up and walked around her studio, dress swishing, channelling Barbara. Kathy sat back down, took three deep breaths and let her mind go. By venturing into her and Barbara's inner worlds she hoped to figure out what to do with Sheena.

It didn't take long. As the words came to her, she spoke them aloud. "Sheena is not you. Sheena is the opposite of you. Her experience is the opposite of yours. Do the opposite of the opposite to make things right. Sheena shall learn the lesson you are trying to teach."

Kathy felt Barbara's presence and was profoundly moved. She thanked Barbara and opened her eyes. The message was cryptic but, no doubt, a pencil, paper and a list would help her come up with the answer. As always, the dressing and undressing took forever in relation to the event itself. After another shower and some vigorous scrubbing with make-up remover, she was back into normal clothes and ready to start thinking.

She poured herself a large glass of white wine and opened a bag of crisps. On a large piece of paper on the floor, Kathy wrote her name at the top and Sheena's beside it, creating two columns. She then started to list all the items she could think of where she and Sheena were polar opposites. It didn't take long to find the biggest opposite of them all. Kathy, by nature, always thought of romance first. It was, after all, the almost exclusive focus of the revenges, and in that department, Kathy was always the dumped and Sheena did the dumping.

"Well, isn't that just peachy. Of course, she's a dumper. Doesn't care about anyone but herself. She's like all my exes. Now, if my objective is to get my own back on the dumpers, then how ..."

A light bulb went off in Kathy's head. She'd need time alone in Sheena's flat. The room of doom beckoned.

90

↩

Kathy was up at 8 a.m. and hanging around with the door to her studio open, hoping to hear Sheena leave so that she could sneak into her flat. Sheena rarely locked the door when she left, trusting soul that she was. *Shame she lost her job*, Kathy thought. Eventually she decided to skip work, claiming terrible toothache, and get her fancy-dress costume for the Grand Reveal. After that, she'd have the rest of the day to wait on Sheena leaving the house.

Sheena saw Kathy leave. A quick call to Jack established that Kathy was meant to be at home with toothache. Sheena decided to follow her. She could see Kathy at the bus stop and hung back, hiding behind a hedge. Thankful, for once, that the same number of buses seemed to move in packs, Sheena hopped on the one behind Kathy's. It would require split-second timing between seeing Kathy get off her bus and jumping off herself.

Sheena saw that Kathy had alighted from her bus just as her one was closing the doors. After frantic bell ringing and a few choice words from the driver, she managed to get off and follow Kathy down the street, ducking into various shop doorways and squeezing behind lampposts. Sheena had watched her fair share of detective movies and was confident of her ability to be invisible. Seeing Kathy go into a fancy-dress shop, she was left in a bit of a quandary. She wasn't sure whether she should hang about outside or risk sneaking in to see what Kathy was up to. It could be as innocent as choosing her fancy dress for the Grand Reveal, or she could be meeting a fellow conspirator. It was a labyrinth of a place and perfect for clandestine meetings. Impatient, Sheena decided to chance it and sneak in.

She followed Kathy up and down the racks of costumes, ducking into the clothes racks as Kathy changed direction for the umpteenth time. After twenty minutes of spying on her checking out Superwoman, ABBA, Cat Woman, the Roaring Twenties and the Queen of Hearts, Sheena was bored and needed the toilet, but Kathy finally made a decision.

Kathy left and Sheena decided to get her own costume while she was there. Just as she had taken out the cash to pay at the desk near the front door, her eye caught the inimitable shadows of the duo Shug and Charles. Sheena ducked down behind the counter and handed up the cash to the startled shopkeeper. She put a finger to her lips and whispered "surprise party". The shopkeeper was relieved.

With a "hello there" from Shug and a nod from Charles to the shopkeeper, the duo started down the aisles. Sheena could hear them.

Shug was insisting, "Come on, Charles. It'll be guid for ye. A bit of fun. Here, you could be Batman!"

"No way."

"Harry Potter?"

"You are joking."

"Here, I've found it! Obelix!"

"I don't have the stomach for it."

Chapter 90

"But ye're a big man. A bit of padding round the costume and ye'll be perfect."

"I'll be roasting."

"No, you won't, it's summer."

As the argument continued, Sheena slipped out.

91

↬

Back at the flat, Sheena sat down with the list of names in front of her. Fifteen people and fifteen phone numbers. It was going to be a challenging afternoon. She wasn't sure how they'd react but it was clear that no one was going to be happy. She planned to tell them that they'd been had, calm them down and convince them to a bit of light revenge. As expected, it went down like a lead balloon.

Sheena chose David, Kathy's last ex to start with, guessing that it might be the least stressful call and get her into the groove. David was fit to be tied.

"That woman'll be the death of me! I'll kill her!"

"I can assure you that she won't be the death of you and you're not going to kill her. Anyway, what did you do to deserve it?"

"I don't know! I wrote her a letter."

"A letter?" Sheena was astonished. "Who does that? We're not in the Elizabethan age." She mimicked the queen, sarcasm personified: *"By royal decree you will get out of my sight, be sent to the tower and beheaded forthwith. Yours truly, Queenie."*

David huffed with exasperation. "It was the easiest thing

to do. Honest. If you know her, you'll know her temper. I wouldn't have got a word in edgeways. Anyway, I gave it to her and she read it and then we went for a drink."

"You went for a drink?"

"Stop repeating everything I say! Yes, we went for a drink and then I had a date so I left and I haven't seen her since."

"So, you had a date. And you gave her that little nugget of information while you were having a drink with her after you'd dumped her?"

"Eh, yes, that's about it. Doesn't sound too good now that I come to think about it ..."

"You fucking muppet! You deserved all you got and more!" Sheena took a deep breath. "Anyway, you can get some revenge of your own by attending a fancy-dress party in full attire including mask. That way Kathy won't recognise you. It's on Thursday. Attendance is obligatory so no argument. I'll WhatsApp you the invitation. And you'd better fucking be there or you'll have me to deal with!" Sheena slammed down the phone. Shortly after, she realised that she'd skipped the step where she was meant to calm him down. "Oh well, can't win them all," she muttered to herself. "Now, who's next?"

92

By 4 p.m. she'd talked to everyone except Shug's ex. She was wrung out. The level of vitriol which she, in her role as messenger, had received was, in her opinion, utterly unjustified. However, through a mixture of cajoling and completely unveiled threats, Sheena had, pretty much, guaranteed the presence of every person she'd spoken to. Her main worry now was how on earth they were going to keep the peace.

To get some fresh air and give her phone ear a break, she decided to go and visit Mrs McNally at work. Shug told Sheena that she worked at Greggs in St Enoch Square and got off work at 5 p.m. Considering Sheena could do a bit of shopping at the same time it made the trip extra worthwhile. And, she was curious to meet the woman who had married Shug.

Sheena walked into Greggs and ordered a sausage roll. She was starving; having to deal with all that emotion had given her an appetite. She asked for Mrs McNally and a petite woman in her fifties came across to her at the counter.

"Aye, hen, that's me. What ye after? Hope ye're no sellin' somethin' coz I'm broke. Unless I've won the lottery?" Mrs

McNally smiled and looked around for hidden cameras. Her smile was friendly and she had the air of a woman younger than her years. Her hair was black with a few white strands at the temple and it was scraped back into a tidy bun. Sheena took to Mrs McNally immediately. She had a warmth about her that was attractive.

"Actually, no. Sorry!" Sheena smiled back. "I'm here to talk about your husband."

The smile disappeared. "That wee toerag! I'll kill him when I get ma hands on him!" She shook her head ruefully then turned and smiled at Sheena. "Enjoy your roll. I'll be oot in five minutes. We're just closin'."

Sheena went outside and sat on a bench to enjoy her sausage roll and the sun, when it chose to poke its nose from behind the clouds. Mrs McNally sat down next to Sheena, stretched her legs and untied her bun, shaking her hair out with her fingers. As her long, straight hair settled down into a slightly unruly mop, she suddenly looked ten years younger and extremely attractive. *How on earth did Shug manage to get her to marry him? She must have had the pick of the boys when she was younger*, thought Sheena.

"So, whit's up noo?" Mrs McNally gave Sheena her full attention.

"Well," Sheena was hesitant, "I heard about an incident with a cow?"

Mrs McNally smiled and shook her head. "Aye, I knew that wiz him. I can laugh about it noo but he nearly had me arrested! It wiz no' very subtle, considerin' he caught me with the milkman." Mrs McNally shook her head again and smiled. "No' very subtle at all. But when I got over the shock and all the busybody neighbours had found somethin' more interestin' tae talk about, I could see the funny side. And I deserved it too. If it made him feel better then that's fine."

"So, you know it was revenge, then?" said Sheena.

"I'm no' daft! Of course, it wiz. Plain as the nose on ma face." She turned to smile at Sheena.

Sheena found Mrs McNally so pleasant and open that she ventured a question that had been on her mind. "Mrs McNally, could you tell me more, if you don't mind, about you and Shug? He's such an, emmm, character."

Mrs McNally laughed. "You can call me Betty. Aye, he's a character all right! I remember when we met. Right full of himself he wiz. He wiz learnin' tae be a carpenter. Full o' big ideas of makin' exclusive furniture for the rich and famous. And then he'd be rich and famous too." Mrs McNally looked into the distance, watching the past scroll by. "We met at a dance. He wiz no oil paintin' even then, but he wiz charmin' and old-fashioned and had ambition. I liked that. I wiz young and wanted so much oot o' life and I dreamed of livin' in a big hoose." Mrs McNally looked over at the shop. "And here I am, workin' at Greggs sellin' sausage rolls all day long and still livin' in the same housin' scheme."

"So, what happened? Shug's a carpenter?" said Sheena.

"No, he gave that up. He didnae have the patience fur it. I'm no' that sure he had the talent for it either. We'd got married and I wiz right disappointed because he had nothin' else goin' on. He ended up duckin' 'n' divin', lookin' fur the latest scheme tae make money. He wiz no' that great at that either, tae be honest, although he'd never admit it. He's a bit of a dreamer and never settled tae anythin'."

Sheena looked at Mrs McNally in surprise. She didn't expect Shug to be the dreamer type.

"At the end o' the day," Mrs McNally paused, reflective, "he's no' the man I wanted him tae be." And, after a moment she added, "And, he's no' the man he wanted tae be either."

Sheena could see a tear in her eye. Mrs McNally looked away for a moment before continuing. "We wanted children but it never happened. We never talked about it."

Mrs McNally looked down; her thoughts had turned inwards. She took off a shoe and rubbed her foot. Sore from standing all day. She did the same with the other foot. Sheena waited, patient.

"I think I gave up on Shug a lot earlier than he gave up on me. We were in a rut. Bored. Nothin' new, nothin' interestin' ever happened. Just the two of us in that wee hoose tryin' tae make a livin', each wan dreamin' o' a better, impossible life. We'd practically stopped talking. We argued so much that I spent more nights in the huffy room than in oor bed."

"Sorry, the huffy room?" Sheena asked.

"It's the spare room. If wan o' us is in the huff, we go and sleep there tae get away."

"Ah." Sheena smiled.

"Now, I know that sleepin' with the milkman is no' exactly goin' to help me lead a better life but he wiz there, and he stopped on his deliveries tae listen tae me. I had no one tae talk tae. There's no privacy in that scheme." She shook her head. "And here I am, talkin' yer ears off and I don't even know who you are. Ye've obviously met Shug. How's that?"

"Don't worry, I imagine you've had a difficult few months with the fallout over your ... milkman adventure." Sheena smiled at Mrs McNally. "The thing is, a *friend*," Sheena made inverted commas of her fingers, "not a close friend, got a group together to get their own back on their exes or anyone who had annoyed them. Shug's a part of that group and has been helping out in the revenges. I found out what was going on and me and my friends decided to give them a taste of their own medicine. We've been meddling in their revenges and generally messing things up."

"Sounds like ye've been havin' a bit o' fun yersel'!" Mrs McNally laughed.

"Well, to be honest, yes." Sheena grinned. "The group had planned a Grand Reveal fancy-dress party with the idea that the exes would attend and the group would reveal themselves, tell them they'd been set up and that what had happened to them wasn't real. Just a bit of revenge."

"Sounds like a recipe fur disaster."

"That's what we thought. We're talking to everyone, like yourself now, and we're turning the tables on the group by having our own Grand Reveal party and inviting them along."

"Sounds like yer jist as bad as each other." Mrs McNally shook her head.

"Well, not really. I've just spent the day on the phone with each one, attempting to manage their anger so that the event, when it happens, will be relatively peaceful."

"Hahahahaha! Yer dreamin'! Ye'll need a team o' bouncers tae separate people. Charles—"

Sheena jumped up, alarmed. "What? Where?"

"Are ye OK? Ye look like ye've seen a ghost."

"Sorry, nothing. Go on." Sheena fought to get her heart rate back to normal.

"I wiz sayin' that Charles is Shug's bodyguard. Well, no' really, but that's how he's presented. He's Shug's best friend. Anyways, I think ye've met him, judgin' by yer reaction?"

Sheena nodded.

"He could dae bouncer duty fur ye."

"Good idea, I think. I've only met him once and it didn't go too well. But I imagine he'll help Shug out." Sheena handed Mrs McNally an invitation. "Would you like to come along to the party? See Shug?"

Mrs McNally took the invitation. "Charles checks in on me every now and then so I know that Shug has found a woman he really likes. If she makes him happy, that's fine wi' me. If wan o' us is happy, that's a lot better than where we were before. You know?" She looked up at Sheena, her eyes shining.

"Do you still love him?" asked Sheena, quietly.

"Aye, I do love him but I don't want to be with him now. Oor time is up. I've moved on. I don't know if I'll ever meet someone else but I'm gonnae try."

"Will you come to the party, anyway?"

Mrs McNally got up to go. "Ach, I don't know. Probably no'." She extended a hand. "But, pleased tae meet ye. I'm glad you're sortin' out that group ad I've no doubt ye're capable o' it. Sounds like a nice collection o' nutcases. All the best."

93

♻

While Sheena was with Mrs McNally, Kathy was in the room of doom rifling through boxes of files, looking for old diaries. She sprinted back upstairs, got out a pen and paper, and settled down to her research. It took her a couple of hours to trawl through each diary, day by day, year by year, and pick out all of the male names. A few included surnames and some had phone numbers. Sheena had a remarkable number of exes which made it easy for Kathy to contact fifteen of them without having to dig too deeply. She then sent Facebook messages, emails or WhatsApps with the following message:

> *Hi,*
> *I think you may remember me, but it may not be a happy memory. We may have gone out for a long time. It may have been a short time. For me, it was an important time, even though you probably can't see that right now. And it's all my fault.*
> *I'm getting in touch with you now, because I joined AA and I am following the Twelve Steps, one by one.*

Chapter 93

As you may know, one of the important steps is to make amends with people I have wronged. I wish to do that face to face so that you can know the sincerity of my apology and understand that I am getting better and better every day. For reasons which I cannot divulge right now, I cannot go out and I humbly ask that you come to my flat tomorrow, Wednesday, at 7 p.m. so that we can speak in person.
Yours, humbly,
Sheena
P.S. Please RSVP to the person who sent you this message on my behalf.

All fifteen confirmed.

94

⮂

Kathy had one more item on her list for that evening, and that was to shout at Shug. She stormed into the pub and into the group's regular spot in the snug.

"Since when do you get to organise group meetings, Shug!" Kathy roared.

"This here," said Shug, "is an informal meetin' of people in the group. It's no' a group meetin'. Ah have an invitation for youse all." He handed out Sheena's invitation tickets to the party.

"What's a melder?" asked Joanna, looking at the ticket.

"Nothin'. Never you mind. You're all invited. See, it says fancy dress. You've all got yer outfits for Friday so you can use them for Thursday too. Twice the use of the fancy dress. It's like half-price."

"I don't think that's how it works, Shug," said Kathy, lamenting the fact that she seemed to be the only one with any brains in the group.

"Who else will be there?" asked Stuart.

"Just us and the melders. It's a special invitation because it's their centenary. There's no' many melders left, it's a dying art, so ah convinced them the party wid be more fun if we were there. And ah gave them numbers so ye have to go. It's free and there'll be alcohol and food."

Everyone agreed that a pre-celebration to their main event sounded like a great idea.

"Are the melders interesting?" asked Joanna.

"Handsome, by any chance?" asked Stuart.

"Beyond yer wildest —" said Shug before he was interrupted by Kathy.

"So, what happened at James's house and where have you been, Shug?"

"Nothin' and decoratin'."

95

On Wednesday evening, Kathy needed to keep Sheena in the house and gain for herself a front-row seat to her planned event. She had a karaoke machine that her parents had given her one Christmas. Sheena loved karaoke but didn't know that Kathy had the machine.

By 7 p.m. they were all set up in Sheena's kitchen and giving it laldy, belting out 'Total Eclipse Of The Heart' when the doorbell rang. Sheena opened the door and found herself facing an old boyfriend. Someone she hadn't seen for about five years. He marched past her into the house.

"So, here I am. Where's the apology? I want to hear it. You stupid, vapid, mean woman, dumping me the way you did."

Sheena didn't even have time to reply when the doorbell rang again. Another ex-boyfriend marched in. She hadn't had contact with him since she stood him up ten years ago. She could see that he was still angry.

The doorbell rang again and again. Ex-boyfriends were piling in, all shouting at her. Her dentist appeared and, realising that the message hadn't really been meant for him, extracted a quick and slightly hysterical apology from

Sheena for being rude to him when he extracted a tooth, and then left. By this time the living room was full. Three had made themselves comfortable in the kitchen and were comparing notes and helping themselves to Sheena's beer. Sheena stopped answering the doorbell with the result that five wild-eyed exes were now banging on the living-room window. It looked like a scene from *Shaun of the Dead* with Sheena's zombie exes advancing on her, angry and unstoppable. She grabbed a paper bag and ran into her bedroom to hyperventilate in peace.

And still they came.

Someone opened the front door and left it open. They kept coming. Kathy was fascinated by the wide variety of men who'd now taken over the flat and were drinking and eating everything in sight. Sheena's exes came in all shapes and sizes – and all were equally pissed off. It occurred to her just how like Jack she was. Kathy had always felt uncomfortable around Sheena, blaming her for not telling her about Dan, but it wasn't only that. She wondered if it was because Sheena seemed to have had the same habit as Jack: trying out someone to see if they fitted, without having a specific type. But then, it wasn't the anatomy experiment like Jack's girlfriends during his student days. Kathy left the noisy flat that was rapidly turning into a party and sat on the stairs to think.

She was startled when she realised what was going through her mind. It dawned on her that Sheena was nothing like Jack or even to blame when it came to Dan. It was that she and Sheena were the same but opposites. Just like Barbara had said. But in a much more profound way than Kathy had thought. Mirror images and both unlucky in love. Both trying hard, in their own ways, but failing in their own ways, to meet The One. Kathy's head dropped into her hands. She felt a bit guilty for this heavy-handed revenge. And yet, if it didn't serve Sheena, at least it had served her.

She walked back into the flat and, looking round, saw that she had a choice. She could either leg it while Sheena was bunkered down in her room, or get rid of these men before they ate her out of house and home. Kathy settled on the latter – and then legging it.

96

With all the activities surrounding the alternative Grand Reveal, Sheena wanted to meet Shug and Charles properly before the party. She already knew the event would be stressful and an apology might get Shug and Charles on her side. Shug needed the key to the club so he could decorate it for the party, having already made miles of paper chains that he knew wouldn't be needed on Friday. The chances of the group's own Reveal actually happening were now a million to one.

Sheena invited them both to her place despite still feeling a bit shaky from the avalanche of exes that had landed on her doorstep the previous night. She hadn't yet figured out how that had all come about, but she had her suspicions.

She had hoped for back-up to avoid facing Shug and Charles alone, but no one was available due to everyone else, unlike her, being gainfully employed. It was left to Sheena to depend on the faithful company of The Wee Besom. She girded her loins and waited for her doorbell to ring and for The Wee Besom to loudly announce their arrival.

Both Shug and Charles looked grim as they walked in.

Sheena invited them into the living room and offered tea from her grandmother's best Queen's Coronation china, and chocolate digestives which The Wee Besom already had her eye on. They sat down. Charles was almost prim in the way he had his huge hands folded on his lap. Shug sat on the edge of his chair, knee bouncing and patting The Wee Besom's head in rhythm.

Before Sheena could say anything, Shug opened the proceedings. "When James handed over the invitations for the group yesterday, he made a point of telling me who ye were. He told me he recognised me from your description. Ah'll no' take that as a compliment. Ye hurt ma feelin's that day. Ah was havin' a difficult time and you were insensitive tae say the least."

Sheena stuttered. "I'm so sorry. I was having a difficult time myself and it all came out at the wrong moment. You see, I'd just had my fortieth birthday and—"

"Ye're tellin' me that your birthday is comparable to the loss of ma wife and ma marriage tae the milkman? Is that it? Is that it?" Shug looked agitated.

"No, I didn't mean it like that at all! I admire you for how well you handled it. I'm just a mess. I'm sorry. I really am. Could we just forget it happened? Please, I got fired, after all."

Charles picked up a china teacup. It looked like it belonged in a doll's house as it was swallowed inside his giant fist. Sheena relaxed, slightly.

"OK," said Shug. "Ah've had time tae think about it. Let's call it water under the bridge. We've bigger fish tae fry tonight. There's no' much time tae decorate. Ah'd better get crackin'."

Just as Shug stood up, Sheena glanced through the bay window to see Kathy approaching the path to the front door.

Chapter 96

"Oh, shit. Hide!" Sheena shouted.

Shug nosedived behind the couch with a speed and expertise which suggested this was not his first tango. Charles, amazingly nimble for his size and, without spilling a drop, hid with his teacup behind the door. Never one to miss an opportunity, The Wee Besom nicked a biscuit and ran into the kitchen.

97

James desperately wanted to get back in Lizzie's good books. Any grief from a girl and he would normally have dumped her immediately. But Lizzie was different.

The last time he'd upset her he'd bought her flowers. And had them thrown straight back in his face. That was a confusing moment for him. Flowers, as far as he knew, were all about contrition. As Lizzie pointed out, that was just the point. Every time she'd look at the flowers, she'd be reminded of what he'd done to upset her. She made it clear that he had to learn two things. One: flowers were for when he wanted to surprise her, or please her, or when she'd done something that he really appreciated, or when he thought of her. And two: don't upset her.

As he learned these valuable lessons, he realised that Lizzie was teaching him to be a man. A mature man and a thoughtful man. And he liked it, even though it wasn't always easy. She kept him on his toes.

They met for a coffee. As he nervously stirred sugar into his flat white, he started the conversation. "I've changed."

Lizzie looked up. "Oh, have you now?"

"I'm more mature."

Chapter 97

"Since when?"

"Since I met you."

"That's not exactly true."

"Well, it's been a process. You've changed me. In a good way."

"Aw, really?"

"Definitely. Honest. Now, please, can we go back to where we were?"

Lizzie paused and searched James's face for the precise level of contrition and commitment she was looking for. "OK. But you're on probation."

James had been unconsciously holding his breath. His shoulders dropped as he relaxed. "OK. I can do that." He looked for a change of subject before she changed her mind. "Now, what costumes shall we wear tonight?"

"Fancy his and hers outfits?"

James looked alarmed but smiled and said yes.

98

As Kathy walked up the path to the front door, she caught sight of Sheena looking out of the window. Kathy waved and Sheena gave a weird, nervous little wave back. *Odd*, thought Kathy.

Having run to her own front door and listened to Kathy thump her way up the stairs and slam the door to her studio, Sheena, for once happy for Kathy's evident lack of a stealth mode, handed Shug and Charles the key and directions to the backgammon club, then ushered them out.

She took The Wee Besom for a walk in the late afternoon and decided to pop into the club to see how the preparations were going.

Paper chains were clearly Shug's thing. They criss-crossed the ceiling, hanging from the lights, around pictures and over doorways. Christmas decorations that Shug had found in a cupboard festooned every other available surface. Nothing matched and the overall effect was rainbow chaos.

Sheena looked over at Shug who was grinning from ear to ear, clearly in his element.

"You should become a party decorator!" Sheena shouted.

Charles was testing the sound system. The Wee Besom

rushed around trying to grab paper chains out of Shug's grasp. He broke off a section and made a collar with it and put it on her. Sheena left them to it. As she turned the corner towards home, she bumped into Kathy who was going to the shops.

Kathy really did not want to see Sheena as she wanted to avoid any discussion about who might have been responsible for bringing Sheena's exes to her house.

"Kathy, could we have a chat about last night?" said Sheena.

Kathy quickened her pace. At that moment, The Wee Besom, who'd had her head stuck in a bush sniffing heaven knows what, reappeared, showing off her paper-chain collar. Kathy stopped and stared. Shug had already shown off his decorating skills when they discussed their plans for the Grand Reveal. This was only the second time in this current century that Kathy had seen a paper chain.

"What's that she's wearing?" She pointed suspiciously at the paper chain.

Suddenly Sheena was the one who wanted to avoid a conversation. Dragging The Wee Besom away as fast as she could, she muttered, "Sorry, got to run! Places to go. People to see."

99

↩

Kathy admired herself in the wardrobe's full-length mirror. Her final choice of costume was a far cry from Barbara Cartland but she felt absolutely right in it.

She had chosen Morticia Addams as her style icon for the evening. The dress was jet black and figure-hugging right down to the feet where it splayed out and was almost mermaid-like. She couldn't really walk in it so she sashayed. The long-sleeved blouse, made of the same material, flowed down below her waist, the hem scalloped and decorated with silver thread motifs, and buttoned up the front. The shoulders and sleeves had ethereal tendrils of fabric hanging down and on each hand the fabric was pulled over her middle finger.

She styled her jet-black hair completely straight and parted it in the middle then carefully applied Morticia-like make-up. As no one, including herself, had ever seen her sashay, she thought that was probably disguise enough and she swayed her hips in wild exaggeration.

She was enjoying this dress rehearsal for the real thing. Shug was right: getting to wear the outfit twice was like getting it for half price. She picked up a velvet evening bag and took one final look at herself in the mirror.

Kathy was ready. If only she knew.

100

When Kathy arrived at the party, the room was already busy. She could have kicked herself for not checking what the rest of the group would be wearing. She advanced into the centre of the room looking for a friendly face or, at least, a recognisable body.

Sheena had passed the word round about what Kathy would be wearing and when she walked in, heads turned. Kathy felt the attention and a weird atmosphere but she didn't know what to make of it. She'd never met a melder before. Maybe they were a cult.

In the right mood, Kathy enjoyed being the centre of attention but, right now, she felt conspicuous. Looking at the front door, considering a quick exit, she noticed a curious couple arrive hand in hand. It was either Tweedledum or Tweedledee, she could never tell them apart, who waddled past her accompanied by a petite, female Asterix. She wore bright-red trousers and a belted top, a mask with a large bulbous nose and blonde whiskers topped by a winged hat. Kathy watched them curiously, then it dawned on her who it was. Tweedledum, or Tweedledee, let go of Asterix's hand and gave her a slight push towards a giant Obelix.

Charles was wiping the sweat off his forehead, the padded fat suit a sauna, contrary to Shug's reassurances. As he was putting his handkerchief away, he looked round and saw the tiny Asterix pad towards him. A huge grin spread across his face. He swept his wife up into his arms and whirled her around.

"Oi, ya big lump! Let me down! I'm getting dizzy."

Charles gently let her stand on her own two feet, himself slightly dizzy with happiness. He couldn't resist taking her in his arms in a perfect ballroom hold and they danced a waltz around the outer edges of the dance area regardless of the blaring disco music. As they finished, a round of applause broke out.

Shug was very, very nervous. He'd married young and had never really figured out the female psyche. He wasn't sure if it were even possible. He didn't want Ella to push him out of her life and didn't have high hopes for anything other than a friendship but, even if it didn't develop into a romantic relationship, he'd still be the happiest man in Glasgow. A couple of days earlier he'd sent her a package with a note which simply said:

> *Dear Ella,*
> *Will you be Tweedledee to my Tweedledum?*
> *On your terms, hen.*
> *Shug*

As Charles went into his own world of joy at his reunion, and Shug continued to glance anxiously at the door every three seconds, Sheena watched events unfold from behind a column at the far end of the room. She didn't want Kathy to see her just yet. Her choice of costume, having seen Kathy choose hers, was identical but different: Sheena's was pure white. She'd straightened her blonde hair to within an inch of its life and parted it in the middle. She wore the full Morticia make-up, and her mask was identical to the one that Kathy had. Her high heels were killing her already.

The boys had arrived and claimed a corner next to the beer. William was dressed as a mad zombie doctor while Dan and Jack played zombie car-crash victims, their faces covered in fake gashes and blood. They moaned and tried to smear fake blood on anyone who came between them and the beer table. They wheeled around drip bags of beer, drinking it from attached tubes and offering it to whoever who walked past. How Kathy didn't recognise them was a miracle.

Sheena watched Kathy cross the dance floor to talk to Charles but he was so engrossed in his wife that Kathy had no choice but to leave them to it. Then she went for Tweedledum, but stopped short as she saw a red-trousered, yellow-topped, blue bow-tied Tweedledee stride through the crowd and stop in front of Shug in his identical costume.

Shug had been inspired. The costume covered Ella's assets and allowed her to be invisible for once. Ella was delighted. She gave Shug a big fat-suit hug then stood back.

Shug stared at Ella for a moment. He could barely believe that she'd actually come. All he could think of to say was, "You dancin'?"

"You askin'?"

"Ah'm askin'."

"I'm dancin'."

He held out his hand and they waddled off together to shake their fat-suited booties.

From Sheena's vantage point she could see Kathy wander around trying to strike up conversation with, amongst others, one Elvis, two Spidermen, six zombies, one Trump and one Obama. Those two were having an amiable conversation, much more amiable and Sheena would be sending them to get a room. Kathy tried to express an interest in melding. Oddly, no one that she spoke to seemed to know what a melder was. Kathy was starting to feel uneasy. Even Sheena could sense her discomfort from her vantage point.

Costumed guests continued to arrive and the disjointed conversations became animated as the booze flowed. The music was turned up and the makeshift dance floor filled up.

A resounding wolf whistle rang round the room as Dr Frank-N-Furter walked in. High heels, suspenders, the lot. He was holding hands with a woman wearing a Susan Sarandon mask and dressed as Janet. It took Sheena a moment to realise that it was James and Lizzie. One glance at James's eyes through his mask and Sheena could see his mortification. *Ah, the things you do for love.* Sheena smiled. James had obviously met his match. They joined Jack and William, who promptly fell about in hysterical laughter.

Dan was next to arrive and, to avoid recognition, had remodelled his ABBA costume into Elton John. All he had done, really, was add a mask and funky glasses.

Sheena could feel the tension rise as the alcohol removed inhibitions. Now was the time. She went into the kitchen and brought out bags that she'd put there before the party started. She picked up the list she'd made of the fancy-dress costumes and handed one bag each to her gang and had them pass them round the GIVE! victims. The music stopped and the victims milled around until they were standing in what vaguely looked like a line, isolating Kathy's group at one end of the room. A long drum roll sounded, getting louder and louder and longer until Sheena screamed, "GO!"

The victims, including Jack, Dan, James and William,

whipped off their masks to the collective gasps of Kathy's group, and started pelting them with rotten tomatoes and putrid vegetables that the greengrocer next door had given Sheena.

The drumroll continued and turned into a cacophony of cymbals and drums and every type of musical instrument in total discord while the victims shouted insults and Kathy's group cowered, covered in revolting, stinking vegetables, in a corner.

Sheena made the cut motion with her hand across her throat and the music stopped. The victims were red-faced and panting. Kathy's group stood in collective shock.

One person, dressed as a milkmaid and wearing a cow mask, separated themselves from the victim's group and marched up to Shug. Mrs McNally held a rotten tomato in each hand and rubbed them all over Shug's face then stood back to admire her handiwork. They stared at each other for a moment until Shug roared with laughter and took Mrs McNally in a bear hug, smothering her in rotten vegetables.

Each victim walked up to the perpetrator and had it out with them. Charles got between a few potential fist fights. Insults were thrown but no one was hurt. Sheena handed out spare bags of vegetables and a general bunfight ensued.

After a while, the atmosphere changed and there was a general consensus to stop, with a few notable exceptions of "Best fun I've had in years", "That'll show them" and "Can we do it next week? I could do with the de-stressing."

Kathy was stunned. She recognised this as the Grand Reveal, but not hers. They'd beaten her to it. No one had pelted her with vegetables. No one had come up to her. Not Jack, not Dan, not James, not David, not even her brother William. She was isolated. She felt that more powerfully than any accusation or recrimination. She turned her back as the tears stung her eyes. This wasn't what she'd wanted. This wasn't redemption or revenge on her terms. From Kathy's perspective, everyone else appeared to be in the process of reconciliation and yet, here she was, the one who had helped them, but she'd not managed to help herself.

Ella was in no better position. She stood there watching Shug and his wife, heads together, talking, laughing. She felt like an idiot. Taken in by a stupid costume. At that point, Shug turned round and took Ella's reluctant hand.

"Ella, ah'd like ye to meet ma wife." He looked at Ella, realising that she needed the reassurance. He was amazed, and happy. "It's over between us. We met when we were teenagers. She's been ma best friend for thirty years. We've both moved on, but ah'm no' goin' tae give up that friendship. OK?"

Ella nodded. She didn't trust her voice. Shug nodded at Betty who melted away, and Shug started to sway to the music. "Dancin'?"

Ella smiled a little tearfully. "OK."

Dan ran home and brought The Wee Besom back to the party. She pranced about in her element, so many new best friends to make.

Kathy turned back to look round the room. She saw how the atmosphere had changed between her group and their victims. She had a lot of questions, but decided to take a moment to be proud of what she had managed to achieve before it had all gone pear-shaped and she'd got her own deserved comeuppance. Her eyes swept the room, and rested on what she now recognised was a kindred spirit. Sheena, Kathy's mirror, Kathy's opposite opposite, had on the exact same, but opposite, costume.

Admitting to herself that she'd been bested, and in admiration of Sheena's equally devious abilities, Kathy, carefully stepping over the rotten vegetables, walked over to her.

"I assume this is all your work? And everything else that has happened over the past few days?"

Sheena, ready to kick off her shoes and make a run for it, nodded.

Kathy nodded back and paused for a moment. Then, in the time-honoured tradition at the end of a football match, Kathy took off her black blouse and handed it to Sheena. Sheena took off her white blouse and handed it to Kathy. Now they were both black and white, and white and black. The opposite opposite, making them the same.

Just at that moment Matt walked in, late to the party. Mask in hand, he was a gladiator, his bare, muscly chest, glistening, abs tight, biceps to die for. Kathy gave him the once-over. "I would just love to run my hands over that body."

"Mine," said Sheena. "I saw him first."

"No, you didn't!"

"I met him before you."

"He owes me."

Jostling and elbowing each other, Kathy and Sheena walked, and then jogged, and then sprinted across the dance floor towards Matt.

101

Kathy tapped the shiny brass name plaque three times for luck, as she did every day when she walked into the office.

The receptionist was busy taking calls. "Getting Even Agency, how can I help you? ... Certainly, I'll put you through to one of our specialists ... Getting Even Agency, how can I help you?"

As Kathy walked through reception, she smiled at the life-size poster of herself and Sheena on the back wall. It was a photo from the night of the Grand Reveal. Arms linked and grinning from ear to ear, Kathy was in black wearing Sheena's white blouse and Sheena was in white wearing Kathy's black blouse. And then, with a reverent nod towards the framed photo of Barbara Cartland – nobody dared ask why that was there – she turned to Sheena who was busy carving a notch into the latest of a series of bedposts that they'd fixed to the wall.

"That's 188 cases," said Sheena, focused on getting the notch exactly in the right position at the top.

"Make that 189," added Kathy.

"It went well?"

"Stonkingly, amazingly, diabolically, fiendishly well." Kathy grinned. "189. Not bad for six months, eh?"

Sheena stood back to admire her work and they high-fived. "Not bad at all."

Kathy turned towards her office just as The Wee Besom shot past. The faintest rustle of a biscuit wrapper had woken her from her slumber.

"That dog is getting fat."

Sheena followed her gaze as The Wee Besom's rump disappeared round the corner. "I know. But what can you do? We can't ban biscuits. They're the lifeblood of the agency."

Kathy popped her head round the door of Shug and Ella's office. Ella's stomach protruded massively as she turned to face Kathy.

"So, how's it going? When did you say it was due? And how many have you got in there, again? Are you sure it's not quadruplets?"

"Still only one and still due in three months." Shug gazed adoringly at Ella and stretched his hand across the desk. Ella took Shug's hand and gazed back with equal adoration.

"Oh, you two – for heaven's sake, get a room." Kathy opened the door to her own office across the hallway. No sooner had she sat down at her desk than a loud bell rang out. The receptionist was clanging the large handbell they kept for auspicious occasions.

"Oyez, oyez, oyez!" she shouted. "The sausage rolls are in the house!"

Mrs McNally popped in every Friday afternoon with a tray of Greggs sausage rolls and stayed for a chinwag.

Bottles of wine and beer were opened and the Friday celebration of their week's achievements had begun.

Chapter 101

Everyone crowded into reception. Charles and his wife, who was in charge of spiritual development and counselling, stood at the back, smiling and clinking beer bottles.

Stuart walked out of Sonia's office holding an ice pack to what promised to be an impressive black eye – a present from someone none too chuffed about his ex getting even. Sonia followed him and picked out a sausage roll just as Sanjit arrived.

The Wee Besom sneaked closer to her goal, crouched, alert to every movement, as if the tray of rolls was a flock of sheep. She kept one eye on the rolls and another on everyone else. She held still, waiting for her moment, and then, in a flash, grabbed a sausage roll and scarpered, with a chorus of "Ya wee besom!" ringing in her ears.

Sheena held out her glass to Kathy. "To getting even."

"And living happily ever after," responded Kathy with a grin as they chinked glasses.

Thank you for reading

It would be very much appreciated it if you would leave an honest review of *Getting Even* wherever you bought the book. Thank you!

If you'd like to know more about the author, follow the link below and you'll find everything you need on this page: www.guid-publications.com/gillian-pollock.